Rooftops

Darren A Franklin

ISBN: 9798343658996

Cover design by: Art Painter
Library of Congress Control Number: 2018675309
Printed in the United States of America

For Louise, Mhairi-Louise and Rachael.

Words can take you places.

PROLOGUE

The moon was sitting low in the sky, its light casting a dull white aura over the rooves of the city. You could still see the patchwork of a thousand stars in the sky all adding to the illumination of the normally heavy darkness that weighed down on the city.

A line of small, golden lights snaked through the gaps in the rooftops, splitting in different directions like a stream of lava pouring from the crevices of a volcano over and around the disrupted architecture of the city.

But unlike the volcanic lava flows, this stream of gold had a purpose. The lights were torches gripped in the fists of vast numbers of intense and purposeful men, dressed in the blood-red livery of the City Guard. They moved with speed, the whites of their eyes matching the cold steel of their spears and swords as if chasing some elusive prey.

And that prey was a mere hundred feet ahead, high above them. Two figures were running along a precarious, red tiled roof, leaping over the narrow gaps between buildings and in some moments seeming to fly over unfathomable precipice.

Their goal survival, but their minds focused on the avenues before them. They are driven by fear and panic, moving fast, faster than the precarious nature of the ancient rooves should allow.

The two hunted figures are young, one so young that the other clasps his hand tightly and must carry him over the highest hurdles. For them no torches, no weapons, they seem to progress with the confidence of the night fox or frightened rat. Their heads are hooded like thieves in the night, their faces black with the soot kicked up by their pounding feet.

Their hearts thump and their breaths strain, gasping for the energy giving air to sustain their flight. Their urgency is driven by not just the torches below, but a growing number appearing on the rooves behind them.

The elder of the two figures glanced back at the chasers, and then forward; they were running out of roof. Ahead lay a canal, cutting through this part of the city, its breadth wider that anything they had overcome so far, but on the other side a pathway to the Great Dam, to the docks and boats. There lay probably the only real chance of escape.

Reaching the edge of the precipice, the older youth realised that his plans were doomed to fail. He might make the leap but for his brother it would be impossible. Could he make the leap carrying his brother? He had done that once before but not this far, not even close.

He looked back on the pursuers, then looked down. Fifty feet below the waters of the canal, dark and uninviting with the stillness of death. He could hear the voices of the hunters now and feel the tremors in his brother's hand.

"I can't do this!" the small boy whispered; his eyes red with tears. The boy is young, no more than seven years old, exhausted and obviously terrified.

"We must make it to the Dam, Ark. There's no other way." There was a hint of anger in his voice, "Just a few more metres and then we can steal a boat and we will be safe." His brother attempted to encourage him, but he knew this was impossible. He tried not to sound angry, but he was not immune to the fear, and he struggled with his emotions. Ark began to shake. Tears began to appear in his brother's eyes.

Ark looked down at the water and gripped his brother's hand and in a moment of bravery said, "We will be safe, come on." and stepped forward.

His brother looked back to the rooves. There was now torch light appearing on the Dam in the distance, streaming along the walkway. The glimmer of the flame reflected in armour on the bodies of the men, meant that these were more soldiers.

6

The Dam was no longer the answer, the gateway to the sea was compromised. Its dockyards, on the seaward side, harboured the great ships that transport goods and people to the rest of the empire but now it was a barrier to their escape.

It had been a miscalculation anyway by the youth. In daytime there were boats in the docks, but at night the boats had to moor at least five hundred yards out to sea. Even if they reached the docks, there would have been no boats.

The approaching guards from his rear, were too close now. Ark and his brother began to run parallel to the canal towards the rear of the Great Temple, aside from the Citadel the largest building in the city. Ahead of them was the tall spire of the temple.

As they ran an idea formed in the older youth's mind. "One last leap" he shouted as they neared the end of the current building, and then together they launched themselves out across the two yards of air before landing flat against the temples tiled roof.

Both the fugitives grabbed hard at the tiles and seemed to stick like glue. A few feet above them a flurry of birds flew frantically from their night-time perches, scattering filth, dirt and discarded feathers down onto the brothers.

Both then climbed the twenty feet up the weather-beaten spire, its damage and erosion providing foot and hand holds for the two. The chasing mob, alerted by the birds, made their way to the edge. Some prepared to jump in pursuit whilst others launched a flurry of spears. They whizzed through the air and rattled against the spire, but well beneath the feet of the ascending pair.

The higher altitude seemed to make the wind more robust, and both held tight to the flagpole crowning the spire. They regained their balance and then shifted around the spire to be on the side that was out of sight of their pursuers. They sat in their own silence for a few seconds, the first moment of relief that they had had for hours.

The elder brother pulled back his hood and took a deep breath. His dark face was crowned by the feint wisps of hair hanging down from dark black locks that covered his head. His eyes were red, not the red

7

of tiredness but red in the pupil, with dark cavernous wells under dark eyebrows. When he grimaced his teeth were white, clean white and gripped in determination.

Ark could have been his twin, but younger and not so gaunt and worn in the face. There were still signs of childhood chubbiness, but the same red eyes, and the same grimace.

The brief respite was broken by the sound of guards landing on the spire. The older brother looked down, where the same canal weaved its was along the side of the Temple and its surrounding houses. It was still directly below them but now they were another twenty feet higher. "We have to jump, don't we?" Ark asked.

His brother avoided looking at him. "Jump, and then swim for the sides" he said, knowing that they were nearing the end. He took a deep breath and grabbed Ark under the shoulder and hoisted him up. He looked down, and the side of the temple was a seemingly endless drop to the canal below. The moon seemed brighter from here and in its half glow the blue ripples of the water could now be seen.

The elder brother, licked his lips and closing his eyes, whispering possibly a prayer and then looked at Ark. "Are you ready?"

The tears had dried in Ark's eyes, his face inanimate with fear. Staring straight ahead into space, he seemed almost catatonic, avoiding seeing the edge of the rooftop and the waters below. He did not answer. The older boy knew his brother was too afraid to jump. It was dark and the night was silent, amplifying the noise of the mob so it sounded like some angry beast desperate for food.

Across the roofs more golden torches, rising from the edges of the roof like dark shadowy, wiry demons lit up by the flaming torches and the slow rising of shouts of anger. Staring into his brother's eyes, the elder squeezed the boys' hand, "We must jump, or we die. Do you understand?"

With one final breathe he stepped off the edge into the air. He felt the weightlessness and then the tug as, still gripping his brother's hand, his momentum was stalled. Ark hadn't jumped! He was no longer holding his hand!

The rush of air disorientated him. He tried to look back but there was only darkness. Then he feels it: the impact of the water crashing into him and then darkness. He is alive but sliding and somersaulting like a rag in the water. The current takes control and he rushes away from the landing site. The waters crashed over his head and he fought his way to the surface, driven by the desire for breath. He gulped the beautiful air in sharply and then again.

Disorientated, he tried to stare up at the Temple. He was too far now to make out nothing except torches and dark shadows on the rooves above. but could only see a collection of torches and bodies up where they had stood.

"Where was Ark?" He strained his eyes, wiping water from his brow. Nothing and then for a brief moment he thought he could see him. Huddled a few feet below the spire, on a boarded window ledge, cowering like a scared cat.

Instinctively he screams: "Stay! I'll come back! Stay!", but the words are swallowed up by the water and as he emerges again, he is in darkness, drawn away by the current.

Ark curled up on the ledge, shrouded in the shadows, lit sporadically by the eerie light of flaming torches hurled from above into the canal waters below.

So, Ark sat, until the yelling slowly died away and the waters had washed away all remnants of the night's adventures. Ark sat, not daring to move. The nights shadows moved across the rooftops, until a faint ebb of dawn poured slowly over the roof above and entered his sanctuary. He sat, whilst the waters came alive, with the dawn traffic of cargo boats and the calls of their drivers.

Ark sat through the morning still hidden. Safe. Then the afternoon and then the night came again. No-one came, no torches, no mob. He was back among the darkness.

He sat for days, not daring to move, gripping tightly to the single thought: I heard him, I heard him. He said he will return. My brother will come back."

I

Havar the Baker was busy the dawn was still to rise over the city, yet he had been up and about since the night guards called their final "All's well!" from the Tower of the citadel.

Every day this was Havar's routine. He would wake before dawn, before anyone else, to bake the bread cakes that were a staple for the city. He set up the display outside the front of his shop with brown bags of bread cakes ready for the customers who were always in a hurry.

Today, Havar followed his ritual the same way as always. He placed at the bottom of each bag the cakes left over from yesterday. Havar knew that his customers would eat one or two fresh ones from the top of the bag as they headed to work and eat the remainder at lunchtime. They would blame their toughness on the passing of the day. Yesterday and been a good day and only half of today's bags had one or two of the older cakes in them.

Havar began to whistle a popular tune that had been bumping about in his head since his son's birthday party last week. He scattered some flowers around the display. Then a stray cat let out a wail, reciprocated by another a few streets away. Instinctively Havar leant over his stall to guard his precious wares. "Cats! Huh!" he grumbled to himself.

He checked all around himself, even back into the shop, and not until he was completely satisfied all was clear, did he continue with the display.

"Now a touch of heather", carefully he placed the heather in several spots to add colour to the display, "...and there, excellent! Havar you are an artist!"

He walked slowly backwards into the market square to get a wider look at his creation. There was no-one in the city who took more care over his displays than Havar the Baker.

He lifted his head to see a sharp line of orange breaking from behind the shadowed crest of the Great Dam, that stood towering over the city. Dawn was breaking and another profitable day was about to begin.

The orange line became a golden crescent, and he shielded his eyes, and blinked for a few moments. He blinked again and rubbed his eyes to clear the dark patches. Always the same, he thought and rubbed his eyes as one persistent dark shape wouldn't go away, annoyingly just above his display. Then Havar's brain started to catch up with his eyes. The dark shape was not going away.

"What is that?" he thought. The dark shape was not a result of the sun...it was a crouching animal! Right in the centre of his display – his beautiful display!

"No!" he yelled and launched himself at the stall. The animal turned its head and faced the scream, turning slowly and calmly. Its face was black, black as soot and two piercing white eyes stared straight at him. Havar stumbled forward and leapt at the cat, for surely that was what it was?

The animal sprang up in the air, leaping five or six feet clear of the stall and grasping with its outstretched arms the metal flagpole that marked the baker's shop. Havar continued forward now losing control of his body and flying at the space where the animal had been, crashing head first into the breaded cakes destroying the display.

Wood, heather, cakes and bags crashed around him as he fell, some flying high above him. One found its home in the palm of a small, grubby hand extended from the dark, curled up form perched upon the baker's sign.

Havar lay flat out on his back staring at the beast. What he saw he could only describe as a small gargoyle eating half a cake before dropping the final half down into Havar's lap, smiling. He then leapt up to the rooftops and disappeared.

2

The sun finally broke clear of the Great Dam as Havar sat amongst his broken cakes. The small dark figure scurried amongst the rooftops of the greatest city in the world, leaping between buildings before disappearing amongst the confusion of the chimneys, dens and tiled roofs; lost in the maze invisible even to the birds.

The Great Temple is one of two structures that rise above the rest of the city, the other being the Citadel of Korsch. The Citadel was directly opposite the Great Dam at the southern end of the valley, nestled into the mountain range surrounding the city. It was not only walls was the main building fifty yards back from the walls across an elaborately tiled an immense edifice but also far more ornate and elaborate than any other structure in the city, including the Great Temple. It was surrounded on the non-mountain sides by a great wall of over 10 feet high sporadically interrupted by circular guard towers.

Beyond the courtyard. The building seemed to be a random collection of towers, verandas and curved walls all glistening white in contrast to the patchy browns of the city. What really stands out, though is the windows, hundreds of windows.

There are two unique features to note inside the walls of the citadel. Firstly, the Great Gate on the eastern end of the courtyard. This is the entrance to a huge tunnel passing through the mountain range to the plains beyond, seldom used now because of the dangerous nomadic tribes beyond. In the western corner was the three locks that guided the mountain rivers into the city's canals. One of the most spectacular sights of the city is watching the locks open and close as canal boats ferried goods from the Great Dam up into the bowels of the Citadel.

Beneath each window were broad balconies, usually with ornate barriers and lush with greenery and foliage. In the very central tower high above the other balconies stood a loan figure, leaning on the rails and staring out towards the city.

The city is laid about before him, stretching from the citadel walls to the docks of the inner lake. The city, a patchwork of rooftops, the multiple colours contrasting the snowy whites and greys of the mountains and the deep blue of the ocean. A carpet of browns, beiges, blacks, and yellows like all the leaves of the forest have fallen in one day. A city unplanned, that had grown like an untended garden, seeking dominance wherever space or light allowed.

The scene is so crushed and contained that there is no sign of the rivers and canals running through as prolific as the lanes and passageways between the houses. There was no sign of the aqueducts that feed from the hidden reservoirs inside the mountains, nor of the myriads of people that live contained within these patchwork houses.

To the left and right, the mountains curve around what was once a simple bay, but now they are a claw clasping a multi coloured and textured metropolis. From the east to the west for miles, the city within is a a collection of buildings of all shapes and sizes. There is no space that is not man made and where the mountains begin to climb, the houses follow in a ragged pattern, seemingly defying gravity until eventually they concede to nature.

A cloth merchant would liken it to a bride's wedding quilt, with thousands of tiny patches joined, of varying sizes, colours and shapes, pieced together, not over a lifetime but over generations. No design just whatever scrap fits in whatever gap.

The mountains caged the city in at his sides, but the stopper is the great wall curving outward from the eastern to the western tips of the mountains. A wall set back from the city, separated by a great lake. A hundred metres at its base. The wall is old and huge and completes the encirclement of the city started by the mountains.

This is the Great Dam and it does not protect nature from the city, but the city from nature. Beyond the dam is the ocean, the deep blue, stretching thousands upon thousands of miles to the next land mass. And it sits fifty metres above the level of the city, holding the sea back and there are those who spend their lives praying that it will forever hold its mark.

The Duke of Korsh was born here but never ceased to be amazed by the magnificence of the Dam next to the tragedy of the city. Yet today his eyes were not fixed on this, but rather on the dockyards and city paths leading down from the Dam to the thousands of bodies swarming the docks like an ant nest turned over or a beehive disturbed.

"Ishman, come here. Look the crowds! Are they not greater still than yesterday? Is it not at least twice as much as the day before?" he asked, not even turning from the view. The Duke looked out of the sea of people amassing around the docks and did not acknowledge the figure behind him emerging from the room behind the balcony.

"Ishman, are they ours or the city guard?", he turned to Ishman whilst still pointing down from the balcony.

"City guard, sir. There are two thousand today, Duke, a thousand yesterday." Ishman replied.

"Yes, I thought so. Damn mess. When will it stop? It's clogging the city - I feel like a prisoner in here."

"They are of the second echelon, sir. Noble families, and wealthy, back in the capital. The Council stresses that we must accommodate them."

"The Council?" the Duke's head seemed to sag. "Yes. Ensure the guards are careful, I see them pushing the crowds, I don't want some third uncle of the Emperor ruining my life." He continued looking. "Wait a second. Are you sure that they are second echelon? Those on the first two boats aren't. There not even third!"

Ishman lent forward creasing his eyes to try to see what the Duke was seeing.

"Stop the ferries, no more!" yelled the Duke.

"The Council would need to vote sir..."

The Duke's body clearly sagged now, the contempt he held for the Council could not be hidden. For the last ten years he had been Duke, elected by the city elite to rule until death, but he never felt truly in control. The Council provided the balance of power. The body of twenty Lords, from each Guild, Church and other eminent entities were elected by their own members and had to ratify every significant decision they made.

They were a hangover from the founding of the city, and abolished by his predecessor, Duke Hala coincidently a decade into rule. Duke Hala had been a tyrant, of that there was no doubt. Even the Duke had to acknowledged that his power needed reigning in. He had mysteriously died in his sleep following a final year of rule that almost brought the city to a revolution.

The climax, the day before he died was the slaughter of the Xari at the Great Dam. For a moment the Duke pictured the horrific scene in his head and struggled to shut it out. One of the worst days of his life...but not the worst.

The Duke had come to power, and had ruled not without his own challenges, especially in this last year. His first year was a whirlwind of reforms, one being the reappointment of the Council. Over the last few years, though, he had begun to wonder if Duke Hala had been driven mad by the Council itself.

"Just issue a memo saying we are changing the entrance criteria to ease pressure and any funds will go to the Council regeneration fund. It will pass."

The Duke's face clearly showed his forty-five years. His once handsome chiselled features now more like a quarry near the end of its usefulness. His eyes, red with dark markings beneath them, signs of his constant insomnia. His hair, well cut and styled but the dark brown locks now fully invaded by the grey of years.

"Is there anyone of significance we need to bring into the citadel?"

"Yes, actually there is, sir." The aide pulled from his cloak a bound parchment and handed it to the Duke.

The Duke, surprised, took it, and as he began to open it, asked "and who is it, the Emperor?" He laughed.

"Almost", the aide's delivery remained dour. "Guardian Rahim and the Emperor's youngest daughter Lady Francesca."

And there it was again. The vision of that day at the Great Dam. Duke Hala's massacre of the Xari. The Duke standing on the dam, next to him two monks, one well on in years, stoic, calm, the other younger, smiling.

"Rahim has been here before." Ishman began.

"Yes, I'm aware of that". The Duke left it at that. Guardians were trouble. Pure and simple. No questions. They were trouble.

"He has been in service to the Emperor's brother for the last few years." concluded Ishman. In simple terms the Guardians were clerks to the government. In all but name they ruled on behalf of the imperial family. As children, their parents would send them to one of three university retreats for the brightest and most able children, there they would stay until there're late twenties when they would be sent to mentors in governments departments.

They lived like monks, although very little is known of the teaching practices and the lives spent there, as all are sworn to a vow of secrecy.

The Emperor's brother, Yon, was responsible for the management of the temples, and interactions with the various religions across the empire. Outside of the army this was the most important department, but Yon was typical of most of the imperial family, in that he spent his time focused on the pursuit of pleasure rather than the complexity of government.

And so the Guardians, had become as powerful as the Imperial family itself.

"Which brother?" the Duke asked. "Brother Yon? "The aide nodded in reply "Why has he come here?" Ishman gave no answer. Just shrugged and motioned to the paper.

"Which one is Francesca?" The Emperor was renowned for his legion of children. The daughters, of whom there were fifteen, were barely known, the sons numbering twenty were hard to name other than the five crown princes like Yon. The Duke picked up the paper and began to read, speaking aloud when he came to the reason for the visit:

'So, in line with the Emperor's request wishing to understand the empire and it challenges, he also wishes all of his children to see the empire and all its richest, whilst providing a positive figure for each community to align its aspirations and commitment to the empire..."

...can you believe this?" the Duke shook his head.

"What he really means to say is, 'it's all gone to the dogs in the heart of the empire and I need to ship my offspring to multiple places of safety, hoping to the gods that one of them at least survives!'. It shows just how unimportant we are, we don't justify a one of the princes."

"You may be correct sir, but I'm sure you would prefer a young fledgling running around the walls of the citadel than one of the princes taking over the gates."

"Indeed." The Duke acknowledged the aide's wisdom. He picked up a paperweight from his desk, a glass cube carved like a dice. He rolled it over in his hand. The Duke appeared deep in thought for a few moments, as if considering something. Ishman had seen this many times before, and it usually led to an idea that no one else had considered.

Th Duke was a smart man, a lifetime of politics had made him cynical but aware of how to play the system. He was handsome enough, with his well-groomed wavy blonde hair and blue eyes, and this with his genuine love for the city and its people made him a popular ruler. Then, again anyone following Duke Hala would be considered perfect in comparison.

After a few minutes he spoke, "What is on the agenda today, we need to welcome him to the citadel. Setup a dinner for this evening – keep it private. "

His words were interrupted by the loud explosion of the midday cannon. The Duke stopped speaking and looked back over the balcony. "Look now, at that rabble. What are the guards doing? The crowds aren't moving quickly enough! I want the docks clear! And Ishman, no one is admitted to the citadel, unless I express it."

Ishman nodded, turned and strode away.

3

In the dock area of the city, the area had exploded with the unexpected number of arrivals at the port on the seaward side of the Great Dam. The arrivals had been ferried through two great stone chambers high at the dam's top and then if permitted made their way down through various cavernous tunnels to the dock area, level with the inner lake.

Those with luggage could pay to be lowered on platforms attached to a pulley system that travelled down the face of the Great Dam and then walk along a number of wooden paths that crossed the lake to the docks themselves. On the Eastern corner of the Great Dam huge platforms lowered goods and produce shipped in from the empire and raised up produce for export the other way.

On any normal day it ran well, although slowly for those progressing down the fifty-metre drop by foot. Today, though the stairwells and docks were jammed solid.

Famine and plague had wreaked havoc in the empire in the last year and the city seen a steady stream of people fleeing the other cities. This was not unheard of, intermittent plagues popped up every few years. In fact under Duke Hala, this had led to the closing of the pass through the mountains to protect the citadel. It had worked so well that it was never re-opened and the current Duke hadn't reversed the order.

Travelling slowly down on one of the larger platforms was a group of twelve elaborately dressed soldiers, in golden helmets carved with eagles, bright red cloaks, and gold breastplates. The sun reflected off the combined breastplates making a golden glow that could be seen from all corners of the dockyard. It was like the sun was falling slowly to earth. Beneath their gold helmets, the soldier's faces were all the same, not just their expression, but their eyes, mouth and features.

These were Imperial Guards. They were surrounding two figures. One was as tall as the guards but had a long spiny neck and thin face, crowned by only a small ring of hair. His face was almost a mirror of the eagle heads on the helmets of the soldiers, his thin body wrapped in a cloak, blacker than the night. This was Guardian Rahim and next to the Golden Guards he seemed like a different species.

Beside him stood a young girl perhaps ten or eleven, cloaked in a purple cloak, with a happy smiling face, crowned by beautiful golden hair, almost as perfect as the gold of the guards next to her. Where her companions were stoic, she was wide eyed, animated and full of excitement. Her arms were pointing at the city and the dam, constantly leaning to view more, but continually checked by a dark claw like hand that reached from beneath the Guardians cloak. "Restraint, Princess Francesca, restraint" the Guardian commanded.

Over five thousand people were flooding onto the dock from the staircases. It was like market day in the city square, except they all had one purpose and one direction. Soldiers were containing the crowds funnelling into the two main pathways out of the docks, and into the queue for the city barges that ferried people up the river into the heart of the city. Wealthy Families tried to break out of their funnel towards the city barges but were pushed back. Old ladies fell, well-groomed gentlemen remonstrated, small children cried.

The economy was booming with the expats being generally from the wealthy end of society and bringing back savings and wealth to spend in the cosmopolitan city. Children and the poorer ends of the social mix would sit on the dock and make a day out of watching the arrivals. They called it the "carnival" as the wealthy always arrived in their best wares, with a rainbow of colours and glittering jewels. A few of the children would watch find a particularly well adorned lady, and then sneak off to spread the word to the street gangs further in.

Garik was standing to attention on the walkway that the platform was descending towards. Rich and privileged guests would have an escort to take them from the docks to whatever location was assigned to them, and as a commander in the Citadel Guard he and his six men at arms were up next.

"Here we go. Look lively, their lordships are on their way down."

24

When he arrived at the docks with this assignment, he thought it would be a huge problem ferrying the dignitaries passed the unwashed masses on the docks, so had brought a few more men along. Now looking at the golden warriors on the platform, he felt inferior and even worried for the poor plebs that they would pass through.

Standing next to Garik, was Will Gascon. This was his first time carrying out this duty. To get to this position had taken three years of saving up to pay his enlistment fee, three weeks of training, and then making it into uniform. He knew there would initially be the boredom of guard duties, but he expected his first real soldiering to be in the colonies or if he was lucky in the marines guarding the trade routes, not escort or crowd control. In his hand he held his highly polished spear, and at his side his short sword, given to him by his uncle who had recently retired after twenty years guarding the Duke.

With precision and control the platform pilot landed his passengers at the foot of the Great Wall and onto the walkway. As the gate opened on the platform, four of the golden soldiers, in a precise and single motion made their way to the front, stepped onto the walkway and stood guard with their spears.

Before Garik could say or do anything, a whistle came from someone remaining on the platform, and the four guards lined themselves up to make a single file corridor for the others to walk down. More soldiers walked through adding to the line each side, and eventually followed by the only two remaining guards, and then the Guardian and Francesca walked down.

"Welcome!" saluted Garik in his most professional way. The men at arms copied, to varying levels of commitment but Will was precise as he had ever been.

"Yes, yes," said the Guardian, in a deep, almost echoing voice. Then he nodded to one of the golden guards on the edge of the line. The figure stepped forward, and then in a precise and authoritarian tone barked at Garik a set of orders:

"Go ahead, and clear the dock area, at the double. We will form a guard around the Honoured as an inner shield. Go now."

Garik was about to speak up, and then thought better of it. Twenty years' service had not made him an idiot. He looked back over his shoulders at the crowds, then at his men at arms, and finally back at the golden guards.

"Right, men, let's do as the golden nugget says, and clear a way for our guests." He drew his short sword from his belt and raised it in the air, turned and marched towards the crowd. The men at arms looked at each other and then followed suit, raising their spears in front of them.

They made a formation like the point of a spear and begun to penetrate the crowd on the dock. At the pinnacle was Ursun, who was a giant of a man, mostly pure fat, but enough muscle to be able to stand his own against anyone else in the guards. Will and Garak were in the next row, and as the crowd pushed against them, they each used their spears held across him like a fence to push back the crowd.

"Hey watch it! We're citizens, not dogs" a young man bellowed.

"Hold steady!" called Garick. As they penetrated the crowd the formation became a line of twenty soldiers from dock to the nearest building, the Guild Hall, their spear points and bases touching to form a makeshift, but solid fence. Then marching down the newly formed avenue came the golden soldiers.

"Hold Steady". Garik was an experienced soldier; his grey hair and worn face were the epitome of story books soldiering. He looked like he had slept every night on the battlefield and when he smiled the scar on his cheek would send a shiver down your spine. You felt you could pull his face away if you just grabbed a lip.

Garick, was calm and controlled. His body large, and dominating, but he looked every inch a controlled military man. He was a commander but still bunked with his men in the barracks. Will had wondered – but not quite had the nerve to ask- why he had never moved into the officers' quarters or even the Citadel itself.

Still, he gave Will confidence and as the golden guards passed, he pushed back a complaining man with the side of his spear. One of the colleagues plugged the gap, whilst Garik guided the party into the Guild

Hall. Then like a pea bursting from a pod, a small figure ducked beneath the spear and ran towards the Guardian.

Will was caught flat footed, but Garick extended his stance, leaned to the right and all in one instant reversed his spear so the edge extended to catch the shoulder of the escapee. He then hooked the spear beneath the runaway's armpit, tripped him to the floor, whilst his left had extended to hold back the shoulder of a lady who had threatened to fall away from the crowd.

Guardian Rahim and Francesca and a handful of the Golden Guards stood at the door watching.

"Whose boy is this" Garick yelled.

A few faces in the crowd looked but the crowd's momentum moved them on like a river rushing pass. The boy lay on the floor trying to get up, but the spear had skewered his shirt to the wooden decking below. Garick gave Will and another soldier a quick movement of the eye, then stepped out of the line as the two soldiers filled the gap.

Garick then squatted down and looked at the boy. The boy's face was smeared with dirt, his clothes quite tatty, unlike the barge refugees. His face was red with fear, his eyes white amongst the dirt of his face.

"A bloody thief!" Garick exclaimed with disgust, and he looked to his side and spat. "I should have just skewered you and had done with it!" Garick released the spear and the boy reacted, but the spear was quickly levelled across the boy's torso pinning him to the ground.

"So, what have you been up to?" Garick asked but not expecting an answer. He reached into the boy's pocket on the inside of the boy's vest and pulled out two small purses. Garick held them up to his face and shook them. The clinking of the coins inside seems to make the boy wince.

"There yours, just let me go" he cried.

"Too right... they're mine." Garick then exerted his weight onto the spear and its edge moved up to the boy's throat.

"No..." the boy was now choking with the hideous smile of the devil himself grinning over him." Spittle came out of the boy's mouth.

"Let him go." A calm, deep voice broke through the bedlam. Garick looked up and the Guardian was hovering above him. Garick eased off and the boy grabbed his own throat and coughed. Garick sensed, a smirk from the Guardian, and so Garick gave the child a push, then hissed: "Clear off."

The boy didn't need telling and fled off into the crowd.

Garick stared hard at the Guardian, standing a few inches from his face. Will could physically feel the tension. Garick was dangerous and could explode if necessary. Garick could kill this man, but surely, he wouldn't. He was a bear in a cage that only a fool would let his guard down with.

"That's none of your business!" Garik growled. One of the golden soldiers began to draw his sword.

"The Guardian raised his hand to sop the soldier, "No." Then leant forward, his hawklike nose almost touching Garick's, and his eyes like red fire in a black pit. His claw like hand grabbed Garik by the shoulder and squeezed. Will feared the worse.

"Everything is my business", the Guardian hiss. "Leave the boy and take me to the citadel, now."

Will had never seen Garik scared. He had, literally gone white like the grip of the guardian had sucked all the blood out of him. The crowd had come closer and begun to surround them so that there was only a couple of metres space between them and the door.

The Guardian finally let go of Garik, and he continued the motion of the arm into a wide arc with his palm facing out to the crowd. Will had never seen anything like it. With the motion, the crowd suddenly shifted as one body backwards. Garik fell to the ground, and the Guardian turned and marched into the warehouse leaving Will and the guards standing.

4

Way above the docks, a figure watched the whole confrontation. Hidden in an alcove of the roof of the Guild Hall, curled up into an anonymous form of black and hidden in shadows was the beast. The only colour breaking the darkness was two site slithers: the creature's eyes.

They had watched, unblinking, but now were flitting left to right across the whole dock, like a hawk. Every day the beast came down to the dock and watched from its hideout. Watching from the moment of the first arrivals to the last travellers disappeared into the jungle of the city. And he could pick out what he was looking for as easy as an owl could spot a mouse beneath the leaves.

An hour passed before the crowds had thinned out leaving only the flotsam and jetsam of dock workers, beggars and the slow stragglers who had made the long walk from the top of the Great Dam. The hanging platforms were no longer being raised and lowered, and the sun was beginning to touch the top of the Great Dam, casting long shadows across the lake. The shadows were more than welcome to the beast: the shadows were the pathways that made his travels easier and safer.

Ready to make his departure from the Guild Hall, the Beast suddenly caught sight if something amongst the stragglers. There was a small gang of boys under the boardwalk by the lake, sharing their earnings from the pickpocketing. One of them was the boy that was nearly killed by the guard.

Most of the guards were long gone now, with only a few remaining on top of the Great Dam. The gates that lead to the paths up the side of the dam were being closed when a last figure forced it was through and began the descent down the final steps to the dockside. For anyone else the figure would just be a small dot, but for the beast he could make out every detail.

The figure was bald with a long brown robe, obviously a priest, or at least a monk, like those of the Great Temple. And the figure was old, or so he presumed as it walked so slowly.

The beast's eyes locked on the figure, as it descended and eventually took the final steps onto the dockside. The figure was larger now, and the beast could make out his face, clearly. The face was strange, face heavily worn, and darker, darker than anything the beast had seen before. He looked at his own, brown-skinned hand, but this man's skin was darker still, like the soot from the chimneys.

The beast adjusted his position, showing more of his own form. To only the most perceptive the movement was invisible, but it was enough for the old man to stop in his tracks, raised his head and looked directly at the beast.

The beast could see the old man's eyes, now notably white with no discernible pupil, and in doing so his heart stopped for a second, and he felt the air catch in his lungs. Instinct kicked in and like a startled bird he bolted from his perch and leapt for the roof above the Guild Hall. The figure had seen the manoeuvre and what he perceived was not an animal, but a human, a long black human.

The beast grabbed at a guttering above the hideaway and swung himself onto the sloping tiled roof. He rolled into a prone position and then leapt across the roof, disappearing into the shadows.

The old man had seen it all and slowly his head adjusted to the invisible spaces where he sensed the beast had fled to. Now he was the watcher, but finally the beast was gone. He smiled a row of young perfectly white teeth, and the white eyes saw a faint pupil emerge that seemed to suddenly twinkle.

He slowly shook his head and slowly made his way across the dockside. It had been many, many years since he had been in this city, but his memory was good and very little had changed.

Still, when reaching the main thoroughfare, he paused and looked around. The Great Temple was the tallest structure in the heart of the city, with only the citadel higher, but that was far to the back of the city.

And so, it was easy to see the spire from anywhere where a clear view of the sky could be found, which meant the docks and a few rare gardens of the middle classes. Although the crag and its citadel housed countless temples, this structure was built amongst the people. It celebrated the deliverance of the people from the great sickening, centuries before.

The old man remembered the first stone being laid. The stone was shipped from the distant corners of the Empire, contributing to the twelve great spires soaring sixty metres into the sky, each spire meaning to represent the supplicant hands of the dying populace pleading for salvation.

The spires stood above the body of the temple, housing hundreds of steps spiralling around its outer skin and deep within its body. At the very tip a chamber opens to the elements, where the priests would pray every month in unison.

The old man spotted a spire, nodded and then made his way down a dark alleyway passing the small group of boys that the beast had spotted earlier. Strangely they had not noticed the old man and so they instinctively reacted as he went past, ducking low into the doorway of the adjacent warehouse.

***

The beast fled across the rooftops not daring to stop until his lungs began to burst. There were several hideouts amongst the forest of tiles, spires and chimneys, and he finally stopped at the one he trusted most. On the long roof of a two-storey brick factory, which looked out over the piazza in front of the Temple, he had constructed a makeshift tent of two old wooden doors resting against a great chimney. The constant smoke from the brick baking fires added another layer of protection.

His hideout His mind battled with a thousand thoughts, and now safe in his haven he began the task of organising them: "Who was the traveller? How had he seen him? Where was he from?"

The beast new little of the world. He had been living amongst the roofs for longer than he could remember. His memories were vague, shadowy images, sometimes he was not sure if they were just dreams. The questions about the traveller were the same question he could ask about himself.

The days he had spent watching the docks, were as much about learning about himself as it was about the world around him. He knew he was different, and he was looking for someone like himself. He had come to terms with the knowledge that he was not like the people of Kursch, but he still struggled because he had seen no-one arrive in the city like himself. Did this mean that there was no-one like him beyond the city?

He had studied his own reflection countless times, in the pools of water formed upon the roof. The most obvious thing that separated him from the people of the city were his eyes. Looking straight on, the eyes sat a little further away from the top of his nose than most people, far enough that it would make people uncomfortable.

The beast identified more with the birds, his neighbours. In fact, he was more like a hawk. The eyes were unblinking as well, not for a few moments but for hours, only blinking if something was coming towards him.

Beneath the layers of dirt his skin was darker than those of Kursch, though not as dark as the old man. His hair was black, and very long. So long that when running the roofs, he would tie a knot in the back, and when hiding could actually pull it over himself like a cloak. The clothes, black and brown with dirt, were stolen from houses; he had not taken shoes though, he had never worn shoes.

***

The old man was deep in thought as well. He made his way through the city as the sun began to set, the last light like a gold pebble balanced on the top of the Great Dam. In the alleyways and pathways, it may as well have been night. Darkness had crept into every nook and cranny. The alleyways were empty as most people had hidden behind their doors; night was a time of fear.

The Traveller had no fear though. His pace did not change, and he had purpose. He never looked up for signs or reminders but seemed pulled by a magnet around the maze of alleyways. Eventually he emerged into one of the few open spaces in the city: the Great Temple piazza.

The piazza was dominated the amazing edifice its base surrounded on three sides by buildings, some touching the eastern facade like wild ivy. But on the Northern face, facing the docks was the imposing Temple entrance. Two sets of grand oak doors, each set in the shape of an archway, each three metres high and either side of these two smaller replicas. High above the doors was a relief carved with scenes from the history of the city. If you looked closely, you would see that many of the images were badly eroded, with soot and city grime clogging the deepest cuts. Twenty tiers of stone steps took you from the doors to the piazza.

The piazza by day was a bustling market, but with the darkness descending the stalls had been packed away and the only movement was the rolling of tired papers, and rubbish.

The market didn't have a fixed time to close, just shutting when the foot traffic slowly ebbed away. Today, though was a holy day and so had not opened.

As the old man tracked through the city, the Temple Bursars emerged from the two small doors and from the outside closed the great doors using a special hook that attached to rings in the centre of each door.

The small white cloaked figures were frail, and slight compared to the size of the doors, but with the slightest pull the doors seem to swing with great ease, and close precisely without a sound. The two figures then returned to the side doors and disappeared.

The Temple's original and purpose was to provide a place for the populace to pray to the gods. People could come and go as they required, only coming together as a mass on the monthly worship. There were no priests, no scheduled text or creed. Everyone prayed quietly for their own needs, creating a constant low, almost mystical hum. The Bursars lit the tower flames and locked the doors and for those outside this was where their duties stopped.

On reaching the piazza, the old man stopped and stood for a few minutes, like he was taking in the full scene ahead of him. Rain had begun to fall, and the first drops bounced off his body. The colours of the square had disappeared with the last sunlight, just the dark greyness of the surrounding stonework of the piazza.

Eventually, he looked up and headed towards the Temple, eventually arriving at the doors.

The rain was now lashing down, bouncing in puddles across the uneven parts of the piazza, his cloak soaking up the wetness. The old man didn't mind the rain, but the dampness would become irritating soon.

Despite the rain the old man pulled down the cowl from his head, revealing his full baldness. In doing so, some rain ran into his sleeve, and so the figure shook out his arm. Suddenly from the sleeve a flurry of colour escaped. Three butterflies, red and yellow escaped from beneath the cloak and flew up through the immediate sky and into the eaves of the Temple and amongst the eaves, gargoyles and guttering they flew and then disappeared inside the Temple.

The old man looked up and smiled. He cleared his throat and then began a low mantra, almost a chant in an indistinguishable language, and forcibly placed the palm of his right hand on the great door in front of him.

A gentle tremor could be felt in the door, until it became a rumbling sound. The sound became a crescendo until there was a thunderous roar like a stone battering ram hitting thick beams of oak.

Inside the noise resonated around the Temples chambers like some titanic musical instrument.

The Bursars inside, looked up with a sense of terror: only the gods and the priests could open the doors. Either the gods were here in the city, or worryingly priests from the North were here. The Temple inside was a huge space, with just a scattering of small carpets that the Bursars and priests sat on. There was no altar like the eastern temples had, but rather all prayed to the circular sky painted above their heads in the central dome.

Standing, watching the entrance was a collection of monks, one slowly stepped forward. He looked nervous, but taking a gulp proceeded towards the door. The others bean to follow him, but sensing this he turned briefly raising his hand to halt them. Shaking his head at them, he turned and carried on walking.

The doors were shaking, not dramatically like in an earthquake but a fast subtle throbbing accompanied by a noise like the whole Temple was about to collapse.

Fearing a cataclysmic collapse of the Temple, the monk grabbed at a thick rope hanging from high in the ceiling, next to the doors. The monk grabbed it and looking back at the monks with one last look he began to pull down on it. Slowly the great door began to open.

The monk was Ravo, the Chief Bursar and eldest of the monks. He had been chief bursar for the last five years after the death of his predecessor, and in all that time he had experienced nothing like this before.

As the doors opened, he closed his eyes. Surely if this was a god its presence would blind him? The door opened a few inches, before the rumbling suddenly stopped.

Ravo opened just one eye first. As if that would protect him or at least leave him only blind in one eye. The door was only slightly ajar and so there was nothing to see beyond the door. He opened both eyes and saw a small red butterfly, like a rose petal floating on the wind.

It fell slowly to the ground in front of Ravo's feet, and instinctively he pushed his palm out to catch the butterfly. Then suddenly a swarm of thousands of red butterflies swarmed through the door into the space of the temple. The priests ducked down, as they filled every corner.

The other monks through their arms up as if to will them away as if caught in a swarm of locusts. Realising that the flaying was useless the monks fled to the only clear space, in front of the great doors. Ravo stood and watched, his hands out in front as if in supplication, but as a perch for twenty or thirty red wings. The red mass pushed towards the great doors and seemed to corral the others into a huddle in front of the door. And as they huddle the doors flew openly completely.

"By the Gods!" screamed a single voice, breaking the silence. The monks fell to their knees and the butterflies appeared to disappear into the Temple's rafters.

The silhouetted figure stepped forward. Every monk, including Ravo's head was bowed.

"Whose Temple is this?", a dark, hollow voice rung out like a bell from the cloaked figure.

Silence. None of the monks looked up.

"Anyone?" the voice asked again, but this time with a slightly less commanding tone.

"Yes...of course my Lord" stammered Ravo, but looking up he regained his confidence "Of course, it is your Temple, my Lord."

The hooded figure seemed to ponder this, his eyebrows coming together as if he strained to comprehend. Then he smiled.

"No, no it is not mine" the old man spoke and then let out a slight laugh.

He stepped out of the doorway into the light of the internal lamps. His weary form was now clearer to the monks. The great doors shut behind him.

Ravo looked up, his hands still in supplication to the old man. Ravo was confused. Was he a god? He did not recognise him from the images they worshipped.

"I am Sern. I am a traveller from afar and I seek shelter and sustenance."

Ravo knew these words from the Book of Xa. They were the words spoken by Xa, when he arrived at the first city of men.

"You are Xa?" Ravo stammered.

"I am a traveller, from afar and I seek shelter and sustenance", the traveller repeated. "That is all you need to know. Enlightenment is a gift of the future."

***

Far above the city, the beast saw the great doors of the Temple shut as the traveller entered. Looking out of the rain-drenched piazza he had seen the old man appear. At first, he thought he had been followed, but then he realised that the old man was making his way to the Temple. The beast waited as the figure went inside.

The beast knew how to wait. The night descended and moonlight bathed the piazza. The watcher sat until even the moon was clouded and true darkness came. A stray dog entered the square and fed at some scraps at the Temple steps before moving on.

5

There had been one other person in the piazza that night, one other person who had followed the old man from the dockside to the Temple.

He had watched the old man pass his gang as he left the dockside, and once they had recovered from the instinctive reaction to scurry into the shadows, he had decided to follow the old man.

He didn't seem the type to have anything worth stealing, but something intrigued him to follow.

Lilkin was more than just a waif of the streets, one of far too many that roamed the city, homeless and parentless. This had been his life for as long as he remembered, he had arrived alone in the city a refugee of the Empire and survived through wit and chance. Over time he had met others and a gang had formed as much for protection as for any other purpose. The dockside was his territory and this gang, his gang had been revelling in the increase in visitors.

It was the gang that had named him Lilkin. An abbreviation of "Little King" the nickname they awarded him as ruler of their little empire.

Like the beast, Lilkin had learnt to live in the shadows, and to have a keen eye for an opportunity. They had had a reasonable day today and stole enough to merit a small celebration later in their den beneath the docks, a dry haven safe from prying eyes. But for now, Lilkin had another interest.

The Temple was a little out of his territory, the domain of far older gangs, but they wouldn't feel threatened by him. When he saw the old man enter the Temple, he was a little disappointed assuming that the mysterious one was no more than just a monk. They were usually penniless.

Turning to leave the piazza, though he caught a glimpse of something high up on the factory roof. For a moment he assumed it was just a cat, but it wasn't. It was the beast. He was sure of it.

He had a fascination for the beast. He had seen it once before, a month ago, but not as clearly as this. Everyone feared the beast, but he wasn't afraid, he just hated it. It had been stealing and encroaching on his territory and he wanted rid of it.

He watched as the beast watched, eventually settling into a crouch on the floor, wrapped up warm like one of the many night beggars. The city at night was very different from the day. The hustle and bustle were gone, the rich and purposeful were long gone, back to the safety of their homes. The night belonged to those with more nefarious objectives. Thieves, vagrants, drinkers at the ale houses, those who perhaps didn't want to be seen in the daytime.

His gang, all children would not be out stalking or stealing. They were too easy prey for the deadly night hunters, especially with so many arriving from the greater Empire, residing in inns, hostels or the poorhouse accommodation provided by the Duke.

But Lilkin was strong, confident and his years much closer to the age of the drinkers and other vagrants. He was lucky tonight, as the moon provided more light than normal, allowing him to watch the beast.

Minutes went by, and eventually the beast moved out of sight. Lilkin sat for a further hour hoping to see the beast again, but eventually he gave up. The beast was gone, but perhaps there was something in this sighting. He would return, and maybe keep a closer eye on the piazza.

***

Inside the Temple, the traveller had been shown to the monk's dining area and sat at the high table usually reserved for the senior monks and provided with bread, fruit and a cup of wine. The other seats were filled with five of the most senior monks, including Ravo. They sat and watched the traveller eat, all waiting for the traveller to say something or Ravo to direct the conversation.

Ravo was waiting, though; he was waiting for the traveller to finish eating and then he would interrogate him and interrogate him he would. He had overcome his initial shock and awe, his was now filled with doubt and concern. He had offered the required food and comforts as demanded by the Book of Xa, there was no point taken the risk with something so easy to give. If this was a vagrant, then he could be sent on his way quickly enough.

But he wasn't a vagrant, Ravo knew that. The man knew the holy book and his voice had the power and authority, a certain resonance that he had seen in the most holy and experienced monks. Ravo himself had never been given the gift. No this was not a vagrant, but he could not be a God.

The Gods had not walked the earth for hundreds of years. In Ravo's own moments of doubt he had wondered whether they had left these lands forever, given up on their pitiful creations. Yet, he was a believer. There were tales of his own ancestors having been in the presence of the Gods. No, the Gods had not gone but waiting for the moment of need to walk the earth again.

"And do you not think this is a moment of need?" Ravo's pondering had been broken by the traveller. Had Ravo spoken out loud?

"I'm sorry?" was all that Ravo could blurt out.

The traveller stared straight at Ravo for what seemed like an eternity, until he broke the spell by placing another piece of bread into his mouth. He ripped the bread from his teeth, leaving a morsel to chew on. When he had finished, he smiled.

"The answer to your question is that it is not relevant if I am a god or not. Your generosity is befitting of the gods and that is what matters. In harbouring me and feeding me you have performed the duty required of any godly person. "

He paused.

"What I ask now, is beyond the godly, and is in your gift should you wish to provide it. I require lodging for tonight, and maybe beyond.

Does your godliness stretch to this?" The words were warm and any doubts Ravo had that this stranger was not holy were disappearing.

"Of course!" he responded and signalled to the other monks to stand. "We will prepare a cell, immediately" He waved his hand and the others took that as a signal to depart the room and presumably prepare the cell.

"Can I ask, will you be joining us for night prayers?"

The traveller wiped his bowl with the final piece of bread and lifted it dripping the last remnants of soup back into the bowl.

"Of course." He replied.

6

"First of all, I must give you my condolences". Rahim sat opposite the Duke. The Guardian's smile was wide, completely out of keeping with the sentiment.

"Your loss was tragic. I never met your wife or daughter when I was here before, did I? " he continued. His speech was slow, methodical like each word was vetted and checked before it passed between his lips.

"Yes, I remember you and I appreciate your condolences…. but that is the past. How fairs the North?" The Duke was keen to change the subject.

The three were eating in the Grand Hall alone They were sat opposite each other with Francesca in between, to the Duke's left. The room was enormously spacious, and their voices echoed.

"You see Francesca, it was very sad." Rahim looked across at Francesca. "The Duke's wife she died. In childbirth I believe?" he looked at the Duke for confirmation.

The Duke gave a barely perceptible nod.

"Yes. This was a true fairy-tale. The Lady Jane was beautiful, and their romance was quite the love story!" The guardian seemed to ignore the Duke's obvious discomfort.

Francesca lent over "Do tell?" she pleaded with the Duke, but in a calm caring way. She placed her hand on his, gently.

For a few moments the love story replayed itself, but the darkness returned. "I think not…" he started

"And of course," Rahim continued "a beautiful child was the completion of that story…"

Francesca had not stopped looking at the Duke.

"But then Francesca will tell you, empathy, consideration not my strongest point. He looked to his side to the pretty girl next to him."

"And she was so like his wife, or his wife as he remembered as a child, when they grew up together. The wave of sadness pacified him. He could never be angry when he thought of her. He smiled at Francesca.

Her skin was incredibly pale, and immediately the Duke wondered if this was because she'd probably spent most of her life indoors, or whether this was because of her ancestry. All of the royal family were direct descendants of the Gods, and her paleness certainly matched the traditional images that ordained the Temple. He wondered if that would change after any time, down here in the warm, hotter southern city.

Her hair was blonde and tied back from her face into a ponytail. Her neck slim and pure only broken by the large diamond hanging from a silver chain around it.

But it was her eyes that stood out. They were blue, like many in the North, but the blue was the colour of the calm seas in the southern bays; almost translucent. And beyond the pale blue, like diamonds on the seabed her eyes sparkled. Real sparkles, like there was something beneath the blue, not just the sun reflecting the light.

And at that moment Francesca gripped his hand, just a little tighter.

"And of course, she died as well. Tragic. Very tragic." Rahim broke the spell.

"I think that is enough, Lord Rahim." Francesca smiled and turned to him, continuing to squeeze the Duke's hand.

The Duke had only known this young girl a few minutes and he was completely mesmerized. When she smiled, he broke his gaze, almost embarrassed, and looked down at his hands. The brown tanned pinkness of his hands now felt grubby and dirty.

"You are too kind Princess." The Duke faltered. "But it is long past, and you should not worry yourself."

"Don't be silly" she said in a childish, almost giggly way. "I'm not a Princess yet, and I do not need to be bowed to until then. Just call me Francesca." She sat as she spoke but did not blink or break her smile.

"Yes, yes, of course, milady. Yes, of course."

"She would not actually be a Princess until she reaches sixteen when she will be eligible for marriage or public position." Rahim added.

"Let's eat Duke, shall we?" and then almost sarcastically, "What passes for quality food in this backwater?"

The Duke was taken back, but held his temper, sitting back in his chair and waving his right hand to the waiters to come over, which they dutifully did on masse bringing silver trays laden with delights.

The Duke instinctively directed the conversation to Francesca. "Of course, fish is the mainstay of the city, we have a huge variety that I'm sure you will find delightful. There is gull's egg as well, which are gathered from the cliff edges along the coast. These are wild gulls, but we do have a breeding farm near the base of the dam that provide a cheaper, but less flavoursome variety.

Francesca smiled, and the Duke thought she was about to speak, when Rahim exclaimed through clenched teeth: "You eat birds!"

"No, of course not – well at least not here in the citadel. We had a problem for a while with young street urchins shooting gulls with slingshots from the rooves when they nestled in the higher towers and spaces, I'm sure that wasn't just for fun."

"We eat just the eggs, and as close to freshly laid as possible, and no longer than seven days laid."

"How do you know there seven days old?" Francesca asked.

"That would be the colour milady. They are laid white but begin to turn brown after seven or eight days." Much like northern visitors, he thought to himself.

"Do please try them."

"I think not," Rahim interrupted. "ma'am, it is important that we defer any risks to your health and I think the spawn of a flying rat would be a step too far. I see there are some fish cakes there, am I right Duke?"

"Yes, of course. They're delightful."

The meal then continued, drifting easily into long periods of silence, only broken by queries on the foods laid before them. Rahim was not giving much away, and so the Duke decided to dive in with the obvious question, not knowing how Rahim would respond.

"So how is the north?"

Rahim did not break his stride with his eating, but Francesca for the first time broke her elegant composure.

"Dreadful, my Lord. Truly dreadful. They say the dead walk the streets in the eastern cities and that the plague will engulf the whole world within months."

"Not quite, Francesca. That is just the idle speculation of the gossiping classes in the salons and drinking establishments. The Emperor has closed the borders of the east, so there is no news other than that from the Emperor himself. The plague is contained in the east, I can ensure you."

"Not everyone in the north can agree with you then" the Duke returned. "We have boat after boat arriving at the city and I'm sure other southern cities have the same. Very few are from the east, but rather from the North and western shores. They must be afraid of something, to give up their homes and livelihoods."

"Nervous types, that is all. Before the Emperor closed the border, rumour and ludicrous tales flooded the lesser parts of the city. The weak and feeble minded are easily afraid, and their ignorance has driven them here." Rahim responded.

"I assume that is not the case for you Rahim. Tell me, what has brought you south?"

The silence was crippling. Rahim was just staring at the Duke, like a snake. Food dribbled from the corner of his mouth. His hand crushing the fork within it, and the blood vessels rose in his neck.

The Duke did not waiver.

Then a tuneful, sweet laugh broke the air. "You are funny, my Lord. The Emperor asked Guardian Rahim to bring me south to see the great cities before I become a Princess. It will help my brothers, when one of them comes to rule"

She leant forward, like a collaborator about to shed a secret. "But I know he is scared and just wants me safe."

"The truth is that the Emperor's counsellors ordered you to be removed. The princes have also been sent to cities. This is not out of fear of the plague, but rather to bolster the morale of the citizens in the outlying regions ahead of the rumour and farce of the current environment." Rahim explained.

"Well, I am grateful, that you chose this city, which is remote and distant from the heart of the Empire and protected from the plagues and the nervousness of the ignorant populace of the north." The Duke said with all seriousness.

"Tell me about the city, I have heard an incredible story about how it came about." Francesca beamed.

The Duke smiled at her excitement. "Well, every city has its legends, Francesca, but Kurch is special indeed."

"It is said that from the mountains that surround the bay, a tribe of people emerged. This was long before the Great Father made the Gods and established the world, we live in. The mountains were taller then and the world a dangerous place."

Rahim turned his eyes to the ceiling, whether it was contempt or to ease his digestion the Duke could not tell. Francesca gave him a stony stare.

"Who were they? The people"

"They were the Xari. The first people. They numbered just a few hundred, a tribe who had fled across the desert from the north into the mountains.

"Who were they fleeing?"

"She is humouring you, Duke. She knows this legend probably better than you," interjected Rahim. Francesca smiled and slapped his hand then stared into the Duke's eyes. Those eyes were bewitching.

They were fleeing the er.... I don't recall, "the Duke scratched his head. "They were fleeing the Great Serpent!" Francesca completed, pleased that she knew so much.

"That's right...The mountains were snow covered at that time of year, but they had no choice but to go on. They were unaware of the great pass that would have guided them under the mountains into the bay.

"Great Pass?" Francesca had not heard of this.

"Yes, it runs from the north under the western peaks and comes out.... well, look I'll show you." The Duke stood up and took her hand and guided her to the window. The hall was high enough in the citadel to be able to see across the courtyard and over the citadel wall.

"Do you see" and he pointed to where the citadel wall met the mountain. On the city side was a set of large doors, each as wide as a cart, and as high as two people.

"Just there, those gates. That's where the Great Pass comes out."

"But of course, "interjected the Guardian, "This would all have been under the water, so they would have had to have been very good swimmers."

"He is right" the duke agreed. "There was no great dam then and so the sea came right up to the mountains."

"And that's what the tribe saw..."

"Yes, Francesca. They sat huddled together on the mountain side..."

"What is now the royal high gardens, is it not?" interrupted Rahim.

The Duke seemed to pause and looked lost. "Yes. Yes. The legend believes so."

The doors to the hall opened and in came three servants, their mission to remove the cleared plates of dinner. The diners all sat silently, watching the servants fulfil their task. Only Francesca smiled at them as they left the room.

Francesca then took over. "For three nights they waited. The Great Serpent did not come, and so they were safe, but with nowhere to go. And then the Great Father sent a meteor passing through the heavens. It stayed in the sky for five more days until, and I like this bit, the meteor glowed from the sun, and it shone a beam of light down onto the waters of the bay. Right to where this citadel sits. Is that right?"

"Well done. Yes, that's what they say. And the Great Father spoke to them through their leader." The Duke continued the story. "They must mine the mountain. Dig caves and prepare great stones. He gave the dimensions and sizes. Only when complete would he send them the means to make this their land.

This they did for one hundred years. Many died, but the tribe grew. They carved the great caves that are within the mountain, and they made the great stones.

And then the meteor appeared again, and the Great Father spoke for the last time. He told him, that a great storm would come, but they were not to be afraid. The seas..."

Francesca continued in a booming deep voice "the seas...would leave the bay, leaving a fertile and safe plain. Four of my angels, Gafael, Gartuli, Sark and err...I can't recall...."

"Gaal" Rahim said.

"Gaal. They will build a great wall to hold back the seas! And that's what they did. The four came and using the great stones built the Great Dam."

"But that's not the end. Is it?" Francesca smiled coyly.

"Gafael found something where the meteor had shone. And he dug deep", said the Duke.

"Tell me what they found? No-one seems to know?"

"No one does know. But they finished the dam, opened the Great Pass and left to go north, taking whatever, they found with them. They fought the Great Serpent and his servants and then settled as our true Gods, and the Great Father was heard of no more." Rahim finished.

"And the tribe prospered." added the Duke.

"Until the Gods wiped them out for their hubris, pride and arrogance," said Rahim. The story seemed to have morphed into a verbal battle.

"For their worship of the Great Father." The Duke jabbed back.

"As I said...their pride. And you, Duke. Do you worship the Gods, or the Great Father?

The Duke recoiled, "Milady, you never ask a man who his god is, that is not polite and can be very dangerous in the wrong company."

"Don't be ridiculous, it's fine," Rahim pulled a strange, disgusted expression then smiled. "I follow Sark, as I'm sure the fair Princess does. The Great Father is long gone."

"So, he has no followers here?" asked Francesca.

"To be honest, I'm not sure he has any followers at all," said the Duke.

"Except the Klarion." said Rahim

"The Klarion?" Francesca

"Yes. They are a tribe from the desert. The Duke knows them well." Rahim looked to the Duke.

"Now their story is very interesting. They are nomads from across the Great Desert, north of the mountains. You sometimes come across them on the edge of cities where they come to trade. In fact, Kosch was a regular trading destination. They would bring all sorts of things from the north to the city, although the sea trade has put quite an end to this." The Duke seemed happier with the direction the conversation had now gone.

"Why do they worship the Great Father?" asked Francesca.

"The Klarion believe they are the descendants of the Xari. Those who escaped the...." replied the Duke.

"It is called "the culling" said Rahim "the legend continued you see. The four angels as, they returned hundreds of years later, led by an army

50

of immeasurable size. They swarmed through the Great Pass and massacred them. None escaped, but no one can be truly sure. The city was then sealed by the followers of the four."

"Can I meet them? Guardian? Can I meet the Klarion?"

"Francesca, there are none in the city...are their Duke?" answered Rahim. Rahim knew very well there were none, thought the Duke. He wiped them out.

"It's a sad tale, Francesca, but yes there are no longer any in the city. Duke Hala, my predecessor had them all... removed," said the Duke.

"Removed" nodded Rahim.

At this point the servants returned with the main courses, set them down in front of the diners and then left the room.

"There must be some left? Where did they all go?" asked Francesca.

The Duke mind flashed back to Duke Hala and the Great Dam. The line of a hundred and twenty-seven Xari stood facing the city along the walkway of the Dam. A hundred and twenty-seven. He had counted them all. He could remember the faces of the first ten vividly, after them he had stopped looking at the faces full of fear and counted their legs.

"So how are you finding the fishcakes?" the Duke asked.

Francesca was prodding them with her knife but had made no attempt to eat them.

"Could we get you something else? What would you like?"

"I would like to see a tribe!" she said calmly without looking up.

"I will bring you a selection of fruit!" the Duke continued. "It's shipped from the north so were low on oranges, but the apples keep well."

He stood up and walked to a side table that was piled with fruit and breads. He threw an apple at the surprised Francesca, who caught it excitedly and began to laugh. The meal carried on, with very little dialogue beyond the odd comment on the weather and the décor of the room.

The Rahim chirped in "Would it be an imposition to find someone to show the Princess around the Citadel tomorrow?"

"Oh, and the city!" beamed Francesca.

"I would not suggest this right now. Settle in, get to know the Citadel first. Yes Rahim, my man Ishman will show you around."

"Oh, not me," Rahim explained, "I think I can remember things. No, I was thinking of sitting in on the council, I believe there is one tomorrow?"

How do you say no to a Guardian, thought the Duke. He didn't trust him or like him. "Of course, I will make sure the clerk summons you."

"Good, it will be most interesting."

7

The Great Council was held in the Citadel in a building adjoining the outer wall. The Council was scheduled to meet every month but could be called by the Duke, or with a member's petition, whenever needed.

For the last few years, the Council had followed the same monotonous agenda items: trade requests, the Emperor's edicts, petty thieving – significant crime was not that widespread. The last few Councils though had started to be dominated by the news from the north of the Empire and the spread of a great pestilence.

Outbreaks of an unknown plague had been initially reported in the cities furthest north but in a matter of months it had spread further south and to all corners of the Empire.

Reports included the numbers of dead and the Empire's attempts at halting what was now being called "The Wraith". Gossip and rumour were racing ahead, spreading its own panic and of course driving refugees south acting as a vanguard of terror. These refugees had come to dominate the Council meetings.

Each session began the same, with the Warden of the Chamber marching ceremoniously down the Grand Hall to the Council chamber doors. In his hands a silver key, the length of his arm, carried on a tray across both of his arms.

Each step the Warden took was an elaborate elongated exercise, where the leg was raised, to its maximum height and then straightened before the Warden then leaned forward to allow the extended leg to hit the ground. The following leg was then dragged to stand parallel.

The doors to the chamber were built by the same architect who built the grand doors of the Great Temple within a few months of the Temple's doors being complete. The Council doors were impressive, the best decoration and carvings seen in the city. Matching the splendour, the four permanent city guards on the chamber dressed in red robes carrying ceremonial curved swords, hanging from their shoulders across their chests, and in their hands twelve-foot lances.

After five years of service, a guard was eligible to a six-month posting on these doors; within the first week all regretted the posting, the only entertainment being the tramping of old Lords in and out and counting the soldiers in the mural of the Great Battle of Aldermar Plains on the opposing wall. On the first day, most questioned why they had the lances, which when lowered touched the mural and thus would be completely ineffective as a weapon. The old set up was about pomp and splendour not practicality.

A few yards behind the Warden followed a huddle of twenty Lords most bent over with age, staggering snail-like towards the chamber. They all wore dark red ceremonial gowns although discoloured with time and dust.

The Warden ceremoniously opened the door, and in walked the Lords. Following behind, was an even greater number of people led by the Clerk of the Chamber. He carried in his hands a small table piled with papers, and behind him the clerk's assistant carrying his chair. As they reached the door, one side swung shut. The clerk setup his chair and table facing the crowd, and then said "First?"

The crowd was a collection of people coming to petition the Council, with complaints, requests, and reports. A mix of dignitaries and soldiers and guild members. Rarely did the lower echelons make it this far, mainly because only twenty-five people were allowed, and the higher echelons were given the primary positions. Additionally, most clerks were not unknown to except payments to ensure a petition is heard.

The clerk acted as the gatekeeper to the Council. He owned the list of who could speak and who could not. The list today was the usual mix of complaints and claims and the Commander of the Watch reporting on events of the week, but most of the petitions were personal requests for family members to be allowed into the city as part of the great migration that was underway.

The clerk sat in silence for an inordinate amount of time. The clerk's assistant counting to a hundred before tapping the clerk on the shoulder; just enough time for the Lords to settle in their seats.

Today saw the continuation of an unofficial custom, the Duke striding down the hall at the last minute, through the petitioning crowd parting like standing corn beneath a reavers scythe. His tardiness reflected the disdain he felt for this Council, this session and the obvious waste of his time. As the clerk stood up to make comment, the guards stared down at their feet, and the Duke strode through the open door.

The chamber inside was lit by a myriad of placed torches that created a mix of bright light with sporadic pockets of darkness. The Lords sat in two rows of five opposite a further two rows of five. The six-foot gap separated by a marble floor stamped with the symbol of the city. Set back from them but in the space between was the plain un-ordained seat of the Duke.

Not a head was raised as the Duke strode across the marble floor, swung around and sat in the chair, not a head turned or reacted. The Lords had played this game too often to give the Duke the pleasure of a shocked reaction.

"So, are we ready to begin?" he bellowed out, opening his arms to the floor and looking dramatically to either side at the Lords.

The Duke feigned an interested smirk waiting for a comment. The silence was broken by the clerk's nervous announcement:

"The Commander of the Watch, my Lords".

Proud and confident, the Commander marched into the chamber, reached the edge of the benches, stopped and stamped his legs together. His uniform was plain, indistinguishable from any other officer except for the five golden lions embossed to his bronze chest plate. They matched the symbolic markings on the floor in front of him. Slowly he removed the plain leather gloves on his hands folded them together then unclasped the satchel hanging beneath his arm. He placed the gloves inside and withdrew a rolled piece of paper, with a plain leather band round it.

The Duke's patience was being pushed to its limit. His eyes staring forward, locked onto the Commander, but his right hand was beginning to drum the arm of his chair. The Commander unravelled the paper and raised it to the level of his head, obscuring it from the audience.

"Week twenty-seven of the Year of Gaal. Fifty-four arrests for violent conduct; one hundred and seven arrests for drunken behaviour. Two illegal drinking houses shut down...."

The Commander then continued with an unbearably dull list of city related activity, including number of traders in debt and bankruptcy orders. All the Lords struggled to maintain some level of attention, until the Duke heard something hidden in the mix. "Wait, four arrested for ill-prophesising? Explain."

The Commander, had rarely, if ever, been interrupted. Afraid of the Duke and his reputation, he looked towards the Lords. The Duke did the same. And there amongst the Lords, was the Guardian. The Dukes felt that his mouth must have hung open. Damn, he was here. The Duke felt transfixed and the Guardian turned his head —just slightly — and met his glare. It felt like a lifetime and then he blinked, and the spell was broken. He took a deep breath. "Speak up, Commander; let's not be afraid of the one thing that may have been of interest within this dull splurge of irrelevant numbers. This is your moment to get some excitement into what appears a miserable life!"

"Yes sir. Yes. Let me look back. Yes, yes, four arrested for ill-prophesising. That's right" the Commander's earlier confidence now evaporated.

"We have a crime of ill-prophesising?" The Duke spun his head enquiring at the Lords. The Lords were now looking up. They pulled quizzical faces, and a few leant towards their neighbours, as if to check the answer. The Duke was drawn like a magnet to the Guardian and as their eyes met again, the Duke realised that the Guardian had not stopped looking at him.

The Commander relived the impasse. "Yes, sir, although it has never been used before."

Before the Duke could ask the next obvious question, one of the Lords slowly raised himself from his seat and like a large cauldron slowly bubbling on a loose stand; his voice emitted a low rumble: "City Creed number 5433 states that it is illegal to carry out any act of preaching or sermonising outside of the walls of the Great Temple. Any gathering of joint prayer or worship outside is considered as an act of preaching or sermonising."

The Lord's tone was dull and monotonous, and the Duke seemed to be struggling to concentrate. The other Lords sat slowly nodding like a collection of metronomes keeping time with a soulless dirge.

"City Creed supplemental to City creed Number 5433 was added stating that any written sermonising or preaching was also subject to the above condition." The Duke lent forward to speak...but the drone continued:

"With the enactment of City Creed supplemental B: it is an offense to predict future events with reference to external divine powers, namely personal or public gods; the City Creeds were incorporated into a new law of ill-prophesying, stating that no individual or group through written or verbal sermonising may attempt to influence public action nor attribute future events to the acts of God or Gods or other divine spirits outside the walls of the Great Temple."

There was silence, as the Lord sat down, punctuated only by various subtle, agreeable murmurs.

"This is a joke?" puzzled the Duke. More murmurs and a few gasps. Then silence.

"I think not, your Lordship". Slowly the Guardian stood up. "I am sure that you meant no offense to our revered fathers." Heads turned and more murmurs. "I request your leave to speak. I am sure that the Lords and our gathered audience will permit this break in protocol for a simple guest of the city" the Guardian's arm swung from his cloak indicating the hordes gathered. "Although one who I am in no doubt is more than qualified in this arena."

"Let me explain," he began. "My name is Guardian Rahmin." Everyone now paid attention. "A little-known law among the uneducated and working classes. Very rarely needed with the populaces general distrust of false prophets, and with the Guild of Seers control of all prophesising and prediction."

He gestured with his hands towards an old figure sat in the opposite chairs, a figure round and portly with the golden pontiff on his head denoting his role as Chief Seer to the City. The Seer acknowledged the reference and smiled towards the Duke.

"You see, quite rightly, the Lords had fought against the power of the Gods, fearing that it would undermine civil responsibility and trust in the Lords as primary decision makers on civil matters. Something that, in truth, was never demonstrated by the people of the city." The Guardian stressed the final few words, another dig at the Duke's apparent abuse of power, but it was the other Lords that seemed to squirm in their seats.

"Maybe the creed worked?" The Guardian continued. "The arrival of the Temples residents did raise a more likely risk. Outside of the Guild of Seers, this made very little impression but following some early protestations by the new residents, several charlatans and soothsayers arrived. They have generally kept to themselves, but it was felt prudent that we limit their influence. By containing their prediction of personal events for deluded citizens (mainly visitors and foreigners) this law has never been needed to be enforced. Of course, the main body of the populace looks to that civil prophesying of our eminent Lord and the Guild of Seers."

A final bow from Rahmin and he resume his seat. The Duke looked hard at Rahmin, a predator assessing the danger of bait held out to him. How to remove himself from this potentially embarrassing moment?

"We welcome Guardian Rahmin to our Council." The Duke responded and then gently nodded to Ishman. Ishman, stood behind the Clerk, whispered in his ear.

"Welcome, Lord Rahim. Your holiness" he started. Rahim smiled, a theatrically waved the formality away with embarrassment.

"Yes welcome. You are welcome it's just that" he looked up at the Duke "there is a protocol. The petitioner or reporter makes their statement, and the Council, just the Council make their queries. Not, not the, not you"

The Duke's point was made. The Duke could now be magnanimous.

"Clerk, I think for the emperor's representative we can forego the protocols. Rahim, please come take a seat...." The Duke's canny skills did not desert him and acting on a tiny thought battling away in his mind, he turned to the Commander and asked: "So, what have the four men said?"

"Said my Lord?" the Commander stuttered.

"Yes, what did our latest four hardened religious criminals say that has caused – quite rightly – the full force of the law to descend on them?"

"They said nothing my Lord." The Commander eyes darted backwards and forwards looking for some support from the Lords. "Rather, they wrote something. Wrote on the walls of the Great Temple, that is."

"And what did they write?" Another long silence. A sense of dread seemed to be hovering in the room like a physical presence. All felt it.

"Ezkebal.... Ezkebal is coming...the end of times is nigh." The Commander blurted the last few words out then locked his eyes closed like a child wishing ghosts away from his bed chamber. A deep intake of breath came from a few of the Lords, but generally the mood of the room remained unchanged.

"Is that it?" The Duke broke the silence. "Is that it? Tell me, what is the punishment?"

"Again, the Commander looked desperately around the chamber, hoping that somebody else would answer the question. No-one did. Nervous shuffling extenuated the silence.

"Death" whispered the Commander, expecting something less violent.

"Death for writing on the walls?", the Duke's face screwed up in confusion. "Death?" he almost whispered. Then the voice of the Chief Seer bellowed out with confidence and an unexpected power.

"Death, Lord Duke. The punishment for ill-prophecy is death by suffocation. A fitting end to those who use their mouths to expel such rubbish."

"Except they wrote it!" replied the Duke. The silence finally embarrassed the Seer. "Indeed"

"May I suggest we continue with the briefing as time is precious, although I'm sure the less time we have for the popular plaintiffs the better", interjected the clerk. Even the Duke joined in the scattering of laughter that filled the chamber. The Commander finished off his list and then departed just as quickly.

The session carried on with some minor speeches and commentary from the various Lords before the Clerk announced the next section of the agenda. The clerk exited the room and re-entered to a brief flurry of noise and colour from behind the doors. With him was a well-dressed citizen with a pile of papers under his arms.

"Lords, Citizen Garland, an innkeeper from the docks section. He requests the closure of his current outstanding ban on selling alcohol to city guards."

"Very well, citizen" answered the Duke. "How long has your ban been in place?"

"Sixteen months, sir"

"According to the order, it was a twelve-month ban, Lord Duke" interrupted the Clerk.

"Why have you not requested this earlier, citizen?"

"With respect, Lord Duke, I have posted letters to this affect every week since the ban was due to finish, but they have been unheeded, and the order is still posted to my doors and windows. This is the third time I have come to the council, but the first I have had the honour of being presented, your Lord."

"Clerk is there any reason why this should not be overturned?" asked the Duke. The clerk rummaged through his papers and slowly shook his head. "No, Lord Duke"

"Ban receded" the Duke announced. "Be gone."

The plaintiffs who followed were of a similar style, with requests for closure of a competitor's shop, the repair of a public water fountain, all of which led the Duke to finally lose his patience. "The next plaintiff is the last, Clerk."

A crowd of twenty or thirty stood disappointed as Havar the Baker confidently entered the chamber. He walked in proud, as if he was a foreign dignitary issuing a declaration of war to the Council.

Before the clerk could speak, he began to deliver the speech he had been practising all night and whilst waiting in the queue.

"My Lords, I come to you not just with pleading arms of a poor baker but also with the terrifying woes of my whole community who suffer unimaginable terrors on a daily basis." The baker's arms were cast to the heavens, torture racked across his face. His eyes imploring and downcast, expressing sorrow like an exaggerated clown. Then in a further act of drama he dropped to his knees;

"My Lords, it is an insufferable bane that curses our marketplace and is an abomination of our great city. Grown men scared to maintain their shops after darkness, wives refusing to walk the streets, children cowering beneath their bed covers weeping, afraid that they will not see the dawn. My lords, Lord Duke we are struck by an evil pestilence that is bringing your city to its knees. Help us, save us from the terror of the nights, save us from the watching eyes. Save us!"

With this Havar collapsed to the floor his performance over. The community had chosen well in sending him, he decided. It reflected his superior role in the city traders of the market square.

So, what that he had contributed more to the bribe for the clerk to get him near the front of the queue, and how lucky that he was the last to be heard. He raised his head slowly, dramatically.

"I thank you, my Lords".

The Duke offered a slow clap. "Thank you, Thank you, Mr Baker. At last, some drama and excitement to liven up these laborious Council chambers. Tell me more of your tale of 'unimaginable terrors', please tell us more."

He signalled to the wider chamber, stepped down and offered his hand to the Baker. Havar took it and unsure of what was going on pulled himself up and thanked the Duke.

"Don't worry about them; they just need a good story to liven them up. Go on tell your tale." Reassured the Duke, noticing a moment of nervousness in the baker.

"Well, my Lord, my Lords" the baker voice had lost all its earlier theatre and he struggled to find his confidence. "At dawn yesterday the Beast of the Rooftops attacked me as I set up my stall for the day."

"Attacked you? The Beast of the rooftops. Tell us more!" the Duke teased the Baker.

"Yes, the beast! He knocked me to the floor and then stole food from my stall, before clambering up to the roofs of the city and disappeared."

"What did he steal, Mr Baker?" chirped in Rahmin.

"Cakes, my Lord, I sell the finest cakes in the city."

"Cakes, mmm, this is very serious" the sarcasm and impatience oozed out of Lord Rahmin.

"Go on Mr Baker. You talk of a terror – what is this beast?" the Duke continued to encourage Havar.

"Yes, well. It started as rumour and legend over the last year. Several traders have reported seeing a cat like beast, just larger than a child, who scours the rooftops. You'd catch site of something and on your second look it would be gone. It became our own little local legend, something we began to use as a way of chastising our children...'get to your room or the beast will get you'.

We didn't notice the stealing at first as we suffer this from the urchins anyway – not that your guards aren't thorough of vigilant my lord. But a few weeks ago, I spotted the beast stretching down from the roof of my store and grabbing a whole loaf of bread. It looked at me and my lord it was no cat, but a demon!"

Some of the drama had returned to the baker's performance and he had managed to capture at least some of the Lord's attention.

"A demon my lord. The body of a cat, but it turned its face towards me, and it was the face of a man! Eyes of fire –red, its skin black as soot. Its teeth, that of a ravenous wolf. Dripping from its mouth was rancid saliva. It hissed at me then fled to the roofs."

"Since then, it has grown bolder. Stealing from houses, attacking children and scratching them, it haunts our night times. We fear what is next, the market has seen customers dropping off; we have seen it crouched like a gargoyle on the roofs hissing at customers."

"Well, that is some tale Mr Baker!" the Duke nodded with false agreement "my Lords, have you ever heard of such terror, surely this is of far more gravitas than the writing of a few scrawny words on the walls of the temples? Do you not agree?"

The Duke was enjoying himself now. He had the lords on the back foot. Most were staring at their feet; the Chief Seer was turning a violent shade of red.

"And what is it Mr Baker that you think we should do?". The Baker stood unable to speak. Then slowly and calculated Rahmin stood up. "If I may make a suggestion?"

What's he up to, thought the Duke. "Of course, Lord Rahim."

"Something similar was seen in the city of Korali. It seemed quite a minor thing. A vagabond called "the sleeper" was strangling children in their beds at night." There was an audible gasp of shock. "Only a few deaths, and miniscule compared to the muggings and robberies, and murders that were known in the ghettos, but it was new and did catch the imagination.

In the time of Duke Hala, we saw how easily a normally peaceful people on edge and unnerved by… well, a misguided leader…, could be stimulated to unexpected barbarity by a threat that grips the popular imagination.

Of course, I have just arrived, I bow to your knowledge, my lords, but I will ask: do you want to see the masses storming the citadel walls?"

"I think not," said the Duke.

"Of course, it is. My apologies. Just... the walls were breached at Korali...and...innocents killed. Sons and daughters murdered in the safety of their rooms, citadels and gardens." The final word was preceded by a pause. All knew the inference Rahim was making. The Duke looked furious. The Lord justice stood up." We must act. I propose an immediate enquiry and establish a task force to eradicate the city of this vile menace!"

Rahmin looked hawk-like into the Duke's eyes. Inadvertently biting his bottom lip, the Duke nodded slowly and gestured to the clerk. "Raise an edict!" and then in one motion he left his seat, brushed past the baker – almost knocking him sideways – and headed towards the door, his long red cloak's tail dragging on the floor raising a small cloud of dust. "Session is ended!"

Rahmin, leant back on his seat and smiled, his jaw resting between his index and remaining fingers.

***

Bursting into his chamber the fury had not left the Duke. It was visible in the extreme scarleting of his face, and the whirlwind movements through the Citadel buildings. Slamming the door of his office he yelled at the secretary. "Rahmin! That rich, in-bred politico!", the Duke arms launched his red cloak through the air like a fisherman pitching his net. The secretary gathered in what he could almost stumbling across the desk.

"He has made a fool of me in my chamber! My chamber! I will not let this stand.

My daughter is sacrosanct! Sacrosanct!" The rage was now contained to his face and his fist, as he brought the latter crashing to his desk. The shudder emanated across the desk, and a pile of papers at the side of his desk, began to totter as if about to descend in a cataclysmic manner. Quills spilled out and before the secretary could catch the tower of paper the cataclysm met its peak and the papers collapsed to the floor in waves of parchment in many directions.

8

Rahmin sat down in his chair on the balcony looking out over the city. He was pleased with how much he had achieved in such a short space of time.

He hated this city. It was dank, ugly and foul smelling, compared to the beautiful cities of the north. But it had a purpose. He of all the Guardians perhaps was the safest from the plague sweeping the north; and it was sweeping the north. The Emperor had lost control, and everyone was running out of ideas. Everyone accept Rahim, that is.

He relaxed and smiled. This city was to be his refuge, and perhaps something more, but for that he needed control. Yes, he was a Guardian, but he could not just sweep in a rule the city. The Duke was strong but he had only a handful of guards. As he thought about the twenty or so men he had with him, he looked across at the pile of chests which he still had not unpacked.

He knew the Duke hated him, but he had no right to. The events of the past were not his responsibility, well not solely. Duke Hala was mad, but his views on the Xari matched the Emperor's and more importantly the Gods. He knew this first-hand.

His plan was only partially thought through before he arrived as he would see the lay of the land and develop it from there. He wasn't sure how chasing this idiotic beast would benefit him, but if guards were bogged down in a hunt for a needle in a haystack, then that couldn't be a bad thing. And if the Duke fails, well good. "He can't even catch a cat!" he whispered out loud.

Of course, if the Duke has any sense, he will bury this. He will find some junior clerk to appoint in charge and post the edict on the square of this baker, to keep him quiet.

Slowly he started to unpack the great chests he had brought with him. Most were just clothes and books but there were several older looking chests that he left unopened.

Into the afternoon he read through some of the books and started some correspondence. As dusk started to darken his chamber, he returned to his seta and watched the sunset from his balcony.

Finally, the hunger that he had had ever since he could remember started to come on and he decided that a trip into the heart of the city was required. He gathered his cloak and headed out of his room. He journeyed down the dark, tall stairs into the courtyard and out to the Citadel gates. He would not need a guard with him for this evening, but it took some convincing to make the Citadel Guard open the gate.

"I will only be a few hours, and I assume re-entry won't be a problem?"

"Of course, your Lordship." And out into the city, the Guardian went.

***

The Beast returned that evening and sat watching the Temple into the night. He was used to sitting, waiting and watching. He had eaten only a little and he felt the pangs of hunger starting. He wouldn't be able to sleep without eating, and the markets had all packed up. There was no point checking for fallen fruit as the street gangs would have already done that.

He climbed up the roof and for the first time all day felt comfortable enough to stand fully erect and stretch. He looked around the city. He wasn't high up so could only see the roofs and the mountains. Ahead was the Great Dam, dark and sullen and only visible because of the line of lights on its high walkway.

The city had calmed down from its normal busy activity. He liked the hustle and bustle it gave him something new to think about. The recent arrivals at the dock were colourful and exciting. The different noises and smells, the songs and fights. They were all interesting, but they were not what he was looking for.

It was very late now and the man he had seen had not left the Temple. Perhaps, he misunderstood the look, perhaps it was just...but he couldn't find an answer. He sat longer and then decided he would leave and come back in the morning.

He clambered over the rooftops and headed towards one of his usual hideaways. He stopped further on and leant against a chimney of a tannery. They would have stopped working at this time but the chimney would still be warm from the fires that they left on. He always came here when the loneliness bit. He told himself it was for the heat, but most nights were warm enough, and even when the winter came, he never really felt the cold.

No, he came here for one reason. The skylight. The tannery had a sky light to let the light into the upper workshop below. When the lights were out it was like looking in a mirror. The blackness below reflecting his emptiness.

He had stolen a mirror once but smashed it that same day. His reflection was like a ghost that he could not bear to see every day, but that he was drawn to when the emptiness hurt. He heard laughing in the street below. Late night drunks. His hearing was good, and he could hear the mother yelling at them that they had woken her children. They responded by swearing and laughing.

He leant over and looked in the skylight. Who was he? What was he? There was no-one like him in the city. No-one. Thousands came to the docks, but there was no-one like him. No-one.

His skin was so dark. Not the dark that the dock workers had. That was lighter, sometimes redder. No, his was smooth like the colour of the wood.

He heard a movement behind him. It could be metres away, but it made him turn. He imagined himself more like the birds who flew to the skies before the rains came, than the people below who sensed nothing until it landed on their heads.

There was no-one behind him, but he made his way to the nearest edge. As he did so he could here movement below. It would be the street gangs. Yet there was something different. Something was on the roofs with him. He couldn't see them, but they were close. He decided to move on. He was fast on the roofs and if there was someone up here, he would leave them far behind.

The hunger was beginning to bite. He mainly ate in the early morning, raiding the market or the kitchens through open windows whilst the city dwellers were unaware. Sometimes he had been forced to kills birds and rodents but cooking them was so difficult without shelter from the wind that he hated doing it. Anyway, he loved the bread. The bakers would be shut this late, and so he made his way north of the city towards the Citadel.

The Citadel always had food, but it was tricky. He would need to cross the walls and avoid the guards. The stores were always full and easy to get into. There was one store where he had loosened enough tiles to be able to enter easily without going through the doors. He felt the movement again, but it was further back. He scanned the roofs but saw nothing. He decided he would continue to the Citadel, if there was someone following him, they would need to be wary of the guards too, and probably would be too cautious to cross the walls.

9

Francesca woke looking forward to the day. The first day had been interesting but she had been too tired from the journey. It was great to have met and spoken to someone other than the Guardian, though. The journey across the north to get here had had its moments of interest but Rahim never let her stray far, and they had moved from city to city very quickly, sometimes even avoiding stopping for more than a day.

She opened the curtains to the balcony and walked out to view the city. It was an incredible sight, and she was desperate to explore it. She was being shown round the Citadel today, but without the watchful eye of the Guardian she was sure she could manipulate her guide.

Francesca found this city so unlike hers. There were no great green parks, white spacious houses, or cherry trees. Rahim sees the grubby and dirtiness of the city, but she just saw the opportunities. Her father was overprotective. Actually, her father's advisors were overprotective. Even in the capital she was not allowed out.

Most of her life had been spent in the library, with her tutor or in the walled garden. She would like a garden here. The balcony was large and had seats and plants but if she stretched, she could walk it in three strides. The knock at the door was no surprise. This was the Duke's "Man". His servant she supposed.

"Milady" The man bowed as she opened the door. Ishman waited for permission to enter. Francesca was use to this, but unlike her servants back home, this man seemed friendlier, less scared she supposed. "I wonder if you could tell me something." She clasped Ishman's hand, and stared at him, whilst pulling him into the room, with her widest eyes she could muster.

"Of course, milady"

"You see, I think I made an awful fool of myself with the Duke last night." Whispered Francesca.

71

"Surely not. The Duke…"

"No, I did. You see his wife. His daughter. What happened?" Ishman was taken aback. He quickly formulated in his mind what he should or should not say. "Well, it's no secret milady., but I would not worry about it, it was long ago."

"Yes, I know … but still" she squeezed harder. Ishman knew there would be no easy escape here and after all she was a princess.

"Well let's sit." He pointed towards a stone bench against the wall of the Citadel and they sat down. "Well, it was about ten years ago. The Duke was married to Lady Jane. She was a local girl from one of the merchant families.

"She was pretty?"

"Milady, she was beautiful. The Duke was smitten. It was a great love story. The city was very excited, and the wedding day was spectacular. Hundreds were in the courtyard here, and beyond the walls." Francesca smiled at the word beautiful, excitement building.

"Anyway. The Lady was soon with child, and we all looked forward to the new arrival. The city had been through some tough times before the Duke took over. Very tough times."

"She died in childbirth?"

"Yes. The birth was long and hard. The Duke was away, summoned north, it was a week before he made it back. By that time, Lady had died, and he had a daughter… Grace" Francesca could see his eyes were beginning to fill with tears. She clasped his hand.

"He was devastated. His anger and grief were unbridled. We had to have the funeral of Lady Jane before he returned. As was the custom of her family she was given up to the sea beyond the Dam. The Duke was inconsolable. He demanded that the fishermen retrieve her body. It never happened; he eventually knew the foolhardiness of this. But he did walk the walls of the Dam for day as and nights. He barely saw his new daughter.

"Did she die young, too?"

"Ah, milady this talk is too sad, do not make me recall those days. They were worse days."

"I'm sorry...so sorry. She died of the plague?"

"No. No there was no plague then. It was seven years later. By then she had begun to fill the hole in the Duke's heart. She became his world, but the Duke was overprotective. He would not leave the city, and she would seldom leave the Citadel. The gardens in the mountains were renovated and turned into her own little kingdom.

Ishman stood up and pulled Francesca with him. They stepped back until they could see the mountain beyond the Citadel. "Up there, high up. You can make out some greenery if you look hard." Francesca couldn't see anything, but she didn't let on.

"Can we go there?"

"No. Few go there now. I sometimes do. It's quite peaceful, but it's generally shut off, and the paths are quite tricky."

"Is that where she died?" Francesca took a guess, but she wanted to know.

"Yes. Yes, it was." They were silent for a while. Ishman turned and made his way back into the room.

"I will show you the Council chamber. The Duke is there with councillors as we speak. We will see if we can peak in, shall we?"

"It's just that I don't want to ask the Duke. I think it would upset him..."

Ishman took a deep breath. "Very well. Milady. She was found dead in the garden. She was...she was just lying there, peaceful. Like she was just resting on a bench. She looked so much like her mother. She looked asleep. But she wasn't asleep. Her throat was blue, bruised, her face porcelain white."

"Strangled?"

"Yes"

"Who found her? Was it the Duke?"

"No. It was a servant. A servant of the Dukes"

"Did they find the monster who did it? Was it the servant? A guard?"

"It was the Klarion, milady. People form the northern desert."

"Did they catch them? How did they know?"

The servant paused and considered for a while, looking hard at this impudent but delightful girl. "It was a mystery for a while. Perhaps a guard a servant. But a necklace was eventually found. A silver chain and the Lord Justice and the Duke by chance figured it out."

"Grace had talked of an imaginary friend they she met in the garden. The lady had lots of these imaginary friends; she would have places filled at the table next to her. We all thought it was cute. But this one she said was the colour of burnt bread. She had obviously seen a Klarion from her balcony or on her rare excursions to the city. Well, they all wore silver chains, just like the one found." Francesca held her hand to her mouth.

"The Duke's grief was terrible. This time nothing would stop him. The last of the Klarion had been removed from the city years before, but he sent men to scour the city. A few had been seen in inns and at the docks or peddling to travellers through the Great Pass. There were false alarms and witch-hunts, but they never came to anything. The villain was never caught."

"He must hate them." Francesca commented.

"Yes…there are none in the city and none are allowed to enter. It was enough to stop the Duke sending an army through the pass to attack those that still lived in the desert. But he calmed eventually. His temper can be wild, but it does calm."

"I imagine he would never get over something like that."

"No, he has calmed but he has never got over it. Never."

They made their way from the room and made their way to the heart of the Citadel. Along the halls, Ishman pointed out paintings and the stories behind them. Eventually they made their way to the Council chamber.

The path to the Council chamber took them out of the main Citadel on a high uncovered walkway. Francesca was pleased to have a burst of fresh air, although the wind blew her hair into her eyes, and she had to keep sweeping it away. Both were unaware that in those brief moments in the open air, that they were being watched. Only a few storeys above, laying on the roof of the Council chamber, was the beast.

The night before he had made his way eventually to the Citadel store, eaten his fill then retreated to a safe alcove in the eaves of the Council roof. There he had slept.

And now he was watching. He normally would be well hidden by this time of the morning, but something had drawn him to watching the movements around the courtyard. And now he saw the two walking close by and he recognised the girl. She had been with the soldiers all dressed in gold, yesterday on the dock. He had never seen anything like them before.

They had captured his attention then, but now he could see that she was fascinating. She was so pale, not the olive colour of most of the city. She looked so fragile. And the hair was so golden. And then she smiled. It was like the reveal of a diamond necklace. She sparkled. He watched her as she stood. She suddenly laughed at something and held her hand to her mouth. He watched until eventually they were out of sight.

**

10

The Duke's anger had not lasted long. It had been a week since the Council meeting and although he had screamed abuse in his private quarters about Rahim, by the next day he had calmed down.

Ishman had let the Duke vent his anger, and in the meantime, he had begun the process of organising the hunt for the beast. The Duke had also kept clear of the Guardian, who had spent most of the time in his chamber.

Francesca had started to go a bit crazy being stuck in the Citadel, and this had led to the bizarre image of Rahim's golden guard marching through the city surrounding her, whilst Ishman pointed out the sites. This amounted to basically visiting the market, the Dam and the Temple. It had left her frustrated and, on her return, she had begun to plot how she could get out on her own.

The beast had made a point of being more discreet in this period. Signs had gone up offering rewards for information about him and so he had kept a low profile. For a few days this meant eating birds until he spotted Francesca outside the Temple.

After that he had made his way to the Citadel at night to feed from the stores, but also to catch another glimpse of her. The last few nights and early mornings he had watched her on her balcony and listened to her sing. They were not the usual songs of the city. They were softer, gentler, sweeter.

It had suited him to be away from the main city as much as possible. When not at the Citadel he would be hiding in the high tower at the Temple. He had not seen the old man again, but he had seen a lot of commotion in the market square outside.

Five days ago, hundreds of parchments had been nailed to city squares and thoroughfares, including the market. One had even been nailed to the Temple doors although it had quickly been removed. There were also far more guards on the streets, standing guard or as patrols wandering the city.

Ark had climbed as far down as possible to hear a guard read aloud the proclamation. Like him, many in the city could not read for themselves

"It is announced today the fifth day of Mercy that in response to a serious civil threat an edict has been raised, to investigate, act on and vanquish the said threat. The Council has reported that a dangerous beast has been terrifying the city and that its actions will no longer be tolerated.

All resources will be available to the City Guard and we have appointed Commander Gross to oversee the operation. If you have information that pertains to this matter immediately report to the Excise Office at the foot of the Eastern Stair to the Great Dam. Your vigilance and support are expected.

By order of the Great Council of Kursch."

Ark reeled back in shock. People gathered round the guard and immediately started looking up and down, left and right. Ark scampered along the rooftops as fast as he could, scattering moss and dirt beneath his feet. Loosened slates slipped beneath him and rattled down the roof flying into the free air below.

With a violent crash they hit the cobbles below scattering shards as well as the assembled crowd. Screams went up and shocked shouts filled the air. Ark dare not look back he just kept on running, then leaping between two buildings landing awkwardly on the new roof.

He grabbed at the tiles and pulled himself up, not daring to look back at the noises coming from behind and below. His mind was filled with flashes of the past, of years racing across the rooftops with his brother. The images throbbed in his mind with the pain of each hard slap of his hands and feet against the slates and tiles.

Then he felt something hit him. Stones from below pelting him in his sides and against his head. The crowd of the market were picking up loose cobbles at launching them at him. He couldn't avoid them but fortunately the force of them was weak and barely hurt. When he heard a higher pitched whistle, he spun his body to narrowly avoid a guard's spear flying past and rattling against the tiles and then sliding over the ridge of the apex of the roof then sliding down away on the rear side of the roof.

Instinctively Ark dived after it, disappearing from the sight of the crowd over the ridge. He rolled and rolled before halting his descent by grabbing at the gap in a roof tile. He juddered but stopped, hearing the sound of the spear hitting the ground below.

He managed to clear his head enough to take a deep breath and consider his options. He looked around and spotted he was within two buildings of the side of the Great Temple. He quickly calculated the number and position of the windows on the side. If he made it to the first, he could climb up to the spire.

In a crouching run he made his way along the roof still hidden from the crowd on the market side, although he could sense the alleyways and avenues were filling with voices. He leapt from the first roof across an empty alleyway onto a slightly higher roof, ever closer to the Great Temple.

The end of the next roof was soon upon him, and he leapt across the gathering heads in the alley below to reach the final roof. He no longer stooped but just ran before launching himself with a fantastic leap towards the ledge of the lowest Temple window.

He flew through the air, legs kicking scissor like and arms extended scrambling for the ledge. The fingertips of his left hand caught the ledge and he let out a breath before hitting the wall. The thump knocked the last air out of his lungs, but he clung on. He looked down, and the gap between the building he leapt from, and the Temple was too narrow for a crowd to form in. He was clear if he could pull himself up.

Adrenaline pumped though his veins and he threw his right hand up and used the momentum to pull up onto the ledge. He was soon standing and spinning round he looked down at the market and rooves.

The market was spilling over with guards swamping the usual shoppers and traders. There was still a mix of shouts and screams as panic was spreading like an out-of-control fire.

Ark could wait and hide on the ledge or climb higher. Before long he would be spotted if he stayed put, but if he climbed further, he would be seen.

He leant back against the window, trying to get further inside the stone frame of the window, and the glass seemed to shift backwards. Ark grasped the stone frame, suddenly fearing he would topple in.

The window stayed put, and ark reached to touch it gently. It moved a little, and he could see that the cement surrounding it was crumbling. He wiped away cobwebs and dust and looked inside. It was dark and he couldn't make out anything inside, but he decided to push the window anyway.

The window budged a little, it would require a substantial push to open or full in. He threw his shoulder at the window near its edge, hoping not to break the glass. The window shifted and with a second push it fell inwards. Ark sensed it falling, how far he did not know until a second later it clattered onto a wooden surface. The whole window had fallen in and landed on a high walkway in the Temple. Ark leapt in expecting to hear shouts but there was just silence.

His eyes adjusted to the darkness, and he quickly began to flee along the walkway, before he stopped. He grabbed the fallen window and wedged it back in the stone frame. The glass was broken but perhaps this would fool people for a while. He left the glass on the walkway and made his way into the darkness.

11

The Bursars at the Great Temple were at a loss of what to make of the traveller. Since his arrival he had spoken briefly to Ravi but had since then had locked himself away in the cell that they had made ready for him.

Ravi would be summoned at various points of the day, but no-one else. The traveller did not take prayer with them, other than that first night, when he had lead prayers perfectly. Ravi would exit the cell each time with requests for food, water, and books. One of the junior Bursars had joked to Ravi that he must be eating them in there. Ravi eventually gathered the priests and Bursars together to discuss what he knew.

Some of the priests were frustrated. Here was someone obviously sent by the Gods but for some reason was ignoring them. Others had argued that perhaps he was just a beggar who had once been a priest and knew a few phrases that had got him free room and board.

"He is definitely a strange sort." Ravi began. "First of all, he has asked that he is not disturbed. Secondly, that no-one is informed of his presence until he allows it."

"Has he said who or what he is?" asked one of the Bursars.

"He has just said he should be known as Sern. Listen, I know this is unorthodox, but my gut tells me that he is genuine. I have prayed on it, and the texts and books he has asked for, some are in languages older than time, no ordinary beggar – who may or may not have been a priest could read them."

"And are you sure he is reading them?"

"Just this morning, he called me closer to one of the books open on his table. It was in North script. He pointed and said, "This passage refers to the teachings of Aber, it tells of the tribe recording these teachings. Where would they be? Are they here?"

83

I replied that we have nothing that old, but Aber is the one word I recognise in North script; it's the word for the Great Father, and yes it was written in the book."

"It could still be a trick."

"Yes, but what beggar spends his time reading, and eats so little." There was quiet and a few convinced nods.

"Do you have an idea who he is? He says he is not a God."

"No, he is not a God. My guess is he is a Guardian, sent to find something out."

"Why two Guardians?" asked another Bursar.

"What do you mean?" replied Ravi. Ravi had not been aware of any other Guardian in the city.

"Well, I was talking to one of the bakers and he said that there is a Guardian in the Citadel, from the Emperor." There was quiet.

"I will speak to the Chief Seer and ask him" Ravi finally replied.

"But you said, he said that you were not to tell anyone. If he is a Guardian, then they can cause a lot of trouble."

"There will be no trouble in the Temple. That is the Law. No Guardian would dare break that." Ravi responded, forcibly, raising his tone a few decibels. This was all getting a bit too out of hand, he thought. Life was a lot easier before this traveller arrived.

Then the bell went. Each cell had a bell outside, a legacy of the days when the Temple's western side cells had been used as a hospice. The sick would ring for help.

"That's him, again" said Ravi and he got up and left the others.

The traveller had been busy the last few days. His mission was clear, but the route to completion very much elusive. He had searched most of the northern coastal cities on his journey to find an answer to a crisis that even the Gods now feared.

Many believed the plague was sent by the Gods, but it wasn't. There had been plagues before, but they would burn themselves out, with perhaps a city or two laid wastes. This was different, though. He had not seen the beginning of it, his homeland was immune from such suffering, but when he had arrived in Cartex, his first port of call, he was shocked by the devastation. The city was so ridden with the dying that all order had broken down. The boat would not land, and he was glad. The docks had an eerie silence. Heading south things were better, although some cities were checking passengers as they disembarked.

His mission was simple: find the cure to the plague. The Gods were either cared for their subjects, or more likely were worried for themselves. He was not sure which but that did not affect the mission. He never believed in their complete knowledge of the world, of all its secrets. After all there was life before the Gods.

So, in each city he had searched for answers. He had met the sick, the doctors, the seers, and the prophets. He sought out secret societies, criminals, anyone who could have an answer. He scoured the public and private libraries of each city, digesting page upon page of history, science and religion. He had even resorted to some of the old hags of the forest which had been highly unsuccessful, and his experiences had made him weary of ever engaging with them again. And now here in Kursch, perhaps the oldest city of the Empire, perhaps the city with the most secrets.

And now the traveller had begun to exhaust the parchments and books stored in the Temple. Ravi appeared at the cell door. "What now, My Lord". He only showed a slight indication of his impatience, but it was there.

"Yes. The tribe. What do we know of the Tribe?"

"Not much. This Temple is to The Gods, not the Great Father."

"Milord. "Ravi ventured. "The others they are curious, they are nervous. They fear that you may have…. unknown motives for being here." The traveller did not look-up from a tome he had lifted from the floor and Ravi was sensing he could push more. "I must see the Great Seer this week and I do not keep secrets from him."

After a long pause, and a looking away from his book, the traveller turned and asked, "Who is the Great Seer? What is he?"

"Are yes. The Great Seer is quite unique. In the other cities I think he is the equivalent of a Guardian. Here we are a bit different, but the outcome is the same. He is head of all the religious functions of the city, including the Temple."

"What else?"

"Well, any religion. He defends the rights of visitors who worship other gods. He controls the tithes and who can sell religious artefacts..."

"Is he here? In this building?" The traveller now looked up from the books and directly at Ravi. Ravi found it a bit disconcerting.

"Oh no, no. He resides at the Citadel. He is on the Duke's Council, and he visits here as required."

"But not often?"

"Enough, I suppose."

"I should see him. Can that be arranged?"

"Of course. Of course. I go to the Citadel tomorrow. Come with me and I will introduce you."

Ravi left the room and made his way to the main hall. He could hear rumbling of noises from beyond the great doors, louder than the usual noises of the market. Then he heard a breaking noise from above. He looked up and cursed the junior monks for dropping something again.

12

"Say that again" the Duke asked the Commander standing in front of him. He was sat in the chair of the Council chamber. There was no Council on, but today he had deemed this a better place to meet with the highly strung officer.

"Sir, we have hundreds of people queuing at the Excise Office wanting to provide information in regard to the edict. They just keep coming sir."

"And this is my problem?" the Duke rallied back at him.

"Calm, sir" Ishman touched his arm. "This is ridiculous." Sighed the Duke.

Ishman addressed the Commander, "Why is that a problem, Commander? They will soon disappear when the sun drops, or they get hungry!"

"I have taken over fifty statements just today!" the Commander said, "and dispatched guards to investigate each..."

"But found nothing. I presume." Finished the Duke.

"Yes sir. There are those who had seen the beast; those who knew someone who has seen the beast; those who always knew there was something wrong but had not known what; and those who just lived off the ravings of others."

"Nothing of substance?" asked Ishman.

"No"

"And the patrols?" Ishman continued.

"Nothing sir"

"Maybe we have scared it off." proposed the Duke. "Answer me this. Has this beast actually killed anyone?"

The Commander paused. "Well, yes sir." The Commander looked scared. "It was horrific, sir. There has been a killing. A mother and her child."

"My God!" hissed the Duke.

"The people...well few know. We have shut off the building."

"Who was it? Who was the victim?"

"We don't know yet. They were found in a workshop, the tannery overlooking the eastern canal so I assume she was a beggar sleeping in there rather than someone work late, but I could be wrong."

"Have you seen anything like this before? Anything in the last few weeks."

"Nothing like this. It's not the street gangs' style. Whoever did this didn't hang around for a long time. And the way they died. It was like all the blood had been sucked out of them. They were white and nothing more than skin and bones." The Duke considered this. Word would get out. The city was just like that.

And he was right. City inns and restaurants were packed and had become hotbeds of rumour and speculation. The only other gathering of people was at the docks, and the Temple. The docks saw the normal crowds of people, but, if possible, with an increased buzz. The Temple was a different story. Across the course of the day people had gathered on its steps, initially ones and twos, but now hundreds. The Temple doors stayed shut.

***

For Lilkin, the next few days were particularly galling. People were being too careful. Staying in large groups, checking behind them, and avoiding the shadows. Even the guards were staying in groups and the number of them, and frequency of patrols had made the gangs activity next to impossible.

This has led to more extreme measures. Right now, they were watching the back of one of the inns near the dock side where people were still gathering. The wait had been long, but eventually a figure emerged from the rear door of the inn out into the alleyway. He was obviously drunk and staggered between the beer barrels stored outside. He stopped and leant against two on top of each other and preceded to urinate against them.

One of the gang audibly spat in disgust. To be followed by a group whisper of hush. The man hadn't noticed. He finished what he was doing and then attempted to retrace his steps. Lilkin was ready to pounce, when he suddenly he heard further voices from the rear of the Inn as out came two guards.

Will helped Garick through the door of the inn into the courtyard. It was not often that he saw his superior drunk but tonight the sergeant had really gone for it. After what they had seen today, he wasn't surprised.

It had been Garick who had found the body in the tannery. Sometimes the homeless would go there as the fires were left on throughout the night and the owner was not the most vigilant. Will had always thought that if there was ever to be a city-wide fire it would probably start there.

Garick had taken the hunt for the beast seriously. He was convinced there was nothing supernatural about it and it was just one of the street gangs. The edict had given him the excuse to carry out a personal vendetta against them and he had ordered his patrols to be ruthless in their tactics. The warehouses of the docks and canals were their usual hideouts and he had ordered them to search every one of them. Will wished that they hadn't had been the ones who searched the tannery.

In the corner of the upper floors, they hound found the skeletal body of the women. In fact, they only knew it was a woman because of the small bundle in her arms. A mother and her baby. Will had turned away, but Garick had leant down and checked the details, before sending Will to get help. Will was happy to leave; the room smelt of death.

That evening they had not talked about what they found, but the rumours had spread as others in the inn were recounting the latest horror from the Beast. He tried not to listen, but one-word came up again and again: Vetalas.

"What is Vetalas?" Will had asked Garick. Garick hadn't rushed to answer. He gulped down his drink and said, "Get me another one and I'll tell you." Will obliged but did not keep up himself with this drinking pace.

"See those guys in the corner." He pointed to three grey bearded sailors. "There from Dur. They sail here regularly. That's where the word comes from. Vetalas. One of them told me the story years ago. The Vetalas is a witch or a demon. It lives in the forests of the western steppe. Thousands of years old. They are half bird and half women, and they live in the high trees."

"And they kill?"

"Absolutely. They kill the young and their mothers. Sneak into villages at night and suck their blood."

"By the Gods!"

"Exactly, by the Gods. The legend says that they are the offspring of Aragel. Cursed and hounded out of the heavens for her sins. Most people don't know the full story. The god of the night and of the tears of men. Well, she was the first wife of Ezkebal"

Will pulled a face. He didn't know much religion, but he did know Ezkebel's wife was Aragel.

"First wife?"

"Yes. For some reason lost to history Ezkebel dumped her and took Loane as his wife. But Aragel was jealous of her, and begged Gaal to do more, and to protect her position. And so, Loane was made barren, but not before Aragel had one last.... you know...coupling with Ezkebel. Their offspring was the Vetalas."

"And that's what did this?"

"Of course, not you idiot. It's all nonsense. There are no flying women here, but it does sound like the beast has got a taste for blood! The sooner we catch it the better."

And now they were outside with Garick needing fresh air and to sober up. There was no way he was going to carry Will back to the barracks.

Lilkin cursed under his breathe. Two guards had appeared, and one was now sat on a barrel head in his hands. The other was talking to their target. Hands on his shoulders. It looked like he wasn't letting the man back into the inn. There was some shouting from the drunk man and then unheard words from the guard. Eventually the guard had turned the man around and was pushing him down the alley.

The man staggered down the alleyway into the darkness, whilst the guard went back to his colleague. The plan was back on. Lilkin and his gang kept to the shadows and left the inn area to follow their target down the alleyway.

They waited until the man was a good fifty yards from the Inn and well out of sight of the guards when they struck. Lilkin gripped a thick stick in his hand and stealthily positioned himself behind the man as he leant on a wall.

"Wait!" Just as Lilkin was about to swing the stick down on the man's head, one of the gang touched his arm. "We don't need to do this!" it whispers. "He doesn't have a clue what's going on..." Felix was right. He was the gang's best pickpocket, not something that Lilkin was good at. He relied more on the combination of surprise and force.

He watched Felix, as he slowly took the stick and used the thinnest end to slowly lift the jacket of the man revealing his belt and trousers. Hanging from the belt was his purse. Then Felix nodded at Lilkin whilst he extended his other hand under the purse. Lilkin knew what to do. He pulled out his knife and quickly in one motion sliced the cords of the purse, so that it landed gently in Felix's hand. The man grunted. Felix stepped back. Lilkin nodded, and Felix backed away then turned and stepped back into the shadows.

The man went to turn, coughing and spluttering. Lilkin then grabbed the mains neck from behind and plunged the knife deep into his back. He held it there, and slowly lowered the man to the ground as the life ebbed out of him. As he eased the man to the floor, he saw that he grasped at the wall to steady himself, but in doing so tore at one of the latest edicts pinned to the walls. The edict came free and fell to the floor.

Lilkin looked at it. He couldn't read words, but he could read numbers, and the numbers printed on the parchment caught his attention. He picked it up and read the number: five hundred. Then he followed the other into the darkness.

13

The sun was shining, and Rahim felt invigorated. The journey south had seen his energies slowly diminish but now he was settled in a city he could recoup his strength.

He had kept a low profile for the last few days, just finding his feet and learning about how the city worked. He had neglected Francesca but now that he had the lay of the land, he decided he should reconnect with her.

He had taken the role of her teacher for most of the journey and on the longer voyages he would schedule specific times to discuss important topics. He needed to get the routine back going again. He certainly did not want her spending too much time with the Duke's servants and Gods forbid the Duke himself.

And so, Francesca had found herself sat on the Guardian's balcony on a bench with a table, stylus and parchment. The subject today was trade routes, but trade routes were as boring as it could get. Dur to Xander. Xander to Homsel, Homsel to Zinar. Caravans and ships were boring, Francesca wanted knights, princesses and monsters!

"I heard what happened to the Duke's wife and daughter". She took a gamble with the Guardian.

"Indeed." He replied. The Guardian was used to the princesses' ploys, but perhaps today would be the day when he could start to influence her and lay the seeds for other plans.

"It was the Klarion. I already hate them. He is such a good man, isn't he?"

"Perhaps."

"Very kind, but I see his sadness."

"Yes, of course Princess, but as one of the ruling classes his is not a figure you should be too sympathetic towards."

"What do you mean?" Rahim paused. It looked like he was questioning how much he should say. He wasn't but it was the effect he wanted. "The Duke is a soldier. His whole life was built around being a soldier. He fought in the north against the Klarion and the pirates in the south. Being a soldier is what defined him. He was a popular choice to rule the city, though. Oh, you can forget the Council, he rules the city.

Yet the first duty of a ruler is to protect your people. The Duke failed. The best soldier failed and failed with that which he loved the most. There is sympathy yes, but many began to doubt him."

"Do you doubt him?" Francesca asked.

"Yes, yes I do. His sense is tainted. The city is at its most vulnerable now, from the world outside and the city itself and he is not making good decisions."

Francesca was quiet, this was getting beyond her a little bit. Rahim considered how far he could go as he needed to be careful, but perhaps now was the time. "Francesca, did you know that some measure the passing of time, not in days or weeks but in a different way."

"Other countries, yes."

"No this is different. The Guardians measure time by the Gods. The eight gods each have a time. A period where their influence is strongest. You were born in the time of Fortune. That was a time of prosperity and wealth. All was well with the kingdom. Did you know that in that seven-year period, there were no wars? None"

"So, each God rules for seven years?" asked Francesca.

"That's a simple way of looking at it. The duration is not fixed, and 'ruling' is not really what happens. Imagine the Gods can wish their personality into everyone in the Empire. Everyone gets a slice of Fortune. That doesn't mean everyone becomes lucky or successful, they need to have their own personality in alignment. Tell me who is your favourite God?"

94

Francesca considered. "I pray to Fortune."

"Well, there you go. For you Fortune's years would have been great for you. You were open to her influence."

"What time are we in now?"

"It's hard to be sure, but the Guardians generally agree that we are coming out of the time of Gaal and entering the time of Ezkebel."

"Ezkebel is the darkness, isn't he?"

"Again, a very simple interpretation. Ezkebel is the God of the Hidden Thoughts. He gave the world fear. For the weak and hopeless these manifests as loss, death and disease. For the strong, the ambitious it delivers opportunity. To survive this period, we will need to be strong and open our hearts to the gifts Ezkebel offers."

"I don't think I like Ezkebel." Francesca responded doodling a shadowy figure on her paper.

"Ezkebel is hard to embrace. You need to have a broad view of the world. Fortune concerns itself with the individual, whilst Ezkebel concerns with survival. For example, which of your brothers would you say is the kindest, perhaps make the fairest Emperor when your father passes?"

Francesca considered for a few moments "Ranifess, I guess. He is quiet, but thoughtful, cares about the people."

"Of course, I like Ranifess, a lot. Yet he is fifth in line to the throne. For you to get the best leader then all his older brothers should need to die. Do you want that?"

"No, that's terrible."

"But you want the best leader?" Francesca nodded.

"If I tell you that Ranifess will become Emperor and open the gates to those fleeing the plague, would you be happy?"

"Yes, you see that is what he would do."

"And if just one of those refugees carries the plague and causes the death of thousands including your brother. All gone. Is that not a bad thing?"

"Yes, I guess."

"Well, his brother Togan, would use Ezkebel better."

"But he is a horrible person." Francesca screwed up her face in disgust.

"Yes, yes, he is, but he will use Ezkebel to make tougher harder decisions. The refugees would be shut out and the city would survive. Ezkebel days would pass and perhaps Ranifess would come to influence him, and new cities would be built, and new life come to the world."

Francesca took this all in.

"You see the Duke, is not the right man for the time of Ezkebel. We have plague at the door, death on streets and he is relying on the goodness of people, rather than embracing fear."

"You're scaring me." Francesca felt a colder shudder across her shoulders. The sky seemed darker and even Rahim seemed to be cloaked in shadow.

"Don't be." Rahim pulled one of his rare smiles. "My job is to find the person who can make the difference and meantime guide the Duke in the best way I can."

"And what about me?"

"Don't be scared. Think about what good can come from the bad. Think about opportunity. This city is a haven, a place we can build from. Now get back to your work. Trade routes.... now where were we?" Rahim reached for the book he had earlier put down.

"I will pray to Fortune that she returns soon." Francesca whispered, hoping he would hear, but afraid he would as well. Rahim slowly turned round holding the trade book in his hand. He hadn't heard, thought Francesca. She took the book. Rahim didn't let go, just looked in her eyes.

"Francesca, Fortune will not return for a long time. Pray for the creator, pray for peace, but me I will pray to Ezkebel. It is Ezkebel's time, and he will give us guidance." Rahim left the balcony and went inside whilst Francesca looked at the book. Her masters had never told her about this world. Ezkebel was the darkness that most avoided. You prayed to Ezkebel when you went to bed to stop the monsters coming. She didn't want to be scared. She wanted to be strong. Strong like the Duke.

She started to copy down a map of the north, marking the cities before colouring in the various regions. At least that bit was fun. Rahim then emerged back onto the balcony, looking a little hesitant. He put his finger to his lip like he was thinking about something whilst looking at her.

"I can show you how to pray to Ezkebel. Would you like that?"

"I, I don't think so..." Francesca shook her head. Rahim smiled, that strange smile.

"Why don't we do something special, and leave these books and heavy thoughts? Why don't we go into the city!" he said. Francesca smiled, jumped up and embraced the Guardian.

The rest of the day flew by. Rahim took only one guard with them, and he showed her so much of the city. He was far more relaxed than she had ever seen him. The city and being in one place were good for him.

They had bought fruit in the market and taken a barge down the canals. She loved the noise and the excitement drawing looks from the traders and others, but she never felt afraid. They had been in so many shops that in the end they had a barge on standby to store all the goods she bought.

In the market she got her first real glimpse of the Great Temple. She pointed at the great doors. "What is that. It looks like the temples back home"

"Yes, it's the Great Temple. It's one of the oldest in the Empire" answered Rahim.

"Can we go in?" Rahim shook his head. "You get invited in. This Temple is not to the Gods, it's too the Great Father. Besides, there are a lot of people gathering on the steps there, I sense it could all get a bit unruly. Rahim took her arm and began to lead her away from the square.

As Francesca and Rahim moved amongst the market stalls, she knew the folk were looking at her, but was not aware that one of the watchers had a malevolent desire. Lilkin leant against the wall of the Temple and studied her from afar. One thing crossed his mind: "money".

It would not be easy though. For a start the Golden Guard was a problem, but he would work on a plan for when they came back to the market again. Félix nudged him breaking his concentration. Felix pointed up to the rooves. Someone else was watching the girl. He could see the dark shadow, a movement of hair, and the whites of it eyes.

Francesca and Rahim were now walking out of the market towards the canal side that was at the opposite end from the Temple. They were climbed into a barge overloaded with purchases.

"We could follow in a barge, and accidently collide. Knock the gifts into the water?" said Felix.

"No. She'll be back. I want you to watch that thing on the roof. Get Joel and Gyle to climb up and see if they can follow him. I'll stay on the ground with the others. My bet is he will follow the girl along the canal side. This could be our change to catch the beast, once and for all. I'll take the crew up to the last few roofs and see if we can ambush it."

14

Ark followed the girl as she made her way to the canal and then into the barge. The barge travelled back towards the Citadel, and by hopping between the rooftops of the buildings that edged the canal he could continue to watch her.

The girl had been on his mind ever since he saw her on the walkway. She was beautiful, like a shiny stone amongst the gravel. He had watched the Citadel and followed her progress when she left the Citadel into the city. She was always smiling, happy and laughing. She was impossible not to notice.

He suddenly heard a noise behind him, and he spun around. There was a boy on the roof. He was big, almost a man. His hair was red, and he was crawling towards him. Luckily, he didn't seem too sure on his feet, but could there be others? Ark looked around, suddenly aware that he was in a precarious position. To his left the canal, to his right a stretch of roofs that surrounded the area in front of the citadel walls. Behind him a drop to the square. Behind the redhead were four more smaller but similar types.

The jump across the canal was too far, especially without a run up. He would have to go right, but the gang were fanning out aware that was his best option. Ark leapt across the small gap to the next roof on his right and then ran. The roofs here were, mostly flat, which meant he could move fast, but it also meant the gang would find it easier as well. They began to run, chasing him and attempting to narrow the gap. There was no chance for Ark to cut into the city and therefore make for the Temple or his other hideouts. When this short stretch of roof run out, he would be met by the eastern canal or be forced to the ground.

At the eastern canal he could possibly jump, he would have had the momentum, but the eastern canal had only one small line of houses before you reached the shear face of the surrounding mountains.

Lilkin and his crew kept pace with the beast, never quite gaining on him but not letting him cut into the city. Down on the ground others were following in the square. If the beast jumped down, then they would grab him. Lilkin knew the beast was running out of rooftops!

This was the best view he had had of the beast, and it dawned on him that his nemesis was no monster or animal. "It's just a Xari boy." He screamed. "He is no different from us just dirtier". No there was more to it than that. He watched how it moved. It was like a cat, running on all fours, and then like a monkey swinging between the houses. Whatever it was he knew he could catch it.

That morning Felix had read the proclamation offering five hundred gold coins for the capture of the beast. Dead or alive. One of the gang had commented sheepishly: "Did you hear what it did last night. It sucked the blood out a baby and its mother. I don't think we want to be chasing it." Well, Lilkin didn't know about that, but he did know 500 gold coins would be worth the risk.

Ark had run out of palatable options. He slowed a little and instinctively his body swerved towards one direction: the Citadel. Ark leapt over a longer gap in the roofs and landed solidly. The gap had been wide but only wide enough to slow his pursuers down briefly. Then he saw at the corner of his eye the stable by the Citadel walls. The square was at its shortest length between the city and walls at this point.

Ark started to veer closer to the edge overlooking the square. There were voices down below, shouting, calling out. The same noises from before. There was no choice but to try it. He cut in sharply and accelerated towards the edge. Reaching the last tile, he vaulted into the sky, clearing ten yards before he started to descend. He had jumped over the heads of the pursuers on the ground but was now descending.

He hit the cobbles with a shudder that sent vibrations up through his calves, his thighs and across his spine. He instinctively rolled forward to try to take the energy out of the impact. His hands shot out in front of him and immediately encountered an intense pain as he heard the gruesome snap of his wrist. Then a new pain straight into his arms. He rolled and kept his balance, before being back on his feet and running to the stable. Blood was trickling down his hand, but he dared not look at it. He reached the stables but could hear the voices behind him. Reaching up to the stable roof with his good hand, he looked behind.

At least twenty boys were chasing across the square towards the Citadel. On the Citadel walls the guards had drawn their bows and had rushed to its edges. He could hear an order being shouted at the square. The guards hadn't seen him, though, and Ark used his remaining hand to pull himself up.

Lilkin and the gang halted abruptly as the first arrow imbedded itself in the ground at their feet. He stared up at the beast disappearing over the wall. His first instinct was to point and shout to the guards, but there was nothing in it for him if the guards captured the beast. He cursed under his breathe. "Don't worry boys. His got to come back at some point, and we'll be waiting."

Ark ran along the walkways, heading instinctively for the storeroom, but the pain was becoming unbearable. As he crossed the roof, he saw an empty Citadel balcony. There was a bench, and the plants would give him some cover.

He lowered himself down hanging by his one good hand and then sat on the bench. His heart had started to beat slower, the adrenaline wearing off. Slowly he looked at his hand. On his wrist was a deep gash running up his forehand but protruding from the wrist itself was a sliver of white. Ark felt feint and let the hand fall to his lap.

Ark clawed at his shirt looking for something to use as a bandage. He tried to rip at his shirt, but the clothes were too strong. On a chair opposite the bench was a scarf, and Ark reaches forward for it, but he overstretched and toppled forward, crashing face down on the floor of the balcony.

The air around him starts to dance with stars, and slowly he was overcome by darkness.

15

Francesca closed the door of her chamber, waving away her servants who had carried in all the things Rahim had purchased, and then collapsed on the bed. It had been a good day, no, a great day. She had seen a relaxed side of the Guardian that she had not seen since the trip started. Maybe she was going to like it here. She was exhausted and not unexpectedly soon drifted into a deep sleep.

She was woken by a knock on the door a few hours later. It was one of the servants asking her if she would like to attend dinner with the Guardian? She stood up and went to the door. She was hungry but she didn't really want to spend time with Rahim this evening. She had purchased a set of old story books from the bookseller in the market square and now she was awake she wanted to make a start on them.

"No. Could you send my apologies to the Guardian and just deliver something to the room?" she stuck her head around the door and smiled at the servant. "What would you like, milady?"

"Some soup, not too spicy," she said. "And cake...some cake". She smiled and closed the door. As she turned, she noticed something on the balcony. The curtain was partially drawn and fluttering in the wind. There was a bag or something like a bag on the floor, but the curtains mad it difficult to see. She stepped over and slowly opened the curtains, worried that it might be an animal of some kind.

She clasped the edges of the curtains and there was blood, not huge amounts but a scattering of spots across the floor. As the curtains drew back, she realised the shape was a body. She didn't scream but rather gulped a huge intake of air and clasped her hand to her mouth. It was a boy.

He was lying on his face, his right arm outstretched holding her red scarf. His other was under his body. She grabbed a poker from the fireplace and gently prodded the body. And then it groaned.

Ark felt the sharp edge of something poking at his back. And within seconds he was awake, his eyes opened looking at the dusty floor. Then the pain swept through him again, and he rolled over clasping his arm. Francesca saw a bloodied hand dangle limply from the arm of the boy.

Ark lifted himself up and staggered to the bench, he then realised someone was there with him. His vision was blurred but he could see a red dress. It was the girl! She was standing in the open doorway, with a metal spear of some kind in her hand. Her back was straight, her teeth were clenched, and she looked formidable. Her long, curly blonde hair was blowing in the wind, but her face was stern like a stone statue - like one of the gargoyles on the Temple steeple.

Ark's instinct was to run, and he attempted to stand. But he was weak, and he fell back onto the bench. The pain was excruciating, but he let his broken arm go and raise his right hand as if to fend her off. "Please, please don't hurt me!"

Francesca heard the words and relaxed slightly as she realised, she was not going to be attacked. This was just a grubby, dirty peasant whose attempt to rob her and gone desperately wrong. She took a small step closer, holding the poker out in front of her like the knights did in her storybooks. "Who are you?" she demanded in her most gallant voice.

Ark understood the words, but it had been so long since he had spoken. He didn't answer.

"By the Gods, he is so scared" thought Francesca and then she noticed something. His skin wasn't grubby, or dirty. No, his skin was smooth and clean...but he was brown. She couldn't think of any other way to describe it. His skin was different to hers, to everyone. His skin was brown. And then she gasped, "You're a Klarion!"

Ark finally spoke. "I am Ark. I am Tribe."

"This is incredible". Francesca couldn't control her excitement; she had one of the lost tribes on her balcony! She dropped the poker to her side. and stepped closer. The boy was slightly smaller than her and he smelled of the city. She could see his wrist was badly broken and was surprised it hadn't made her feel sick.

"I am Francesca. I am very important here in the Citadel. With one shout I can have a hundred guards come running with big spikes - lances I mean, which they will skewer you with. So, don't even think of trying to hurt me." He didn't respond. She saw his eyes begin to water.

"Don't be afraid" her voice was now gentle, calming. "I will get you some help for your hand."

"No, no! Ark cried through clenched teeth. "They will kill me…" Francesca remembered the stories of the Tribe, and of the Duke's hatred of them.

"What should I do?" she asked.

"I just need to bind it. Stop the bleeding and it will heal". Francesca doubted that very much. The break looked quite messy, and although the bleeding seemed to have eased, something would need to be done with that bone. "I will tell you what to do," said Ark. "I can fix this" He grimaced. "I need to lie flat, and I need rope."

"I don't have rope" Ark pointed at the scarf as another wave of pain washed over him. "The scarf…."

"Oh, the scarf" Francesca realised and grabbed it from the floor. "What should I do?

"Make a noose…put my hand in the noose." She did as he said.

"Not too tight…not yet." Ark climbed onto the floor and lay flat with his arm flat on the ground. "You need to stand on my hand".

"That will hurt!" Francesca cried.

"Just stand on it, hard. I will pull my arm away from it. When I say pull, tighten the noose."

"I understand, said Francesca

"Have you another scarf?"

"Yes, of course"

"Well, I will pass out, I'm sure. When I do, tie another scarf around my wrist like a bandage to hold it in place, and then let me sleep."

"Of course," she said again.

"And thank you." Ark said. And with that he pulled on his wrist. He felt the bone drop back into the wound, and the in a deluge of pain he blacked out once more. Francesca watched the boy for the next few hours. She left him asleep on the balcony until after her dinner came. Then she attempted to lift him into her room, but he was too heavy. So, she just put a pillow under is head and waited.

When the darkness had come, he finally woken up. He sat up and looked puzzlingly at her and then at the arm wrapped in not one but five of her silk scarves. Some blood had still seeped through but not much.

He sat up on the bench and after few deep breathes, said. "Thank you."

"You're welcome" she answered quickly.

"I should go" he began but before he finished the sentence, Francesca said "No, you mustn't...shouldn't. The guards will see you...you must rest."

"They won't see me", Ark replied. "My arm will be better soon. I heal quickly."

"Not that quickly, said Francesca. Stay until the morning, at least. I could try and smuggle you out." Ark felt the pain still, but his body was healing and healing quickly. He didn't know why but the few injuries he had had, always healed quickly, very quickly. By now the bones would already be re-attaching themselves and the wound closing. He knew this was not the same for the people of the city. Yet the rest would be good and would allow it to heal completely by the morning.

"Thank you" he said. "Thank you, Francesca"

"How did you hurt it?" she asked.

"I fell. Fell from a roof."

"What were you doing on the roof?"

"I was hiding...running."

"Running from what? Sorry. I ask a lot of questions, I know. But that's how you become smart isn't it? Lots of questions and then lots of answers. But you don't have to tell me." They were silent for a while.

"Are you a thief? Ark didn't answer. Francesca tried something different. "So, you are Xari aren't you? That's Tribe isn't it?" Ark again stayed silent. "I thought you were all gone...in the city.... obviously not" she answered for him. I know all about the Xari. Let me show you." She went back into her room. She had bought a book of myths and legends of the city. She quickly found it, blew off the dust and returned.

She opened to the middle pages where she had seen the picture when she had been perusing the booksellers stall. She held up a beautifully painted picture on the left-hand page of the book. It showed dark-skinned figures dressed in furs standing by a sea pointing up at a comet. "For seven days they stood, not understanding the sign in the sky. Many began to question the leaders and even the Great Father himself" she began to read the section opposite.

Ark leant forward and looked at the pictures. He had never seen anything like this, pictures of his people, people with skin like his own. "Of course, this book makes you look silly, like an animal...but I think that's just because the writer probably didn't really know much."

Ark shook his head. It didn't matter. He knew nothing of his heritage, just blurred images. He tried to grab the book with his good hand, but Francesca pulled it away, and pulled a reprimanding face at him. "You don't look like these pictures. Your face is so smooth and your nose, cheekbones are so..." "Beautiful" is what she wanted to say, but that would be strange. "They are sharp not bumpy like in these pictures.

"What else does it say?"

"I've not read yet, but if you stay, I could read it to you." Ark sat back on the bench. "I would like that."

Francesca smiled. "You must be hungry. Do you eat soup?"

16

The Duke poured himself a large glass of wine and put down the quill. He had signed the last document for the day and was ready to relax. Yet, he wouldn't be able to sleep, not with the nagging worry he had that things were drifting out of his control. The beast had turned into a killer. He had issued a reward for the capture hoping that every half-drunk knight and mercenary would solve the problem where the guards seemed to be failing, but now he was full of doubts. Rahim had seemed to back off, but that only increased his tension. But it was none of these things that weighed on his mind, right now. No, he had received some very concerning correspondence. He picked up a letter received this afternoon from his cousin in the north.

"Cousin, I hope you are well. It has been such a long time since Carsine and I have seen you. Too long. Before you think this is another letter imploring you to take a trip North and see us and the children, please believe me, it is not. I write with much sadness and to seek your help.

Riago, the once beautiful city on the hills above the valley of Scalaman has become a tomb. I do not exaggerate when I say that almost everyone in the city is dead. The plague came three months ago, and it seemed like there were only a few small outbreaks that were kept easily under control, but we were wrong.

Three weeks ago, city guards sealed the citadel. We had no reported incidents and thought we were safe. Then a Guardian arrived, and his herald ordered the Duke to ride out and meet him. The Duke reluctantly did, and never came back. The Guardian never entered the city and so, since that day we have been waiting.

I have decided that tomorrow we will leave the city. We have sent birds to the Emperor and to you. If you receive this then know that we have set out and are heading for Feror. We will take the Great Pass through the mountain, if the Gods preserve us.

AR Chmenygt"

The Duke had read this so many times. Riago was the nearest city. Two days by boat up the coast, but a week by horse. He hadn't dated the letter, but the bird had arrived this morning and it was a day's flight. There hadn't been too much bird correspondence in the last few years. He laid the letter down and rifled through his papers until he found a parchment, a report from the Commander. This had sent a further chill down his spine.

That morning a boat had landed out of control at the Dam, drifting in on the tidal currents. On inspection, all the crew and all its passengers were found dead. The plague had reached his city. He had questioned Ishman relentlessly. Was he sure? Who inspected? Where are they now?"

It didn't matter. He had called a Council for tomorrow morning and issued orders to seal the city. No more boats could dock, and the Pass was to be shut. No one in. No one out."

The Duke took a big gulp of his wine and drained the glass, then made his way over to the bed. He would not sleep well that night, as he dreamt of his cousin lying dead in the wilderness.

***

It was late when Rahim returned to his chamber. Francesca had declined dinner with him, and that had left him free to explore the Citadel some more. He had walked the walls and returned briefly escaped into the city.

The city was wild with rumours of the beast, and he had enjoyed the thinking time he needed to assess what that meant to his plan. The Duke had not done as much as he would have expected. He'd hoped for a lot more Citadel guards being sent to the city, but he would need to push the Duke a bit harder.

On returning to his room, he had found a note summoning him to the Council the next morning, urgent business, apparently. Perhaps the Duke had caught the beast, yet he had overheard that a regal bird had arrived from over the mountains, so perhaps there was something important happening in the north. Before he went to sleep, he removed his cloak and began his prayers; these were silent and to

Ezkebel. Hopefully he would have a convert to join him soon, but there was time for that too.

***

As Rahim had entered the gate, he had missed two figures leaving it. The traveller and Ravi had completed their session with the Great Seer and were heading back to the Temple.

Ravi was struggling to contain his frustration at having not been included in the actual meeting. When they had entered the Great Seers offices, he had felt back in control, but when the Great Seer saw the man in front of him, he had ushered him into his chambers and firmly shut the door. They were of different faiths and at times like that Ravi wondered why the Great Father would sanction the existence of the Gods and their legion of sycophants. And so, he had waited outside, for three hours.

The traveller had found the experience as futile and frustrating as his meeting with all the other religious representatives in each of the cities he had visited. They were all the same: holy bureaucrats. Their minds tangled up in the protocols and the messages of the Gods, rather than helping their people connect to their true spirits. He didn't need to read the Great Seer's mind to know his first thoughts. "What does this man mean to my position. Is he a threat?"

At the heart of all men outside the realm of the gods was selfishness. Building kingdoms, processes, walls and words around themselves to protect and advance their own desires. He knew quickly that this man knew little of the true intentions of the Gods, as much as the man sat outside knew the intentions of the Great Father. Both were misguided but both could have something that he needed: knowledge. They knew the writings and histories and they knew the gossip that lived in the city.

And so, he had given the seer his place, and listened. Men like the Great Seer liked to talk. They liked to tell you how important they were. The traveller had spoken little.

"I am a traveller from the North. I seek knowledge and I serve the Gods"

110

Something about his demeanour had made the seer not challenge or ask any deeper questions. He had casually discussed the written teachings attributed to the Gods in a conversational way that the traveller knew was a test of his authenticity. The passages he discussed led the traveller to an obvious conclusion: the Seer believed he was a prophet.

They had discussed the north, the plague and how his colleagues were faring. The traveller had been honest and recalled the names of some of the Seers colleagues. This had led to a few friendly anecdotes. Eventually the Seer had let him leave, but the traveller took with him something useful that may impact his quest. Guardian Rahim was here with a daughter of the Emperor; a beast was stalking the city drinking the blood of new-born babies; writings had been appearing on the walls of the Gods temples predicting the end of the world. The seer had asked if he had written them. The traveller had responded, "The end of the world is always close. I feel no great urgency to tell people that."

The traveller had questioned the seer on the plague. On whether there had been any visions or prophecy specifically about it. The seer had said there hadn't, but that there had been a precedent for this in the last time of Gaal, where the city of Uruqu had been wiped from the earth through a plague of locusts eating the flesh of the city's inhabitants. People had all hid in their homes until the plague was finally raised by the sacrifice of the Kings eldest son.

The traveller had already heard this and new the legend well. The plague of locusts departed, the sacrifices continued through the years of Gaal, until the time of Ezkebel. Ezkebel had flattened the city through a violent earthquake a punishment for the loss of life.

The Great Seer had ended the meeting by saying that he believed we were in a new time of Ezkebel. The traveller had just said "Perhaps". And so, the two men made their way back to the Temple, with the night firmly shrouding them. They passed through the market square, aware of the increased guards around the city.

Lilkin and his gang had made their way back to their hideouts. He was sat with Felix letting his frustration out, leaning against the wall in a space on the Market Square. "That's the fellow I saw go into the Temple" Felix said.

"Another monk, with no pennies to their name. He looks even more like a beggar than most of them do." Lilkin responded. They followed the traveller to the Great Doors.

"I've heard some of the temples were shipping their relics and jewels to other safer ones. Maybe this poor looking monk is carrying a golden chalice, or a jewel encrusted cross." Felix hoped.

"The only thing he is carrying is disease." Lilkin responded. He pulled out his knife and a piece of charred wood. Slowly he began to cut away, carving something, but seemingly with no real focus or purpose. "Read me that parchment, again". Felix, eager to please, dipped into his bag and pulls the document out and reads it aloud."

"500 florins for the capture of the Beast, 500 florins - can you believe that!" Lilkin didn't respond. The traveller and Ravi entered the Great Temple and the doors shut behind them.

"Well, that's them locked away for the night, anyway."

"Not really "Felix spoke up. "The older, dirtier one, he comes out at night. I've seen him."

"You are kidding. What the hell for?"

"Don't know, I've never really followed him, but I've seen it a few times and he goes off in a different direction each time. I bet there's some money in that building, eh. Next time he comes out couldn't we rush the doors?" Felix asked.

"No chance. I don't know what's in there, and we'd be trapped." They sat in silence again. Felix spoke up first. "We don't have to catch the beast"

"What the hell do you mean?" Lilkin responded, angrily.

"Listen, just listen. We might be able to get the reward for the information we have. At least some of it."

"And what do we know that they don't." Lilkin asked.

"Well, I think I know where he usually goes. I mean, I've seen him by the Temple and by the Citadel. Maybe they can stake them out. We know he lives on the roofs. I've not seen the guards searching up there."

Lilkin listened. "Maybe you're right. Get a pencil and a bit of clean parchment, I think we should write a letter to the Duke. What do you think?"

17

Francesca read for hours. The Citadel and the city were quiet, the moon a crescent in the sky. She had resorted to holding a candle whilst she read and sat one on the floor next to the boy whilst she laid on the bed. The light had cast a strange shadow and glow to his features. His eyes were bright and never seemed to shut or even blink, although she couldn't be sure that he was awake as he laid so still.

She had decided to just keep reading until she had finished the book. He never asked a question. She laid the book down and stepped toward the boy. She gently touched his arm and she saw him smile.

"Ark, are you awake?" He nodded. He eased himself up and clasped at his hand. The blood on the scarves had dried in and Francesca hoped that meant that the bleeding had stopped.

"Does it still hurt?" Ark looked up at her and without breaking eye contact, he slowly wiggled the fingers of his left hand. He smiled. "Not much."

"That's incredible" Francesca said. "How did you do that?"

"I don't know, I really don't." And he didn't. He just knew that his body could heal itself in a way he had not seen in others in the city. No-one had ever told him how or why, but he remembered an incident and found himself telling this girl who have known nothing about.

"I remember being in the Market Square. I can't be sure, but I was very young and being held by my mother, or perhaps a sister. I can't remember. But I remember seeing my brother, father, uncles and cousins all in the market square performing. They were acrobats, you see, among other things. They would sing, dance, and do balancing acts perhaps you have this in your homeland?"

"No, nothing like that" she responded.

"Well in those days the city did. My family were performers. Anyway, my uncles and cousins had formed a kind of pillar of bodies," Ark made a triangular shape.

"A triangle?"

"Perhaps, this shape anyway. My brother was climbing on the top, it was three people high, so high. And then I don't know what happened. Perhaps someone threw something, I'm not sure, but he fell, my brother fell and crashed to the cobbles below. There were lots of screaming and running. I was sat on the floor and could see him lying still, there was blood from his head. The men wrapped him in a shroud, and we all were hurried out of the square. We stayed in tents up on the western hills, there are houses there now. I was picked up and carried. I remember the crying and screaming."

"Did he die?"

"Well, that's it, he didn't. I was left all night in an empty tent with my sister. She held me all night, I remember that feeling. The next day I was allowed into my father's tent and saw my brother his head bandaged but sat up smiling. 'don't worry little brother, it's all part of the magic' he said. That's my earliest memory. I've had scrapes and sprains, and they all clear very quickly."

"Are you immortal" Francesca asked.

"What do you mean?"

"I mean can you be killed?" Ark felt a wave of emotion. "I can be killed. We can be killed. They all were killed."

Francesca felt a wave of fear, a sudden sense of danger with the change in Ark's mood. "Things are quiet now. Perhaps you should head back to where you live."

"Yes, I think that would be a good idea." Ark stretched his fingers and walked to the balcony. Ark looked over the edge and then straddled the small wall and leapt to the roof below. He was gone. Francesca shouted "You can come back, though. Please come back."

***

"Just listen!" the Duke had resorted to shouting over the most animated Council he had ever seen. His planned agenda had gone to pot as soon as he announced that the city was to be sealed. It started with calls that he had exceeded his powers and progressed to him being a tyrant. The Guilds were the worst, as they started to understand the impact on trade which had already taken a huge amount of punishment from the reduction in trade anyway. This, maybe, was just an opportunity for them to let off steam. He decided to let them shout it out.

After five more minutes he had lost patience with that approach and signalled to two of the guards to step forward and draw their swords. They seemed to understand and drew the swords dramatically and as loudly as possible. At the same time, he stood up as well and yelled "Listen!"

It worked. The silence was blissful, but it would not last long. He pulled out a parchment. "This parchment has one short statement and a number on it. Yet it is the most important statement that had ever been read in this chamber, in ours and probably all lifetimes since the city was founded!"

That morning the Duke had sat at his desk preparing for the Council, expecting arguments and debates about the closing of the city and this beast problem. Unfortunately, his plans were turned upside down by the single parchment handed to him that morning by Ishman.

He read it over and over again, each time he felt a chill and imagined the candlelight flickered. He was unable to draw himself from the words, unable to move, unable to act. When finally, the spell was broken he rang the small bell on his desk, and Ishman came ominously through the door. "Yes, my Lord"

The Duke went to speak but stopped, sensing too much emotion in his voice. He took a sip of wine then began again, in his normal deep, throaty, authoritative voice. "Are these numbers correct?"

"Yes, my Lord, as of last night. More counts will continue today."

"And where is the main location of the ...outbreak?"

"Main location, my Lord? What do you mean?"

"I mean, is it in the poorer quarters, by the docks? Where is it mostly happening?"

"My Lord, it is ...everywhere. All of the churches are reporting sick coming to the doors...and last night we had reports of bodies .... on the streets." The Duke sat in silence. The parchment read that over two hundred people had reported to the churches, with red marks and coughing. Thirty-seven people had been reported dead. The plague has reached the city.

"Is there anyone in the citadel?"

"No, my Lord." The Duke paused. "Very well, seal the Citadel. No one in and no one out. Are the High priests here or at the Temple?"

"I believe they are here my Lord."

"Bring them to me". And now he read the words to the Council.

"The church report that there have been 237 cases of a mystery illness being reported at city churches, yesterday. 37 of these later died." He let the message sink in. There was an audible intake of breath and even a muffled "By the Gods". Even Rahim face seemed to pale more than it already was.

"Gentlemen, I have no need to tell you that this is devastating news. The plague has reached our city." The noise and debate started up again, but more orderly. Shock had taken the edge off the vitriol, no-one now was questioning the closing of the city, in fact someone even questioned why he had not done it earlier. He let the questions flow before informing them of an additional act he had initiated this morning.

"The gates of the Citadel are now closed. A thousand people live within the walls of the citadel. Sealing it is the right thing to do. If events unfold like the other cities of the Empire, then most will die outside the walls. There is nothing you can do for them now. You all have chambers in the grounds and so will be secure. I assume you all have properties on the mountains or in the city. If you wish to return to them, you may.... but you will not be let back into the Citadel."

"And family...staff...my dogs?" one guild leader stuttered.

"If they are outside the Citadel walls.... then that its where they must remain." The guild leader sat down and buried his head in his hands. Others did the same or stood open mouthed.

"This meeting is over. Go make your arrangements...and your decisions. I have summoned all the religious leaders, some of you here, to a meeting to arrange for prayers to be made for the city. Going forward, I have declared martial law. I am in charge and will only summon the Council as required. Now go make your arrangements."

There were no complaints. It was as if none had heard those last few words. They were already, in their heads, worrying about their own lives and fortunes. They rushed out the room faster than he had ever seen them move before. The Duke wondered how many would leave, how many would stay and abandon family and friends outside the walls. Rahim was last to leave. He bowed his head as he left the room.

"Good luck" were his only words.

18

Within the hour gathered in front of the Duke was a strange collection of individuals. Two were senior priests for the city: Elvin, head of the City Church and Sanid, the Citadel Bishop. The third individual was the Priestess.

The two Priest's appearance were that of wise old men, with white beards, golden robes and skull caps, but the Priestess was very different. She was part of a hereditary sect created before the church was established here; a sect of venerable women who worship the great mountain and dress in a long white robe, and somewhat bizarrely have shaved heads.

Her existence was a compromise to the descendants of the original aborigines who resided in the mountains and the bay before the city was established. There had been an attempt to outlaw the sect a hundred years ago but the ensuing riots and near revolution had nearly brought the city to its knees. Most of the city's underclass were believers and most of the city was the underclass.

She was here because this current High Priestess had the annoying knack of being where she was not wanted, and stubborn enough not to be removed once there. How she got to be here he did not know, but the Duke decided not to question it.

In contradiction to his words at the Council these religious representatives had not been called to establish prayers for the city. What was more important was understanding what was going on in the city and unlike some of the richer cities of the Empire, the church doubled as hospitals for those not wealthy enough for home visits and private care. Therefore, the clergy should have the answers. The Duke came straight the point. "So, is it the plague?"

Elvin spoke. "Yes, my Lord. Some of the Priests who have migrated here in the last few months have confirmed the symptoms".

"I should think so; it was probably them who brought it." The Duke was trying hard to control his anger, he never understood why Priests seeking asylum were always let in.

"This is not so my Lord, faith in God has proved a remarkable defence against the Blight."

"Perhaps. Here are my orders." The Duke began, "Your priests, along with my guards are to establish dormitories in the warehouses down by the harbour. All the sick shall go there, and not return to their homes. The Priests and whatever lay folk volunteer, will look after them. My guards will then visit the properties of the individuals and gather up anyone staying there and take them to a separate warehouse for quarantine. The house will have a red mark painted on the doorway and nail the doors shut. We just have to sit this out and hope it passes. We may even consider burning some of the districts if a large proportion of homes are infected."

The Priests looked at each other. Elvin initially seemed concerned about the role of his subordinate clergy but realised his earlier comments left him no room for complaint. They nodded and confirmed that they would make things happen. The Duke had already briefed the Head of the Guard and the military arrangements were already in place.

The Priestess had been silent all through. Her silence was unnerving.

"And you Priestess what of you and your people?" asked the Duke.

The Priestess seemed to have gone into a trance. The Priestesses were famous for their moments of trancelike state. Then she spoke in a monotone dirge, her eyes firmly shut, then springing open to show only whiteness.

"It is foretold. The ashes of the mountain speak to us. "The dust paints its pictures of what will be and what has been." She then went silent. Legend had always told that the mountains were a dormant volcano, but within certain caves, where the acolytes of the faith resided, there were seams of ancient volcanic dust. The sect used these mixed with blood and water to tell fortunes - their main source of income.

"And what do they say?" the Duke asked.

"We see an outsider. A dark essence. It has come to the city.

It brings death. We see another. It brings life, but in life it gives death."

The dirge was highly cryptic, as always. The Duke shook his head realising that this could lead to hours with the churchmen and his advisors, trying to unravel the mystery. The Priestesses seldom gave any further explanation. "Only the waters will wash away the unwanted. The waters will come when the death bringer is no more."

And so, it went on. The Duke listened to what he considered more cryptic drivel, whilst the other Priests argued why they could or couldn't support the plans. The Duke let his administrators deal with it and got up to leave.

"Your Holinesses, whatever you arrange with my clerks, please bear in mind that what I have stated is not for negotiation. If you do not co-operate, I will find others who will, and you can exit your Citadel chambers at my command."

***

Days went by, maybe two or three. Ark was on the roof overlooking the rooftop garden and sat there reading was the girl. She was in the same dress but sat on a stone bench and was holding a book, reading out loud like she sometimes did. It was almost like she was singing. Ark sat and listened, her back was to him, and on she read with the sun slowly setting.

For the first time in days, he forgot about his worries. He had seen a panic set upon the city, that for a while had reduced the interest in himself. The streets had emptied, and he had heard the word "plague" on the lips of those he did see.

He had therefore a bit more freedom on the rooves and had taken the opportunity to gather supplies to horde away. He had avoided the

Citadel, though, as the guards had been increased, and they had been far more alert.

Today, he had decided to see how close he could get to the stables. He had been successful, although it had taken longer than usual to get there. After gathering some supplies, he instinctively moved towards Francesca's roof garden. After what seemed like hours it began to turn dark and the girl responded to a shout from within. She answered it, running to the door and returned with a lamp. Placing it on the bench the immediate area lit up with a soft glow. It reminded Ark of the fires that were lit when he was young, as the caravans were brought together. Francesca sat down and continued to read.

"What is the story?" his voice was croaky but loud, loud enough for her to spin around.

"It's you!" her face was shocked but happy. "It's you! Oh, how fantastic, the boy from the rooves. Come and sit here.... I can read to you." Still nervous and unsure Ark slowly climbed down onto the bench next to her. He said nothing.

"How is your hand?" Before he could answer, she took his hand and laid it in her lap. The touch gave him a strange sensation: the touch of another human being. Something happened, a sensation, like they were two parts of the same thing finally coming together.

"Your arm, it's healed! She was shocked and grabbed the other hand as if she had made some mistake. "How? You are a strange, strange thing."

"What is your name?" Ark was unable to answer, his mouth suddenly dry.

"Don't worry, my name is Francesca. Fran if you like. The story? Well, that is a very old story. It is about two brothers – Gastax and Distax. The two brothers were princes, being born to the Great Emperor a couple of years apart." Ark listened nodding but not asking any questions.

"The boys were so handsome that the Gods decided to give them both a gift. They argued for days about what would be appropriate with each God offering their suggestions. They finally decided: they would be granted access to the house of the Gods, to live eternally in their company. Only one God objected, Ezkebel, but he kept his own council."

"What does that mean?" asked Ark.

"He didn't tell anyone. He believed that this was too big a gift and that it would lead to problems. And it did!" she smiled broadly. "Ezkebel volunteered to take the gifts to to the two boys, but he would not do so until they had both come of age. The gift would be given by one of the gods whispering the name of the universe into each boys' ears.

Years passed, and the boys grew up but there was a problem. The oldest boy, Gastax, grew strong, handsome and gallant but his brother was very different. He was weak and was often ill, so much so that his parents considered selling him to the Klarion, which was common for unwanted children. They didn't go through with this but did pray to the Gods for healing.

Ezkebel watched the boys grow and kept the Gods informed of the children's progress. When he informed them of the youngest child's problems, the Gods were worried. Unfortunately, they were not worried in a sympathetic way about the youngest child but rather in a cruel and selfish one. Was the boy mute, was he simple? Do we really want that around us in the future. They applauded Ezkebel for his good sense in holding back the gift and advised him that he should give the gift only to the older child.

So, when the youngest child reached 18, Ezkebel visited the Great Emperor and told him of the gift. The Emperor was overjoyed and as expected advised the gift to be given to Gastax. Gastax was brought to the Emperor and Ezkebel, and Ezkebel whispered the words of power into his ear. There was no outward change in Gastax but he felt a warmth inside him like his first tase of the spirits in the inns and taverns that he was known to frequent." Ark was listening intently, drawing nearer to the spellbinding voice of Francesca.

"Gastax lived his life fully, and unlike his father had a definite love and affection for his younger brother. In fact, he felt like his protector and even as a child had got into many fights defending him. Likewise, Distax

125

adored his older brother. He wanted to be like him, but his physical limitations made it impossible. But he was always by his side, and Gastax would have no other person advising him as he fulfilled his role as General in the Emperor's army.

When the Empire went to war against the Archagean rebels, Distax was Gastax's shield bearer and rode alongside him in his battle chariot. Their victory over the rebels was heralded across the Empire, and both brothers were lauded as heroes. Then came the war to end all wars. The largest army ever organised headed out across the plains to defeat the invasion by the Wilder people."

"The Wilder people?" asked Ark.

"The Wilder people. They are like the boogie monsters of all the great stories. They live underground in the mountains and feed on small children. They usually live in small tribes, but somehow, they got together under a terrible king and wreaked havoc across the cities in the shadow of the mountains.

Anyway, there were lots of battles and skirmishes that led to one final great fight between Gastax and the Wilder king. It lasted for three days until finally Gastax defeated the king, but amidst the confusion of the fight Distax had been badly wounded and lay dying. Exhausted and bleeding from multiple small wounds Gastax crawled to his brother, lying gasping with his last breathes in the dirt. Despite his wounds Gastax cradled Distax in his arms and screamed to the Gods.

The army gathered round and joined in the cries and gasped in awe as the heavens opened and a chariot of gold appeared pulled by two golden winged horses. It landed next to the two wounded figures and out stepped a glowing figure. It was Death, the shiny beacon that draws us to the End Lands when we pass away.

Leaning over he whispered to Gastax and spoke. 'Your brother is gone; it is time to let me take him beyond the light" But Gastax said 'No! He must go to heaven as I will when I die.' Now Death new of this deal and had been one of the Gods who disagreed with such a valuable gift, but he had some sympathy for the two brothers. 'Do you love your brother?' he asked Gastax. Gastax replied 'with all my heart'

'Would you give your life for him?' Death continued. 'Of course.'

'Then if you give me both of your earthly souls for a thousand years, I will let them spend half of their day in the End Lands and half in the heavenly skies until the years are spent. Then both I will grant access to the heavenly kingdom.' And so that's what happened," continued Francesca turning a page of her book to a picture of the night skies and the bright adjacent stars called Gastax and Distax.

"You mean Gastax and Gastax are the two stars shining for a thousand years in the sky?" Ark asked.

"Of course! You don't see them during the day, do you? Thats when they are in the End Lands. Ark's eyes lit up with recognition. He knew this and the words start to flood out, like the tears you shed when he realised your brother was gone.

"They are in the skies, at night, above in the skies. My grandfather he knew all the stars, all of them" and Ark leapt up pointing at the now dark sky.

"Do you know the stars?" Francesca asked.

"Yes...some of them" Ark responded. "See there that bright star that is what we call Gaser. Now place your thumb just below it and the next star is Hoolt. The stars all around make a picture, but it is too light right now."

"Your grandfather taught you all this? You are very lucky!" she paused. "Where is your grandfather now?" Suddenly Ark felt like he'd been stabbed with a knife. A sharp pain in his chest. He couldn't picture him or any of them anymore, except his brother. Francesca sensed the change in his mood. "You must teach me. Every night."

Ark nodded, but they sat in silence. A summons from within the Citadel finally relieved the tension. Francesca spoke, "I must go. But please, please come back tomorrow and I will read you more stories and you can show me the stars." And with that she disappeared into the Citadel. Ark sat alone until the dawn.

19

Ark's thoughts were broken by the sound of a boat on the water below. It was now nearly dusk and the noise of oars lapping, and whispered voices were accompanied by the faint glow of lanterns emerging around the corner.

Standing on the brow of the thin gondola style boat was Will Gascon, his arm held aloft with a lantern on a tall pole about four feet above his head. The lantern wobbled awkwardly casting strange shadows. Behind Gascon were six other guards, five staring up the walls into the rooftops, whilst Garick sat steering the boat.

"Keep the boat steady Garick, this lantern is going to smash on to the walls!", Will complained, just as with eerie timing the lantern scraped the wall.

"It's your feeble arms, Gascon. Hold it tighter and use your foot to secure the bottom of the pole." Garick replied.

"My feet are staying exactly where they are…. wait what's that!" Gascon took his left hand off the pole and pointed skyward, before quickly grabbing the pole before it fell away.

"Was it the beast?" asked one of his colleagues. A rumble of excitement spread through the others. Since earlier that afternoon, following the first significant sighting of the beast, the Duke had announced a 10 gold sovereigns reward to whoever could capture the beast. A few guards stayed on duty, but the garrison allowed for as many as possible to scour the streets.

All were silent listening for any sound and squeezing their eyes to see any movement in the faint light. These backstreets and canals were all being searched, but Garik didn't hold out much hope. "Nothing" he said.

"How the hell are we supposed to find this beast in the dark?" whined Gascon. We can't see a thing and if we did how are we going to capture it?"

"Bait" Garik calmly announced. "Any monster or demon out there will see your puny body and see it as easy prey. It will then attack you and whilst it's devouring you, the rest of us will grab it. Simple." The other guards all laughed. Gascon couldn't be sure if he was joking or not. Worst of all they should all be inside right now with their doors firmly shut. The rumour was that people had started to fall sick and the docks had been shut. Still 10 gold sovereigns were a lot of money and would allow him to maybe flee the city if things got too bad.

Beyond the immediate silence was the gentle hum of the city – not the deafening clamour that occurred during the day, as people were locking themselves away. The Citadel had also closed to traffic, how he wished he'd been a Citadel rather than City Guard. After this was all over, he'd have to think about how he could make that happen. Right now, he needed to keep his wits about him, or he'd end up in the water or the beasts next meal.

In the Citadel the mood was tense. People had started to attend the Temples and churches with the Priests running daily vigils that were crammed to the gills. The Council no longer sat but that had just driven the councillors to continually call for individual and smaller meetings with the Duke. The agenda was always "plague" but today he had a meeting that he assumed Ishman had cancelled as it seemed almost petty in comparison.

There had been countless crazy schemes from various subjects on how the beast could be caught. There had even been three different individuals bring in the dead carcases of goats claiming they had killed the beast. There have been a letter claiming the beast was stalking Francesca - that was scary. The Duke had now banned Francesca from the roof garden just in case.

Terrico was an old friend of his fathers who had overseen the Dam for most of his career, being one of the few men who understood how it worked. Luckily, he had established a Ministry for the Dam and trained up an effective team to manage it before retiring. By the time he had retired he had started to lose his memory and lived up to the stereotype of some old professor, so his father had set him up with a workshop in an old stable within the Citadel to keep him busy and safe.

The Duke had always like him, and so decided to humour him today and give himself some well-earned light relief. Terrico entered the Duke's office with a bundle of parchments under his arms, walking rapidly with a servant boy picking up dropped parchments behind him. The boy would force them under his arm as he carried a small bundle of cow hide. Terrico's opening statement was cryptic: "Hot air, your highness"" he stammered. The Duke grimaced.

"Hot air in balloons." They float above the city, and you can hunt the beast from above." The Duke picked his words carefully, "You mean to fly?"

"In a manner of speaking...your lordship...floating really......" Terrico then instigated a flurry of activity, his servant busily readying the animal skin above a small lamp. The Duke was intrigued and in moments he saw a small circle of animal skin the size of a tunic tied at each corner to a circular metal ring. The whole contraption sat above a small lamp opened to allow the flame to be visible.

The Duke's assistants stared on in bemusement. The flame continued to burn, and then something miraculous happened. The animal skin began to rise.... the servant let go, but in his hand, there was a rope tied to the ring. As the skin rose the servant was able to keep control of the contraption. Everyone's jaw dropped, and then suddenly as the contraption reached the roof, it plunged to the ground with a crash!

"That is remarkable!" the Duke exclaimed.

"Yes, my Lord. I call it an 'hot air pod'. We build lots of them with baskets and fires in the basket, that means the hot air pod won't fall to the ground..."

"Yes, I see..." the Duke finished his sentence..."with a guard in who spots the beast. He will need a bell or horns of some kind...will he not?"

"Perhaps an archer sir, who can shoot it immediately", Ishman chipped in.

The Duke considered for a while. The beast may well be the least of his problems, but this technology was very interesting. Who knows when he may need to evacuate the Citadel and this may just be the answer. Meanwhile it would create a distraction fo the city and perhaps draw attention away from some of his other plans. "Make it happen! Get to it! Terrico you may have just saved the city!"

A little encouragement never went amiss.

20

"What is the latest death count?" The Duke had found the days hard as more and more bodies had been reported. The plague was well and truly here. The clerk reeled off more numbers, but the Duke no longer listened.

The Citadel was like a tomb. No one left the Citadel - no-one came in. Everyone depressed, people wandering from room to room like zombies. The only happy face was that of Francesca. What a joy she was. Boundlessly enthusiastic with her tales and songs. In the evenings she would play the piano and for a few moments the Duke's cares would drift away. But even her joy had become muted after his tough actions for her safety. He had had no choice, the roof garden had to be closed off because the slum children had been seen on the rooves. That had changed her mood. She still sung but the vivacity has gone.

"Your lordship, she is here." Ishman announced. The enigmatic Priestess glided in, almost like she was floating on air, and stopped in front of him. No bowing, no polite nod, just a stare and as always it made him nervous.

"Good, you are here...so, let's cut to the chase...you have provided an interesting piece of... verse...."

"Prophecy" she interrupted but volunteered no more. He had called the Priestess back in because graffiti had appeared on the walls of the Citadel, overnight. Scrawled in blood, or possibly, just red paint were the words: "SACRIFICE FOR OUR SALVATION."

The Temple priests had been adamant that it meant that the Gods required a sacrifice, but they were unclear what it was to be. He sat back whilst they debated what should be sacrificed. The Duke had never been overly religious but this would certainly make him doubt his faith. And then of course the Priestess turned up.

"Yes, prophecy...very, very...confusing." He looked to her for more. Still, nothing. "Well, the truth is I, no We need to know what it means."

You pause. "What does it mean?" Silence. Now the Duke was going to hold the silence. After several moments she closed her eyes.

"It can mean many things, my gift is to receive the future, not to interpret it", she finally spoke.

"Very useful", thought the Duke. He continued, "Well, okay...I have asked the Priests and monks, and pretty much anyone who could advise, and they had all come up with some suggestions, all be it, with a common theme. It seemed the answer lay in the Beast. That the Beast of the roofs is the key. Do you agree?"

She spoke, "It could be interpreted in that way." She seemed to think it over. "The Beast must die, or the seas will fall!" At last, something definitive. "You must catch and destroy this Beast...and sacrifice it to our Gods." A long silence. "Sacrifice is always essential." She ended.

"I'll take that!" Enough was enough. The Priestess turned and left. Had he said she could go? It didn't matter, the Duke had heard enough. The Beast must die.

***

Rahim sipped at a glass of wine, swirled it around in the glass and then held it up to the light. The reds danced around creating different shadows and colours. "Blood is life" he whispered to himself. The plague numbers were a concern, not for his safety, but for how it would affect his plans. On the positive side Francesca wouldn't constantly be demanding to leave the Citadel and therefore he could intensify her lessons; everyone would be on edge and no doubt order would start to break down within the walls, putting the Duke under pressure. That was no bad thing.

The downside was that although personally he felt safe, if the plague breached the walls everything could become catastrophic very quickly. Perhaps it was time to begin accelerating the plans, time to act now.

Images ran through Ark's head. Dreams or waking nightmares of the days alone on the roofs after his brother left him. His heart had yearned for his brother for so long but now a new yearning has taken over. His thoughts constantly returned to the roof garden where

Francesca read. Night after night he would return, and she would tell him wondrous stories of the heroes and heroines of the past. In return Ark would tell her of the stars, of the winged horse and the seven sisters, whilst the city below slowly died.

The Duke now saw Terrico's invention as critical. He checked in with Terrico and the team of assistants that the Duke had supplied to accelerate the process. They worked through the days and nights and before long the first batch of "pods" was ready. And so it was, that the city became witness to the strangest sight. Rising from the walls of the Citadel and carefully chosen parts of the city, balloons with guards were seen rising above the rooves.

There were some initial accidents. It took two lost balloons to lead that the balloons needed to be secured to the ground by adequate lengths of rope, but before long the skies were filled with the brave new sentinels.

Ark hid. He hid for days until the hunger became unbearable. His only chance was at night. The balloons were still in the sky, but the guard's torches transmitted a weak light that created eerie shadows. These shadows led to countless false alarms. Tonight, he would have to venture out, hunger making him brave.

Groups of guards would congregate in the street, waiting for an alarm. Ark was hidden in a Temple tower, and there was a balloon positioned just a few feet away. He climbed slowly down the opposite wall, a blind spot for the guard. Reaching the roof of the Temple he began to crawl away from the spire. Here he was vulnerable. The temple was the highest point and if the guard had spun around to face him then he would have been seen.

Ark crawled slowly to the end of the Temple roof. He made the short leap to the building opposite where there were shadows from objects on the roof to help disguise his movements. But on the roof were other things, things that were a greater threat that the guards in the balloons.

Lilkin was also hiding. He was in the shadow of a chimney stack above the old Wayfarer Inn, opposite the Temple. His gang was spread out in similar hide holes across the city. Clasped in his hand was a stick with a knife attached. He was holding his breathe. The air slowly escaped from his nostrils. Draped around his shoulders was a dark, dirty cape helping him to hide but also providing some warmth. And he was waiting. A few cats had spooked him and the rain earlier in the day had demoralised him.

He heard breathing. Very quiet, very subtle, but breathing and it was coming closer. He dares not look past the chimney stack he was perched behind. He would wait until the last moment. He heard steps, not just breathing. Whatever it was, it was very close. His gang wasn't with him. His bravery was being tested. He grasped the spear tighter. His hands were sweaty, his grip was tight.

Closer, the beast was coming closer. A shadow leaked past the chimney stack. His eyes widened. His mouth dried. Suddenly he thrust the spear and the shadowy space.

The spear flew forward and hit flesh. It met resistance but then the spear slid further in. The Beast screamed. Lilkin's eyes misted over. Red - all he saw was red and a bundle of blackness falling on the tiles. Tiles flew into the air and crashed around him.

Lilkin let go of the spear, his insides feeling hollow. In a second the Beast was falling, the spear plunged into its side. It fell down the sloping roof towards the ground. The Beast grabbed the chimney as the tiles ripped away from his feet. The Beast suddenly found air; his last refuge gone. His final journey to the ground five storeys below.

"The beast is dead." Whispered Lilkin.

21

Ark lay there on the ground, looking up at the sky. Forty feet above ruddy, shocked faces stared down at him. They seemed to be shouting but he could hear nothing. Not silence but an emptiness in his head. Then a wave of pain shot through his body like a fire on a spill of oil. And the pain was excruciating.

Hands pointed from the roof, and heads started to appear and then disappear. Ark was in trouble, he knew it. He tried to move but the pain was too much, and a blackness began to appear before his eyes. Then the inevitable happened and shadows appeared before his eye. Figures were now descending upon him, reaching out with their arms. If he was not close to death now, he would be in minutes as the mob would tear him to pieces.

As expected, he felt the touch of hands, but they seemed to be guiding him into the air, and as the blackness began to complete in his head and eyes, he imagined himself floating above the ground and floating on a wave above the cobbles. When he awoke the pain was still there and his first words were an aching scream. He saw the scene around him and fell back into the darkness.

He woke again, and the pain had eased but he struggled to move. Ark realised he was tied down. He looked around and realised he was in a bare room on a wooden cot, and his hands and legs were bound with rope and tied to the bed. In the corner of the room was a man sat in a chair watching him. He was old and worn, like an old destitute beggar. Seeing him awake the man spoke:

"You are a very interesting conundrum." he said, never taking his eyes off the boy. His face was angular like his features had been carved with a knife from an old piece of wood. His skin was pale, almost translucent with the blueish veins showing through. His hair white, but with a sliver thread hidden amongst the foliage. He was the man Ark had seen before.

Who are you?" Ark blurted out.

"Who am I?" the man seemed to be considering the question. "A lot of people have been asking that. Who are you?" Then pausing, but not as if waiting an answer…." Who are any of us? I suppose you are meaning, what's my name? Well, my name is…. not really the right question. It's not really that important. I don't think it will give you any answers. No, my name is not that important. Maybe what is, is my purpose."

"Where am I? How long have I been here?" Ark had hardly heard the old man's mumblings.

"You are in the Great Temple, and it has been 2 weeks since we found you in the streets." The traveller went onto to explain how a temple monk had witnessed the fall and how Ravi had rallied the monks to help the victim. It wasn't until they found the boy that they realised he had been badly wounded in his side as well as damaged from the fall. I must say your healing has been incredible, you had a broken leg and both arms as well as the wound in your side. All are healed."

"Why am I tied up? Untie me!" Ark tried to yell but his throat was dry.

"Here, take some water" the traveller lent forward with a mug of water. "I'll untie those binds. They were just to stop you moving about whilst you were healing. There were times when you were writhing around in a lot of pain."

He held the mug to Ark's mouth whilst he sipped the water then placed it on the floor whilst he untied the bonds. "And how do you feel are you still hurting?" asked the Traveller.

Ark rubbed his arms. "I feel tired. Aching. Sore….but I'm okay. I am in the Great Temple?"

"Yes, and you are safe here. Rest, sleep and we will talk later." With that he stood up and left the room. Ark noticed that a key was turned in the lock after the door was shut.

In two weeks, the city had changed. It was the same city, but it had suffered the ravages of a hundred years in a few weeks. Like an aging face the signs of degradation were clear to see.

Rubbish had built up and found its way into the canals so that a build-up of waste scum layer across the surface of the water. Red crosses marked the doors of households housing the infested. Some of these were broken and collapsed where looters had raided the abandoned homes. Bodies had ceased being lifted and the stench had come to replace the usual odours of the city. The city looked like it had seen the ravages of a besieging army.

Carts were abandoned, wheels broken, and sides demolished where they had been pulled apart for wood and provisions. There were boats floating untethered on the canals and in the great lake beneath the Dam. Scattered across the rooves were the remains of broken and crashed pods. But it was the silence that was most noticeable. None of the sounds of the hustle and bustle of the city, traders calling, kids shouting, people laughing, swearing yelling. Just silence. Except, every now and then the sound of crying or the death knells of the cursed.

Ark drifted in and out of consciousness, sometimes dreaming sometimes awake and recalling memories of his past. He had not been the youngest in the clan. No there were smaller children and babies, but he was the youngest of those who had passed eight caravans to the capital and were ready to earn their keep.

The clan had entered the city from the landward side. This meant that they had had to leave their carts and horses in the outpost on the other side of the mountains, whilst they travelled in on foot and donkeys. This was normal his brother had said. In previous years he had stayed with the caravans, whilst his brother last year had made the journey into the city. In all there were three families travelling in together, one clan.

Ark couldn't recall all the interrelationships, but his mother had tried to explain it, but it never stuck. All that was important was his brother, his mother, father, grandfather and his uncle. Where his father was strict and sullen, distant from both of his children, his uncle was a far friendlier spirit. He joked and sang songs with the boys. His father led the group, and everyone respected him, but his uncle was loved.

By day, his uncle would walk beside him, his brother and the other children, whilst his father and the elders walked together. The women keep counsel in the rear of the walking train. His grandfather would spend time telling stories of the stars, and the histories of the clan. The stories would be full of colour and passion, and no-one cared that they seemed to change every time. On request or as part of a tale he would sing songs and the children would join in with their parts. Even the other adults could be heard humming along on some of the more popular songs.

When they camped at nights, his uncle would rule the roost around the campfire. Flirting with the women and telling his more ribald tales. His father would sit back, always lost in thought, but occasionally cracking a brief smile at a particularly funny joke from his uncle. This is when the uncle smiled the most.

Ark remembered crossing the final peak and looking down on the city for the first time. He felt like a great eagle. The city was stunning, like an opened treasure chest. He remembered standing agape. A hand touched his shoulder, it was his uncle: "Makes you feel like a great eagle, doesn't it?" he whispered in his ear and winked as he walked away. Ark loved his uncle.

Ark spent most of his time with his older brother. His relationship with him was not like that with others in the clan. Other brothers were constantly competing and fighting, a struggle for dominance; but with his brother it was different. Cas was always quieter and supporting of his little brother. When they played, they acted out their uncle's tales. Cas was always the hero, and Ark the villain but Ark never carried the bruises that other younger brothers in the clan did from such games.

It was Cas that he inadvertently clung to as they descended to the city. Uncle was way ahead, goading the other males with the exploits he would get up to with the ladies of the city; his father would be shepherding the group and conversing with guards and other officials we met on the way. It was Ark's brother who would protect him.

The noise of the city was deafening. Ark was used to the unique quite of the savannahs or the eerie silence of the forests. In the forest's Ark could pick out the birdsongs or chatter of the fauna. Here in the city, it was all a glorious mixture of unrecognisable noise. He would catch part of a noise but lose it like an eel between his hands.

And these were the memories Ark had. That night they stayed in a lean-to shelter behind an inn, the only cover the roof above them, the sides open to the elements. The city was warm that night, though. His uncle and many of the males were not around, although he would wake to find their bodies piled around them in the morning. The night was the strangest that Ark had endured. Excited but afraid. Nervous and anxious but desperate to discover more.

"Are you excited about tomorrow?" his brother had asked. Ark just nodded. "Uncle says we will make a lot of money tomorrow, and if the crowds are good then we can expect to stay for another three or four days." Cas's eyes were deep blue like his uncles but there was more of their father's cold calmness in him.

"Of course, uncles share will be spent before the end of the week, and father will be furious, but we will be having enough to by the supplies to see us through winter. Of course, it's been many years since we have been here, father says, and probably since any clan has been here. Hopefully they will not have seen our acts or anything like it.

The city was mobbed, though and father says that there are many travellers who may have seen something similar back in their homelands; but of course, our act is something special". And their act was. At least that's what all the elders said. Ark had never seen anything to compare with it, so was no real judge. His brother described them as acrobats but never in front of father. "Anyone can be an acrobat, we are special, we can fly", he would say. His father would always stare rigidly for seconds until he would show a very rare smile. "We fly, Ark. We fly."

The next day he awoke to the hustle and bustle of the clan preparing for the day. Lari, the Girnata player was blowing into his instrument, ensuring a clean tune would be heard. Fay and his brother Cares were banging the small round drums, the darbuka, practising the intricate rhythms that would accompany each of the gymnastic displays. By the time they came to their great finale, they would be playing at a frantic speed which would help whip up the crowd, ready for the death defining leap that his brother would undertake.

Looking round there was no fear or nervousness. His father sat filing his toenails, an ancient custom that all the males would do. Ark had always believed this was to ensure none of the climbers would stab and sharp nail into the eyes or face of their lifters, but his brother had corrected him and had said it was a religious thing, all about cleaning. This made sense. The males were always washing themselves, especially their hands and lower limbs.

His uncle still slept. He was curled like a pet dog on a blanket, snoring with each breathe. As Ark removed the bowl from his bag, and began to wash his hands, his father gave his uncle a hard but not painful kick to indicate it was time to rise.

Father then gathered everyone together and talked through the plan. Everyone knew the roles in the performances they would give today, but when and where would need to be explained. He addressed each figure and told them their specific role. Each person would have a specific named role. He then explained where we go and the directions. The group then dispersed for final preparations and Ark noticed that four of the group were taken to one side, and his father spoke quietly and firmly to them, to each he handed a bag, bags that Ark did not remember seeing on the journey to the city. The bags were bulging but Ark could not make out the content.

By mid-morning they made their way to the city market, out the front of the Great Temple. And his memories began to change. His stomach making the connection first through a sudden emptiness and tingling. Then his head pounding, and he was back, with his brother being chased by the mob. The same mob, the mob wanting to kill him.

His brother's words were short and sharp, his movements instinctive. Then he was dragged by his brother, his bodies movements in his control, now his body was commanded by the instinct of survival and the familiarity of his life on the roofs.

And now the fear was not the mob. His escape route had become that of that fateful race for survival, and he was heading for the same roofs and the river; the fear now whether he would need to jump again and whether he could. Tile, roof, tile, roof, the details of the world around him a blur. His tough, bare feet taking more pain, his elbows and body scuffing against chimneys and outcrops. His brother's words, pounding like a rhythmic mantra; "run, run, run"

His eyes seeing the escape route, but his mind mixing history and present into twisted tortured images. His brother in the water, the mob behind him...and suddenly he stopped; his feet spewing dust as he slid to the very edge, the very edge all those years ago, and he swung his arms back to stop his body taking that fateful dive into the river below. He was almost airborne, almost floating, but he pulled himself back and fell to the floor.

22

The Guardian looked out from his balcony across the inner city to the sprawling metropolis beyond. In his hand was gripped a crumpled piece of parchment. "Two thousand dead. Two thousand dead". He spoke aloud but to no-one and his eyes creased as if staring into each house.

"This beast is a distraction. The Duke is a fool. The plague is here, and he has no concept of what is to follow." He seemed to smile. Turning from the balcony he made his way to the collection of chests that were stacked with his chamber. Reaching for the smallest he opened it and reached in to pull out a small figurine, an idol of the great god Ezkebel. Lighting a series of candles either side of the figurine he placed them on the floor in front of him.

Then, he reached into the chest and removed a pouch containing coloured stones, each the size of a small potato. He took out the red stone, and placed the others back in the pouch, then leaning to his left, placed the stone, still gripped tightly at the furthest reach of his span to his right. His had pressed hard on the stone as he then traced firstly an arc of red chalk in the floor that became a circle enclosing the Guardian and the figurine.

He methodically placed the stone back in the pouch, shut the chest and placed it outside the circle. Closing his eyes, he then kneeled in front of the figurine and began a slow murmuring. The words, if they were words, were indistinguishable but seemed to have a rhythmic pattern. The Guardian entered a trance like state, as the candles flickered, and the murmurs became a chant.

Minutes passed, and soon became an hour, before the chanting suddenly stopped and the candles went out, burnt down to their metal holders. The Guardian's eyes suddenly opened, and he stood up. He seemed energized, his skin alive with a deep scarlet, like a bruise on the surface of the skin. The colour faded back to his original paleness but there was still a change in the Guardian as he moved quickly around the room and lifted chests down form their place in the pile.

He jumped to the door, opened it and summoned the Golden Guard outside, who nodded his head and entered the room. "Remove your helmet. The time to act has arrived and we must be hasty. It is clear to me what we need to do, and your men will need to act immediately."

"Yes, your lordship". The Guard removed his helmet and nodded again.

"The plague is here and with it is the end of this city. Listen to these instructions and then bring all the Golden Guard to me immediately. Here are four chests, each of the guards must take these chests and place them at these point in the city."

Rahim reached for the papers on his desk, hurling them to his left and right until he found a rolled parchment that he was looking for. He unrolled it and placed a glass paperweight and an empty goblet on opposite sides, the corners curled up, but the content was plain to see: a map of the city. Grabbing a quill from an open ink pot he waved the guard over, splattering red ink across the map in doing so, and marked four crosses at what seemed random points in the city.

"Here, here, here and here!" Take the chests and place them in these places. Remove the lids and place them somewhere dark and out of sight Rachim pointed to the chests, "They are old and worn so no-one will think them of value. After this you and your men are to return to the Citadel. At midnight tomorrow half of your men will seize the inner Citadel gates, ensure the gates are shut, and they will guard those gates until relieved, ensuring they are no longer opened and that no-one gets into the city.

You and the rest of your guards at the same time will wake the Duke and we will inform him that he no longer governs this city, that it belongs to the Emperor. It belongs to me! Go get your men and return as soon as possible, I will prepare the chests."

Of course, this was no new plan dreamed up on the spot. Rahmin never believed that the plague would not make it to the city; he'd just hoped that it would take longer. He always had plans. Contingencies he called them, and when he prayed to his favourite Gods, he saw what he needed to confirm that he was right; he was chosen.

When he travelled south across the Empire, he had seen the true devastation that the plague had brought. By the time he had left the ports of the North to sail around the tip of the empire, he had seen what was to come. The world would be laid waste. The kingdoms and fiefs would fall and nowhere and no-one would survive.

Well maybe somewhere would. Maybe the despised, carbuncle on the base of the Empire, hidden by its mountains and its Great Dam. Maybe, that could survive and if it could survive so would he. Who knew what opportunities could then come from a devastated Empire, a vacuum of power with its kings, dukes and guardians laid waste?

It would need a new saviour, and by the Gods, the Gods were not going to come and save them. Gods who have sat in their heavens forever, who had probably died or just lost interest. That is except for Ezkebel. Ezkebel who did talk to him, Ezkebel who guided him, Ezkebel who had shown him the vision of the future. Ezkebel who had shown him the world at his feet.

It was Rahmin's idea to accompany the Lady Francesca. Not the most important of the Emperor's children, but unlike the crown prince very, much female. The youngest as well, so the least corrupted by the trappings of the Empire. The most malleable, for who can deny that in any new kingdom a malleable bride with the right bloodline might just ease the taming of his brave new world.

And when he prayed, the vision was still there. The future was still his and so the plague had come but the plan would remain.

He used a piece of cutlery to lever off the lids of the four chests that were an important part of his plan. He had seen what the dead from the disease could do and it was essential that the city did not become swarmed with the dead who walked. He had seen it when passing Frizsad. Thousands surrounding the walls trapping its King. He would starve to death, if the plague did not get him.

The death of the city populace did not pose any moral quandary for him. He just did not want them to rise and trap him here. So, he must beat the plague by taking away its fuel. The city must die, but not from the plague. And for that to happen he would need an army. And that is what he brought with him.

Lifting the lids of the chest and removing the straw that padded the top, he could see the first of two hundred figurines, fifty in each chest. Each the size of a finger, each an intricately carved warrior from the blackest wood. Their faces blank but their armour detailed enough to make out individual ringlets, and each baring a shield, a sword and a spear. "My army", he whispered.

He stopped for a moment, lost in his vision and then reached for the chest with his candles, stones and God figures and pulled out a jar full of reddish sand. Then in each chest he emptied the sand until the jar was drained. Then he sealed the lids back on the chests and awaited the Golden Guards return.

These would not help him take control of the Citadel. No army would help him do this, with the vast number of Citadel guards. He would need the Council on side.

Tomorrow he would gather the Lords together, those that he had spent to last few weeks grooming for his purpose. They would be essential to sanctioning his actions or be the first to die.

The knock at the door heralded the return of the Golden Guard. He ushered them in, and they lifted the four chests between eight of them and headed down the corridor. He closed the door behind them and walked to the balcony, surveying the city once more. The dark had crept in, and the night was silent. The winds were still, and the moon shone weakly, not quite full. The city was asleep. He smiled.

**

When dawn broke, Rahmin was already awake and writing. The quill moving ferociously across the parchment. He grabbed the completed parchment with his left hand and directed it into the air whilst he continued to write on the next parchment, not adjusting his eyes: "Take this for Lord Shaancur".

The Guard took it in his hand rolling it up into a tube. The pair repeated this five times and the Rachim said: "Go now, they are to come to my chambers by 11am, today. Make sure they understand." The Guard nodded his head and left the room.

"Now we shall see" Rahmin whispered to himself before nodding his head slowly. The Lords arrived one at a time and entered Rahmin's study. He made each comfortable on the study's balcony, servicing them a drink each, himself. When all were gathered, he began to speak. "My Lords…" he began.

"What by the Gods is this all about!" interrupted the Lord Justice.

"Yes, you will see shortly, my friends. Please take a drink and relax. I will come to my point imminently. "It has been a long time since any of you have ventured north of the mountains, across the seas, into the heart of the empire, I believe?"

Lord Justice went to answer but Rahmin raised a hand. "No need to answer. I know it is. In fact, most of the Lords of this city have never left the city except to holiday on the spice islands to the south, when the city has been just too warm, or the volcano has rumbled to regularly for your liking. I am here to tell you that outside of the city, in the Empire, things are not all they seem. The world is turned upside down, and your sister cities are dying from the plague; and the rule of law…well their rule of law is huddled under the bed until the bogeyman goes away. Turmoil. Yes, the world is in turmoil and its coming to your doors!"

The Lords looked at each other. Lord Shanur nodded. "That my friend is why I am here. To think a Guardian would be seen fit to waste his time babysitting a twelve-year-old. No. My purpose is plain and clear. The Emperor has sent each of us Guardians to the cities of the empire to review, assess and act." Rahmin opened a short parchment and read aloud. "The Emperor's words: 'The cities must be strong, and I need an oasis of safety for the royal family. If they are not so, make them so."

He let the words hang in the air. The Lord Justice was the first to break the silence, "The city is strong. The plague is minimal, and no more refugees are coming in. The Emperor has his 'oasis'."

Rachim slowly nodded his head. "Two thousand dead today, the numbers growing. A city of slums, ripe for vermin and disease to spread at our feet. The Duke...the Duke chasing shadows on the rooftops. Chasing but not catching. Messages of doom on the walls. My Lord Justice, the city is not strong. This city hangs by a thread above a pit of death and decay."

The Lords shuffled nervously in their seats. Rahmin paused and to himself whispered..." time for some butter".

"Of course, you have all worked tirelessly to turn the tide. Worked in spite of the system to make the Emperor's southern gem safe, but there is only so much you can do. Only so much you can achieve without the support of your Duke."

"I think you should get to your point, Rahmin, although I am sure we have all jumped ahead to where we think you are going." Spoke the Lord Justice.

The Great Seer spoke up, "Yes, there are signs, signs every day that doom is upon us."

"Yes. Upon us. But not I think overwhelming us. There is time. Today I have set in motion the solution to our direst need. The Citadel gates will remain sealed. No-one in, no-one out. Tonight, at midnight, the Duke will be arrested. I will arrest him in the name of the Emperor for crimes to be revealed once extradited to the North. I have that warrant here in my hand. Lord Shanur you will call the Council for midnight tonight and ratify the warrant. The Duke will be removed until the extradition can be actioned. Lord Justice you will then have the portals."

The Lords sat stunned. "My friends, we are at a precipice. Your fingers are clutching at the edges. I am reaching down to pull you to safety...but time is not on our side."

The Lord Justice looked deep in thought. "You are already working out how you will benefit, perhaps, you're thinking you'll be the next Duke?" thought Rachim.

"I'm sure the Duke would action anything we asked. What are the crimes the Duke has done?" Lord Shanur stammered.

"You are scared" thought the Guardian. You hate confrontation, you just want to count coin, protect your status, scared of retribution"

"Lord Shanur you are with friends. We are your peers. This is not your decision alone, and the Emperor knows you are a loyal and obedient servant." Rachim spoke directly to the Lord. "And you others" he thought, "Great Seer, you who loves your Gods but when confronted with meeting them soon lose faith."

"Great Seer, you think no-one has listened to your fears, but they have. The Gods have and has made us as your strength. They have sent you a warning that we all must heed. You were chosen and we are servants at your feet. Those the Gods love he sends the truth." Silence. No drinking. No shuffling.

"Your instructions are clear. Lord Justice, at midnight I need you to stand the Citadel Guard down in the corridors of the Duke's apartments. His private guard will be there, but I will...negotiate that. Thank you. Act quickly, act well and know that you are doing the Emperor and the Gods work."

"Ezkebel's work...." Rahmin thought as the Lord's quickly exited the room.

***

Time passed slowly. The way only time passes when you are waiting for something. Rahmin spent the day in his chambers, conversing only with his guards. The Duke spent the morning working through papers in his office, or rather shuffling papers around whilst he daydreamed looking at the sun shining through his balcony doors.

The Citadel was quiet, quieter than normal. What was it? He strolled to the balcony and noticed the birds flying through the sky. The word was that the Beast was dead. The guard had seen him fall from quite a height, but by the time they had got to the street level the body was gone. Probably stripped in minutes by the beggars and low life. But maybe not...The guard had stabbed him with a spear and according to his officer it had probably killed the Beast there and then. The way the guard had described the Beast made him wonder whether there was a big of exaggeration going on; horns, monkey-like but with a bearlike fur, eyes like a hawk.

And those balloon pods! What was I thinking? The site of these falling from the sky, or rather the men falling from the sky and sheets of cowhide floating off into the heavens was comical. If man was meant to fly, the Gods would have given him wings.

Still, it had been a week, and no further sightings. He had sent his guards to mingle in the inns and markets to ask. Still a body would be perfect. If one didn't turn up soon, he may just have to create one.

"Sire". A voice interrupted his thoughts. Spinning round, there was Ishman.

"I didn't hear you come in."

"No, sir." Ishman offered no further explanation, but in his hand were five or six rolled up parchments. "What do you have?"

"The daily correspondence, sir. You will see the latest numbers on the plague, there sir and...some other items that may interest you." The Duke grabbed the numbers first an unrolled the parchment. "It seems to be slowing down a little, although the docks have taken a pounding by the looks of it."

"Yes sir. And you will see a very interesting, an unsettling report from the Commander, as well. Probably just more scaremongering"

"What is it?" he grabbed the parchment with the Commander's seal and read.

"Preposterous. Is the plague not enough for these people? We have got rid of one bogeyman to dream up another. The Commander says that there are reports of grave robbing in the mountain tombs, and even a report of people seeing their plague riddled relatives walking the earth again. Utter nonsense!"

"Yes, Sire."

"The rest are all administrative nonsense, deal with them."

"Just one more, though", said Ishman, pointing with his spindly index finger at a small note rolled over and mixed up with the larger scrolls.

The Duke unravelled it and saw that it was not an official document, but rather a handwritten note, in poor ink and written with a poor hand."

It's not dead. It didn't die. I can tell you where it is.   Lilkin

"An impudent street boy" informed Ishman. The Duke sucked his little finger and thought for a while.

"Ishman, find this boy immediately and bring him to me. A silver coin shown to any street urchin should lead to him. I need him here within the hour. Go"

23

Lilkin walked up the steps of the great Citadel, twirling a silver coin between his fingers, following the stiff, pompous servant through the Citadel side doors. He had been easy enough to find by one of the poor beggar boys on the streets, although this one had not been part of his gang. Hence, why he took the coin off him. Probably a bit petty, as this trip should see him get a whole pile of coins, but habits are habits.

He spat on his hands as he walked and applied the spit to his long hair, pushing it back over his ears. Best look presentable, he thought. The chamber was not one of the great ones, but still impressive, with painted ceilings showing the lesser-known histories of the city and a floor of polished stone, now slightly smeared by his footsteps. "Very nice room", Lilkin opened the conversation as he was halted a few feet from the Duke.

The Duke, reeling he was there spun quickly, gesticulating with the paper in his hand. "What's this?"

"That's, sir is the truth." Lilkin wasn't intimidated.

"The hell it is! A guard speared him, and the beast fell seven stories to the cobbles below".

"I speared him." Lilkin corrected him. "He fell from the roof and then.... well then, he disappeared." The boy's nerve was unbelievable. The Duke looked a him, holding his stare for seconds that seemed like hours. Behind the eyes the duke's brain was filtering a hundred thoughts. "The rats got him", the Duke answered.

"Bloody big rats" Lilkin replied. "Or rat..."

The Duke grabbed the boy by the neck and held him against the wall. Lilkin was shocked but kept his nerve. "What... do... you... mean"

Lilkin pointed at his neck, and the Duke dropped him to the ground. "Speak!" Lilkin still spluttered and coughed, then abruptly swung his open palm in the air showing the silver coin. Then wiggled the fingers.

"You will have coin, your ragamuffin. Tell me what I need to know, and you will walk out of here with your pockets dragging on the tiles. Talk"

"I was there, you see. We've been following the Beast for weeks and know his rat runs. He fell alright, like rain from the sky. And hit the cobbles like."

"SNAP" he clapped his hands together, the noise echoing around the chamber. He lay in a mess, his legs one way, his arms the other. We all looked away. I think Tog was sick. There was blood too. Yes, seeping from under him. Then the strangest thing happened. A monk was there leaning over him. He bent down, and lifted the body up"

"But dead?" interrupted the Duke.

"I, we all thought so", Lilkin shook his head. "It's just something the monk said", he shook his head again, his cockiness gone.

"What did he say?" The room was noticeably silent. "Live. He said 'Live'".

"What the hell does that mean? Live?"

"I don't know, but we followed him, but for an old man he was fast. Within a few yards there was no more blood. We kept up and Togs was closest. He said the monk did stop talking, mumbling a prayer, but in language he didn't know. Through the city we went until...."

"Until where?"

Lilkin opened his closed palm, and the coin appeared again. "I'd really like to see the money before I say that." The Duke shook his head. Torturing the boy would take too long. He clicked his fingers and Ishman came forward, in his hands two leather bags the size of a loaf of bread, heavy with weight of the coins.

"Here". The Duke took them and dumped them at Lilkin's feet.

"Very nice. Very nice. You are a gentleman, sire."

"And..."

"The Temple, sir. He took the Beast to the Temple". Lilkin then grabbed the two bags and started walking backwards very slowly towards the door he came in. He looked over his shoulder at Ishman and then spun on his feet to turn and exit. At the door he stopped. "Oh, and by the way. It isn't no Beast. It's a boy, a Klarion boy."

The Duke stood motionless. Puzzled. "A boy?"

***

Things moved quickly after this. Back in his chambers the orders flew out from the Duke at Ishman like knives. "Summon the Council! Summon the Commander of the Citadel Guard! Get me Rahmin! Get me the head Priest!"

"Yes sire."

"No wait. Wait. Let's think this through. I can't send the guards into the Temple to get the Beast. The Priests will have a fit. The Council won't allow it, I'll be censured."

"No sir, no-one has the authority to demand anything of the Temple, not even the Priests."

"No-one. No-one. Someone. Someone close to the Emperor that even if he doesn't have permission the Council would need to dig through a pile of paperwork to repudiate it. The Guardians can do anything, and let's face it if the Council find out he was wrong, then they can string him up."

"I don't think the Guardian will do it, sir. He is not that arrogant, and he will see the trap." responded Ishman.

"No, you're wrong. He is that arrogant. He would love to be the one who snared the Beast. Summon him for me, Ishman"

***

Rahmin pondered. His plan was coming together but he still felt something wasn't right. Too much was out of his control now. Could he trust the Lord Justice? The Duke is a charismatic chap, and the soldiers seem to like him. What if they turn rebellious? I need a plan for them, I need a contingency. He paced the room, one hand behind is back. Maybe he should have kept a chest of warriors back from the city to help here in the Citadel. No, the use of magic would probably panic the Lords and guards alike and who knows how they would react. Then there was a knock at the door.

It was a Citadel Guard. "You are summoned Lord Rahmin to the Duke's private chambers." Rahmin froze. He knows. Those weak-willed lowlife Lords have squealed. Rahmin looked over the guard's shoulders. His Golden Guards were out in the city planting the crates.

What to do? He slowly picked up his cloak, and in doing so ferreted his slim knife in its folds. "Very well." He was not being arrested, just summoned. Rahmin would see how this played out. The walk was not long, but a thousand excuses and plans went through his head. Contingencies. Contingencies. When he finally reached the Duke's chambers, his contingency was ready, and he squeezed the handle of his knife through the folds of his cloak.

"Rahmin, come in. Sit down. I need your advice." Immediately Rahmin eased the grip on his dagger, his hand hidden beneath the folds. This friendliness was unexpected. "I will come straight to the point. I am in an awkward position."

"Yes, go on."

"We have reason to believe the Beast is not dead. That is it survived the fall," Rahmin's eyebrows rose in shock. "Go on."

"Monks or a monk from the Temple rescued it and carried it away to the Temple"

"My word" breathed Rahmin. "I am shocked."

"The temple you see...it's very sensitive...I can't just go in..."

"Yes. No, of course. Very difficult."

"I, the Council, we'd be heretics" the Duke added, slowly reeling the Guardian in, he thought.

"Yes, yes". Rahmin's mind was working again. Quickly, quickly.

"I just don't think new have the authority to go in and get the thing."

"No…. although if the monks have just rescued a poor soul and have no knowledge of its true nature…well surely they are at risk?" Rahmin was thinking on his feet.

"Absolutely, Guardian. Yes. They are at risk…. It would need an incredibly powerful person to risk the wrath of the…Gods." The silence was long.

"I could do it. I mean I probably have the authority…" Rahmin responded.

"Could you…? Do you think?" The Duke had to hold back a smile. He had got him. He! The Guardian couldn't give up a chance to show him up, show his authority.

"What men could we use? My guards. there are only a few?" began Rahmin.

"Leave that to me. Not the City Guard, they won't do, they are very superstitious bunch. No, we will use the Citadel Guard. I will send fifty men under Commander Valeri."

"Fifty?" questioned Rahmin. "You will need to surround the Temple, create a cordon, plus men to search inside. The Beast will try to flee, so men on the rooftops. I'm no soldier, but I'd say three times that number."

"That's three quarters of the Citadel Guard!!!" exclaimed the Duke.

"Yes, you are right…. but should the Beast escape…we would have caused the potential sacrilege for nothing." The Duke considered. Weighing the options." Yes, one hundred and fifty, but Rahmin I think you need to command them."

"Me, into the city?" He wants to trap me outside…Think, think.

"Maybe I can lose him outside, maybe the beast will kill him" thought the Duke.

"No, you are right. I will lead. But here is my plan. We send the guard out just before midnight. The monks will be at rest and the citadel too. No unnecessary questions. I won't leave with them but tell your Commander to meet me at the Temple. They will surreptitiously circle the Temple approaching slowly. It should all be over in a few minutes. I suggest you keep out of the way, in your chamber. The least you are seen to do with this the better. Yes, I can do this." He then paused to stare at the Duke. "I will do this for you and the for the city, but I will be repaid, and if you fail to back me in the Council tomorrow, I will come for you."

The Duke suddenly remembered he was dealing with a dangerous man. Maybe he had taken on too much here... but then again... maybe this was his chance to be rid of him.

***

Francesca had repeated the same action every day for a week. She would wake run straight for the balcony and look out at the city. After breakfast, she would run for the balcony and look out at the city. She would eat lunch...run to the balcony...eat dinner...run to the balcony...eat supper...run to the balcony...sheep. She didn't bother to see anyone, which means it was the third day when she heard the news: the Beast was dead. Ark was dead.

And then she cried. She'd never cried so much in her whole life. She hated this city, hated the Guardian, the Duke, the people, the plague. Everything. She refused to eat.

The Guardian had come to see her and asked what was wrong, but she couldn't tell him. How could she. That night she had looked at the stars, shining bright. She looked in vain for a new star to see if the Gods had placed Ark in the night sky already. There was nothing and eventually the clouds came over masking the light. It had rained, and she just sat in the rain a sobbed. She must have been carried in by one of the maids, dressed in dry clothes as she woke in her bed the next day.

She awoke with a headache and cough that became a fever and sweats and so she remained for the next two days. The Guardian had quarantined her, afraid that she had picked up the plague, her food just in front of the door. She got better, though the sadness did not pass. She ate but felt no need to let them know she was well. The Guardian visited and looked in on her but seemed happy that she was out the way. Eventually the doctors had the courage to venture in and announced that it was not the plague. By then it seemed she was forgotten.

So, she decided, plague or no plague she would return home. The city could rot. She would see her friends, her brothers and sisters.

***

As the Duke sat in his chambers, musing on the plan he made earlier that day; as the Guardian briefed his soldiers before slipping off into the city; as the Citadel Guard gathered ready to leave the Citadel; as the Lord Justice checked the clocks Francesca instigated her own plan.

Desperately trying to remember the moves and steps Ark took, she climbed onto the balcony rails and stretched for the guttering of the rooftop below. She was as tall a shim, but last time he had almost carried her over. She hoisted her dress – perhaps not the best choice for an escape – and pushed to complete the last few inches.

Her foot landed in the gutter and she threw herself forward onto the roof. Small pieces of twig scattered down to the Citadel courtyard below, but she was secure. She turned so her back was flat against the slanting roof. She took a deep breath. Rather than climb over the peak, she would follow the guttering around clutching the tiles until she was on the other side. She would be visible form the courtyard, but it was dark, and the guards would have to be looking.

She made it to the front and looked down. It must have been a hundred feet to the courtyard, though she could now see the next roof ten feet below, but flatter. She would need to jump as there was a yard gap between this and the building below. She would have to lean forward, and when she did her heart raced as she could see the shear drop below to the courtyard. Below the Citadel Guard was lining up, hundreds. Francesca did not think why. She closed her eyes then opened them; at least no-one was looking up at her.

Just jump. Just jump. It's fine. It's flat. She drew a breath and leapt from the gutter, down through the air and hit the roof. There was a crash, she rolled forward shocked by the impact and lay flat like an ungracious cat. She closed her eyes again, but no-one seemed to have noticed.

The guards far below no seemed to be passing out through the city's gates. That was strange she hadn't seen that before.

She decided just to crawl to the next ledge, away from the direction of the courtyard. Ark had just run and jumped when he reached the edge, but she couldn't remember what was beyond. She reached the edge and just sat, swing her legs over. They were cut and bruised, and her dress was torn.

Below her was a walkway, along balcony running from the library she was sat above across to the Main Hall which adjoined the main Citadel walls. She would be off the roof for a while but getting closer to the walls meant that she could meet a guard, although there didn't seem to be as many as she would have expected.

The Main Hall was three stories high, and this balcony came in at the top floor joining a viewing gallery. This bit was simple; she would join the balcony and walk around the back of the hall. It was what was on the other side that scared her. She remembered that the balcony on the opposite side looked out over the city a story above the top of the Citadel walls. Ark has leapt down from the corner of this balcony to a stable twenty feet below. The stable was for the horses of place visitors who could not bring them inside the gates. On portion of the roof was open to the stars and was where six foot of hay was stored. Ark must have climbed up when he visited, but she almost believed he must have been able to fly.

The gap seemed so small. She looked up into distance. Once this is done, she will be in the streets and be able to make for Ark's den. The Citadel guards were now out of sight, having passed through the gates and across the narrow square. She looked across to the gate. In horror, she could see the Golden Guard emerging on top of the twin towers. If they saw her, and they were vigilant, she would be caught. She looked once more at the gap...and then dropped down from the edge.

* * *

Rahmin had left the city earlier. Nervous of being outside and was heading towards the Temple. He needed no accompaniment, but the Commander of the Golden Guard stayed with him. He had left initially, accompanied by eight of the Golden Guard carrying the four chests, but they had left him once they had reached the start of the city. Two men carrying each chest headed in different directions into the heart of the city. Once the chests were open, they would return to meet him by the Temple.

The first pair reached the back of the Sailor's Inn by the docks and placed the chest behind empty barrels in the yard. They lifted the lid and the quickly left. The second placed their chest under a lesser bridge over one of the tributary canals. The third placed theirs on the opposite side of town, amongst a ghetto of shacks and houses, amongst the highest concentration of people. The fourth, in the foothills of the middle class and wealthy homes that clung to the lower levels of the volcano.

All four chests were left ajar, and heeding their Commanders orders they hurried from the scene towards the Temple. The Guardian was now at the deserted marketplace looking up at the Temple. It was 11.30 and he could hear the dull thud of the Citadel Guard approaching. At the same time, the eight Golden Guards emerged across from beyond the Temple. Seeing them, the Commander waved them over. With the chests in place, the Guardian felt more comfortable that he would not be on his own when he returned to the Citadel.

***

Will Gascon and Garik walked slowly along the dock towards the Sailor's Inn. Their shift was over and late as it was it would be good to have a couple of drinks before returning to the barracks. The night was quiet, and there had been little trouble this evening.

***

Inside the Temple all was silent.

***

Francesca landed with a thud, but nothing seemed broken. A horse stirred but the stable boy remained asleep amongst the hay a few yards away. Lifting herself up she made her way to the stable doors.

164

They were open, only slightly, but enough for her to squeeze through into the fresh air outside.

She could hear the faint sound of the Citadel Guards marching. A simple sprint the hundred yards to the first row of houses was all she needs to do.

***

Lilkin and his gang had gathered in the alleyway running down the back of the Citadel Inn that sat a mere hundred yards from the Citadel gate. They had come waiting to see what move the Duke would make and been rewarded with witnessing the Citadel Guards march pass.

"There must be a hundred of them" whistled Felix.

"At least" said Lilkin. "All shiny and polished. We need to be quick; I know where there heading, and I don't want to miss this show. Who knows there may be some pickings to be made in the fall out?" Lilkin turned and beckoned the crowd of ten motley youths.

"Wait." Felix said. "What's that?" Pointing at the space between the stables and the city proper there was a small figure running across the courtyard.

"Is that a girl?" Lilkin strained to look. "Interesting."

***

The noise had become, if not deafening, certainly uncomfortable, as the Citadel Guard emerged into the marketplace. The shadows had lit up with the torches burned by the Citadel sentinels. Rahmin stepped out of the shadows and approached the Citadel Guard Commander. "Sir!" saluted the Commander.

"Spread your men around the Temple, Commander and then follow me." The Commander bellowed out the order and reams of soldiers spread out in various directions. At this, windows had begun to up in the houses overlooking the market, and a few figures were bold enough to stand in their doorways. "Commander, on my order you are to approach the Great Temple doors, and demand entry. You are to hand them this parchment, which is your warrant. From there, search the Temple, until the Beast is found."

By now a few glints of armour could be seen on the rooftops adjacent to the Temple. The Guardian looked up. "Good, the little ferret will not escape us this time, Commander."

"What if they don't let me in, sir?" queried the Commander. Rahmin didn't really care. As long as the guards were outside the Citadel, that was all he needed. One way or another the Beast would be caught, what was important was the chaos that would ensue. "You have my permission to burn the doors down!" Rahmin spun on his heels and walked away, the Golden Commander falling in line behind.

"Where are you off to sire?" the Citadel Commander seemed nervous.

"I am getting a better vantage point, I think. I trust this can all be left in your capable hands, Commander? Good luck." And with that Rahmin made his way as quickly as possible to the Citadel.

***

The Clerk of the Council made his way down to long corridor with his keys rattling at his side. Very unusual for the Council to be called this late at night, but not impossible. The Duke's father use to call them very late, because generally he slept most of the day.

Whenever this had happened under this Duke it usually had been for very quick things, or to move business out of the following day so that he could go hunting. Well, this time it was actually called by the Lord Justice, which was a bit stranger, but it was probably to handle a last-minute pardon request for someone's execution the next day.

The clerk nodded to the Citadel Guard on the door and he stepped aside from the centre. That was strange; usually there were two guards on. The key was easy to find, being the longest on the ring, and he slowly unlocked the door. It was 11.45 and the council had been called for midnight. He could hear voices coming up the corridor as some of the Lords began to arrive.

***

Francesca ran down towards the nearest house and its looming drainpipe, having just squeezed through a narrow alleyway. She decided to slip off her shoes as she would get a much better grip on the wall and pipe than with her clogs. Shame, they were very pretty but she would probably lose one at some point anyway. Reaching up her left hand she suddenly felt a hand covering her mouth and nose, whilst another grabbed her round the waist and pulled her away from the wall. Her legs dragged along the floor, cutting her now unprotected feet.

***

The Citadel Commander made his way to the great doors of the Temple, up the wide steps, accompanied by twenty of his most trusted men and the two Golden Guards that the Guardian had left with him. Taking the hilt of his sword he bashed the Great Temple door not stopping until the one of the doors slowly opened.

Standing in front of the Citadel Commander was Ravo, spitting flehm, in his fury "What impudence is this! How dare you bring an army to the doors of the temple...!" The Citadel Commander sheathed his sword and raised his hands, palms outward in an attempt to placate the Priest. Sacrilege was not in his makeup and if he could manage this through negotiation, he would be far happier. But that is not what happened. Before the Priest could finish his sentence the two Golden Guards pushed past the Commander, with drawn swords, through the doorway, with one pushing the Priest to the floor.

Ravi let out a scream but before he could recover the Golden Guards were inside seizing the torch from the stands. The Citadel Guards looked to the Commander, who reluctantly nodded, and they followed them into the Temple.

***

"They are here!" the traveller looked up calmly form his cot and looked into Ark's eyes.

"Who are?" spluttered Ark.

167

"Soldiers...and I'm guessing if they have the gall to enter the Temple, they must be from the Guardian. You must leave." Ark stood up. His limbs still sore, a soreness from lack of use, rather than from the wounds. "I'm not sure I can climb..." Ark stuttered.

"I fear this is so. We must find another way."

***

Will raised a tankard in the Sailor's Inn and slowly poured its contents down his throat. Garik did the same with bits of foam sticking to his beard. "Excellent." In the yard behind the inn the old chest creaked, like a boat rocking in the docks. The creaks became groans, like the groans of the mast fighting against the movement of a sail in a strong wind. Then a crack appeared in the side of the chest.

Tiny limbs and arms of reddish brown protruded from the gap, as the wood ripped apart. The lid flew off and the arms and limbs grew followed by the expanding form of first one and then many terracotta soldiers. The box burst into multiple pieces and the figures raised themselves to human height.

***

"Excellent beer." Said Will, "but my last I think".

"Don't be daft", said Garik. "It's your round". Will investigated the empty tankard, shook his head. "I guess so", and he got up and went to the bar. At that moment the world seemed to explode. The wall to his left, seemed to collapse inward, and he fell to the floor, stunned by dust and wood that had flown across the room.

He wiped the dust from his eyes and raised himself onto one hand. Dust was filling the room like smoke from a fire. He could see Garik on the floor clutching a cut head, his helmet lying next to him. Then he looked from where the explosion had come from, through the greying mist, and saw an unbelievable sight. A strange soldier leaning through the cloud to grab the Innkeeper with one arm whilst the other plunged a spear down through his throat.

***

Rahmin had no intention of remaining to see the Temple breached, nor of staying outside the Citadel for any longer than was essential. He rushed back to the Citadel where the gates swung open upon his approach. As expected, when he passed the Gatehouse, he saw four of his Golden Guards. He signalled them to follow him, as the gates swung closed behind him. Everything was going according to plan.

They fell into line quickly, behind the Guardian. They entered the main palace and swept up the stairs almost at a run. A second stairs to the right led up to the Duke's apartments where there would be fewer guards than normal. Reaching the top of the stairs, Rahmin was confronted by a single Citadel Guard, no more than a young boy.

"Halt!" he yelled nervously, adjusting his spear from his side to across his body in a defensive gesture. Rahmin stopped and raised his hand halting his men behind. He looked hard at the boy, then gently flicked his wrist, indicating for his men to move forward. In one smooth motion one of the soldiers drew his sword, the blade rising into the air, and brought it down through the young guard's shoulder, cleaving him in two. Blood splattering the soldier and Rahmin.

Rahmin raised his hand and slowly wiped a piece of flesh and blood from his face, stating with scorn "Please be more careful" then stepped over the body.

The doors to the Duke's chamber was closed but with another flick of the wrist the soldier used the same swing to cleave a portion of the door around the handle and lock. The door caved in with an almighty crash. Warily, Rahim had taken a step backward so as not to be covered in wood this time.

Then with a well-positioned kick, one of the other guards collapsed the door inwards revealing the office, bringing the bulk of the doorframe with it. The Duke had been sat at his desk drafting a letter, when the crashing at the door startled him. He was about to stand up when a Golden Soldier burst through the door. Instinctively he reached for his sword and dived away from the door, splinters showering the room.

Sprawled across the floor he pointed the sword up towards the Golden Guard, when another figure came into view. Rahmin, slowly removed his hood. "Duke, I am here to inform you that you are under arrest..."

169

before Rahmin could complete the statement the Duke lunged forward with his sword. In one swift movement the Golden Guard swung his sword to parry the Duke, knocking the Duke's sword from his hand.

More guards had rushed in with their swords drawn, whilst Rahmin finished his statement: "I suggest you come quietly, my Lord." The Duke squirmed back. He had been outplayed. His mind hammered away to find a way out of this. At least he was alive. He gathered his courage and spoke as forcefully as he could.

"Very good, Rahmin. Very good. have underestimated you." His mind was working, the council will never sanction this. The Citadel Guard will rise up. Then his stomach contracted as he remembered that the guards were mostly outside the walls. Still the council won't support this. "And what make believe charge have you dreamed up, you scoundrel?" he stammered, with a little less conviction.

"Oh, a shocking crime, truly shocking. The Citadel Guard trespassing on the Great Temple. Sacrilege. You will probably be burnt for this...but of course that is for your peers to decide." Rahmin smiled. Two of the Golden Guards grabbed him under the arms and began to drag him out of the chamber. The Duke wrestled momentarily before standing to his feet and halting his struggle. "I can walk. I can walk".

24

Gascon used his elbows and feet to push himself back towards the door of the inn as the stone-faced warrior turned to face him. He could not make out any features, the head was just a helmet with darkness behind the eye slots. The body of the innkeeper had been skewered to the bar, and as the warrior pulled his spear out of the bar the body collapsed to the ground leaving a putrid pile of blood and flesh on the bar.

Behind the warrior, Gascon could see five more hacking at the bodies of the other patrons framed by the rubble and crushed wall that they must have merged from. The warrior at the bar had seen Gascon and strode purposely across the few yards, toward him, both hands raised above his head clutching the bloodstained spear. Gascon could do nothing but raise his hands and close his eyes, turning his head to the floor, but as his eyes began to close, he caught the glimpse of a shadow lunging into the warrior.

He opened his eyes to see the warrior gone, and to his left, the form of his friend Garik astride the prone warrior, with his helmet in his hand, battering the emotionless monster. Will jumped up and ran to help but stopped when he saw a spear protruding from Garik's back and the slow drop of the steel helmet to the ground. Will turned and ran for the door.

Outside the streets were empty, but he could hear from his left distant screams. Not stopping he ran from the screams into the city, away from the docks down the alleyway that ran alongside the Inn. He stopped suddenly as he saw the backs of at least five more of the stone warriors marching with spears away from him. He turned back to face Garick's bloodstained assassin. He was trapped, his only possible escape being the collapsed wall of the inn yard at his side. He leapt over the rubble.

He snatched a view of more warriors inside the bar finishing off the remaining victims. He continued to run to the opposite wall and by placing his feet on the barrels he was able to vault the wall into the yard of the adjacent building. He hoped the warrior was not following.

He took a breathe and tried the handle of the rear door. He was luck it was unlocked and led into an unlit warehouse of various boxes, chest and crates. Shutting the door behind him he felt his way amongst the boxes, like some blind man in a maze, and he dropped to his backside exhausted.

***

Ark and the traveller stepped carefully from their chamber. The voices of the guards could still be heard, and from the crashing noises they were more than heavy handed in their search. "There looking for us," said Ark.

"I think you are right", answered the traveller." Let's head up the way. That's your territory. Are there any nooks and crannies we can hide in?"

"Yes, probably. Over to the left there is the door to one of the bell towers. The corridor to the left leads to a stair that climbs alongside it." They walked along low and quickly, Ark leading the way. They made their way down a walkway with monastic arches on their left that initially opened onto the main hall of the Temple, but quickly ran parallel to the central garden. Keeping low they were able to avoid the dark figures who were in the main halls pushing over statues and moving various benches and altars. Below they could hear the barking of orders. "Where are the Priest's quarters?" ordered the Commander.

Ark and the traveller kept moving, they had just left the Priests quarters on the east side, which thankfully were empty apart from the one they had been in. Over on the west was where the bulk of the Priests stayed, Ark guessed this was because of the traveller taking the east side. He could now here the voices of the Priests and Bursars, woken from their slumbers, mingling with that of the guards. Keeping their heads down they reached the Temple gardens. Looking across they could see figures on the west side but too far away to notice them. They rushed quickly to the end of the garden, towards the corridor that ran east to west behind the garden, and the dark entrance to the bell tower. They would have to sneak at least ten yards down the corridor to reach the east stairs, but hopefully the guards would all be taken up with the Priests quarters.

They reached the corner and Ark peered round. It was clear. Standing more upright they made their way cautiously down the poorly lit corridor towards the door. Then suddenly, a golden figure appeared and the west end of the corridor and looked directly at them. The Golden Guard raised its sword and began to run towards them. Instinctively Ark knew they would not make the stairs. His body made the next decision for him. He made for the door leading to the bell towers pulley room. It was open and grabbing the traveller, he pushed through into the bell room. He slammed the door behind them.

The room was as big as two bed chambers, enough room for four bursars to stand. In the centre were four ropes that hand from the vast empty space above, a hundred feet above were the east bells, and these were the bell ringer's pulleys. Ark looked at the traveller. He shook his head. "You go, Ark. I will stall them."

"But they will kill you" pleaded Ark.

"You will find I am not so easy to kill. Go!" A crash at the outside of the door, was the impetus for Ark to start climbing. He gripped the dry rough rope and pulled himself up. This would take all of his upper body strength. A week ago, this would have been easy, but after the fall, he did not know if he could make it. Hand above hand he was soon twenty feet above the ground.

The traveller had resorted to pushing against the bell room door, whilst the hacking from the other side continued. When Ark had reached fifty feet, the pain screaming in his arms, the traveller looked up, nodded and stood back from the door. Hovering on the rope, Ark saw the door come crashing in and a golden soldier charge at the Traveller. The traveller stepped back almost allowing the Gold Guard to enter. The warrior swung his golden blade at the head of the traveller. Ark had to look away.

***

The doors of the Council chamber swung open, and held between two Golden Guards, the Duke was unceremoniously walked into the centre of the chamber. Arrayed in the seats were all the Council members. Some stared at him, most hung their heads. "Were they all complicit?" thought the Duke.

His seat was empty, but as he was dropped to his knees in the centre of the chamber, Rahmin walked past him and then gestured with a quizzical look to at the empty throne. The Lord Justice nodded, and a murmur rose from some of the voices on the benches. "I'll take that as a 'yes'" Rahmin said, and he proceeded to sit himself on the Duke's throne, but not before waving a hand at some imagined dust that he believed was there. He then gestured to the Lord Justice, who stood up and read out the charge.

"Duke Gardes, First Lord of Karesh, Minister of War and Governor of the Karlen Islands, you are indicted on the charge of Heretical Abuse and Sacrilege of a Holy Site. On the third day of Wintersteen you ordered the Citadel Guard to breach the doors of the Great Temple..."

"Poppycock" yelled the Duke, shaking his head.

"Quite!" bellowed the Lord Justice.

"It was the Guardian who ordered the Temple ransacked. I was in my chamber all night!"

"Silence him!" ordered Rahmin. With that the guard swiped his gauntleted hand across the Duke's face. The noise made many of the Council wince. The Duke swung his head back, the pain excruciating through his cheek and nose. He felt the warm blood dripping from his nose onto his chin.

The Lord Justice continued, "You ordered the Citadel Guard to leave the Citadel..."

"You scoundrel", the Duke whispered under his breath, the taste of blood salty in his mouth.

"He was there!" he now shouted, pointing at the Guardian. "He was with the guard. The Citadel Guard Commander, he will confirm." The guard raised his gauntlet again, but Rahmin signalled for him not to proceed.

175

"Unfortunately, that will not be possible. We are unable to locate the Commander...and anyone outside the gates will not be able to return." Rahmin smiled.

"My lord, it is over..." Rahmin said in his kindest, gentlest voice. "The plague is rife..." Rahmin started his plague speech. It was turning out to be quite useful., "you have lost control of the city and left us vulnerable. Lord Justice move to sentencing."

***

On the streets of the city chaos ensued and an unstoppable army of stone warriors hunted the streets. They kicked doors down and searched homes for anyone alive, and without compassion slaughtered them where they found them. Many of the city's populace fled to the streets, but their escape was always short lived as like bloodhounds, the warriors tracked them down. Will heard the screams from his hiding place and covered his ears.

"Where was the city guard? Why was no-one stopping this? The city guards. Maybe they were fighting back, defending the barracks, defending the Citadel. The Citadel! That will be safe."

The screaming had begun to die down, and Gascon decided he must get to the Citadel. The City and Citadel Guard would probably head there. He made his way back through the maze of crates, back to the rear door. There was no noise from the yard and so he ventured out. There was a distant scream, but it was far off. He climbed back into the inn yard and staring into the remains of the inn he could see countless bodies scattered across the floor. In there would be Garick. He stepped into the ruins and covering his mouth with his hand he stepped through the debris. Then he saw Garick. Laying on his back, his chest was a bloody mess, with flesh and bone protruding from where his chest should be. He was long dead. Nearby were both their swords, laying as still as the bodies around them. He picked up his own, and gripping it tightly placed a gentle had on the cheek of his friend, then headed to the door.

He had a plan. He would make for the Grand Canal that ran from the docks to the inner city and eventually the Citadel. Hopefully on the canal he would be safe, whatever these warrior monsters were, hopefully they were not swimmers. Outside the remains of the inn, he saw the docks were clear of danger. There were a few bodies and scattered survivors appearing to be making their way up the Dam's Mountain stairs. There were a few figures looking down from the Dam.

"Maybe that would be better. Get to the Dam and get a boat away from the city." He thought, "Maybe". But he was a soldier, he was a defender of the city, not a coward. He ran along the dockside and reached the Great Canal at the point where it joined the inner lake. There were plenty of boats tied up and finding the smallest barge he loosened the ropes and climbed down into one. He found the long punt and pushed it against the side and then into the water to give him some momentum. The barge edged forward, into the city.

***

Ark kept climbing. There were shouts below him, and even a vain attempt to throw a spear, clattered against the walls and missed him. He was at the bells, and with a simple swing and then jump he landed on the railings surrounding the bells. He would need to be quick.

This was where the stairs brought you, and he could hear the clattering of armour making its way up them. But this was one of his places. He often slept in the hollows of the bell tower roof and when necessary had climbed down the tower's outside, once even to the ground below, but usually to one of the many drain's outcrops. From here he could jump to a neighbouring roof.

One story up from this balcony was the open windows to the sky, the escape route for the bell's symphonies and now his escape. He quickly climbed up the beams and rafters and was hanging from a ledge on the outside of the tower. His arms quickly began to ache again, but the adrenaline was more powerful, but for how much longer?

He looked out across the rooves, fifty feet below, and saw his normal spot. It was a six-foot leap across and six foot down from him. An easy jump, but this time there was a problem. Standing on the roof was a City Guard, spear in hand. Fortunately, he was not looking up but down into the marketplace then across to another guard, four roofs along. There were now noises from the balcony in the tower and so he had no choice. He began the climb down, aware that although blind to one of the guards, he would be completely visible to the other if he looked up. The darkness would help, but the tower was well lit at its top by torches. Still, it cast some shadows, and where possible he kept to these. He made the first, and then the second hidden from the heads that popped out from the balcony windows.

Placing his foot squarely on the third drain, he saw the guard was still looking down, but preparing to jump he heard a cry from above, and the guard on the roof looked up to see him. Ark was already flying though, and not to a piece of vacant roof but towards the guard. The guard's jaw dropped open, whilst he attempted to swing his spear into position, but he was too late.

Ark landed right on top of him and the spear clattered down the roof. The guard's helmeted head cracked against the tiles and the pair rolled after the spear down the roof. The guard desperately tried to push Ark off, whilst Ark tried to find something to grab onto. As they slid to the roof edge, Ark pulled himself up the body of the guard, so that the guard's lower half rammed into the roof guttering. Ark continued to push up his body until he was almost standing on the guards crumpled heap wedged into the gutter.

Ark could now get his balance and start to climb away from the guard, but in the guard's desperation he grabbed at Ark's foot as he began to slip out of the gutter. The Guard was too slow, though; the downward momentum pulled his hands away as they clutched at thin air. Ark looked round, but the guard was gone.

Suddenly, a spear hit the roof tiles next to him, thrown from the tower above. He scrambled up the roof, expecting another spear imminently, but nothing came. The hollering did not stop though initially from above across the adjacent roofs and now from below. He raced across the roof, with no real direction in mind, just a burning desire to keep the voices behind him. All though his bones ached like a fire, he was still fast, and agile. His mind flashed back to following his brother across the roof tops with the city in uproar. An instinct kicked in, and he headed to the Dam.

25

In the Temple, a Golden Guard sheaved his bloody sword and walked out of the bell ringer's chamber. Through the gap in the door, still standing stunned, Riva the priest could see the feet of the traveller, not moving. "This is sacrilege! Murder in the Temple!" he screamed, throwing a punch at the guards armoured chest. The Citadel Commander ran over to the two figures, "We were not ordered to kill! You are under arrest", and he drew his sword and pointed at the chest of the Golden Guard. "Give up your weapon" he shouted.

The Golden Guard grimaced, drew his sword slowly, and with a speed beyond the perception of the Priest and Commander, the sword arced through the air and passed cleanly through the Commander's neck and then the Priests. Their decapitated heads remained in place and then collapsed with the bodies to the ground. The Golden Guard completed the single swing with the sword returning to its scabbard. His golden arm, now awash with flesh and blood. He stepped over the bodies and made for the main hall.

The main hall was in uproar. The Bursars and Priests stood dazed, some even on their knees on the floor. Some Citadel Guards were still rushing for the tower, whilst others were coming from the same place. The hall was echoing with a babel of noises "Where's the Commander!" "Sacrilege!" "Get the Beast!". The two Golden Guards signalled to each other and marched towards the Temple doors. Reaching them they each took a door and pushed it open, then stepped out to a battlefield outside. Down the stone steps into the marketplace, where once had stood tens of Citadel Guards was a scene of devastation. Scattered where they had stood were the bloodied forms of the once noble Citadel Guard. The market square was awash with blood.

A few seemed to still be standing, but these were not Citadel Guards. Their skin and armour were like dark granite. There were ten of them and they were staring straight at the Temple doors then slowly march forward.

In the cellar of Havar the Bakers, looking out through the small grating, were two white eyes surveying the slaughter. For the first time in many years Lilkin was truly afraid. "What have I done?"

Behind, huddled together, were the rest of his gang. Some of them were crying. Off to the side was Francesca. Her hands were bound, and her mouth gagged with a strip of the bottom of her dress tied across her mouth. Havar's cellar had always been a place to hide until just before dawn when Havar would start cooking in the room above. The gang could all just squeeze through the grating to sleep on cold nights. Now they had headed for here for different reasons. The city was swarming with death and destruction as were mystery warriors indiscriminately killing.

Most of the stone warriors had marched in unison up to the backs of the Citadel and City Guards, and just started chopping away. The Citadel Guards rallied to each other's help, but the warriors were supernaturally strong and within minutes the slaughter was complete. Some of the warriors had broken off initially and begun to raid the houses around the market square. They burst effortlessly through the doors and one by one murdered the inhabitants.

Lilkin had acted quickly. He ordered the gang to lift the various sacks of grain and flour and pile them at the door to the cellar and then huddled silently. This was the best vantage spot Lilkin could think of to witness the storming of the Temple and the downfall of the Beast. But then it had all gone wrong. The marketplace had turned into a battlefield. The stone warriors had marched into the square, the Citadel Guards standing with their backs to them.

They couldn't stay much longer and this time they had a package with them. They had come across her outside the Citadel walls and without any real idea on what they would do with her, had grabbed her. For most of the way through the alleyways she had made an awful racket. Lilkin had eventually had to gag her. Soon Hagar would be moving about unless they were already dead. There was no noise above them perhaps they might be able to stay longer.

Eventually he was courageous enough to look out of the open grate. His eyes were at ground level as he saw the stone warriors marching towards the two warriors dressed in gold who stood on the Temple steps. Behind them they had been joined by ten or so Citadel Guards.

The visors on the Golden Guards helmets were down and they struck similar poses: legs apart, their shields across their body the tops just touching the bottom of their visor, and the long swords gripped in their right hands, the pummel level with the side of their head their blades pointing out across the top of the shield.

Behind them the Citadel Guards were a rabble. They tried to form a shield wall locking shields behind the two Golden Guards, but Lilkin had already seen one of them pull back and disappear through the Temple doors behind them. As the stone warriors reached the Temple steps, two more of the Citadel Guards darted back inside the Temple, and as each warrior stepped forward, more retreated to the Temple, until none stood. By the time the Golden Guards charged to meet the stone warriors the Temple doors had been shut.

The two Golden Guards almost leapt down the stairs swinging their swords down on a stone warrior below. Each sword was parried by the warriors with an alarming metal clang, that made Lilkin wince and close his eyes briefly. The Golden Guard on the left, who had been the assassin inside the Temple immediately through his shield into the wooden face, knocking the warrior back a few strides. The other Golden Guard had not been as quick and was using his shield only to parry a return sideways swing from his warrior.

And so, the duels went on. Both Golden Guards were lucky in that the remaining stone warriors just ignored them, and marched on, some battering at the Temple doors whilst others proceeded around the outside of the Temple searching for victims. The Golden Commander had managed to maintain his advantage higher on the steps and was countering a volley of blows down on his stone warriors' sword and shield, but the other was already retreating under a similar barrage from his warrior. Lilkin was mesmerized.

"What's going on?" Karl asked raising his head from under the blanket.

"The Golden Guards are giving a good try against those monsters...but no, one of them is down...and the monster is about... oh God his blade has pierced right through the side of the Golden Guard! His shield has fallen! By the Gods... he has stabbed him straight threw the throat. The others are hacking at the Temple doors. There's one Golden Guard left, but he looks tired. He has pushed his opponent back to the market square, but .... but he has lost his advantage.... he is down...no...no...the warrior ...oh gods, he has killed him. His dead..." Lilkin span around looking away from the devastation and into the cellar. "We're all going to die......"

Gascon pushed the small barge slowly up the canal. The canal was straight for the first five hundred yards, before it turned sharply to the right at the end of the marketplace, away from it and then towards the Citadel. There was no-one else on the canal, and it was dark and the lights along the houses lit the few walkways that ran alongside the canal rather than water, three of four feet lower.

Some of the torches were out as well, so the canal became a mix of shadowy and sometimes pitch-black passages. What was evident was distant screaming. The noise did not seem to go away just varying in its volume and its length. Some screams were single individuals often whole groups. When it came from windows above the canal, it was quite obviously families.

After the first hundred yards he met the first traffic on the canal, a couple of empty barges, but horribly, scattered with floating dead bodies. Where the wounds could be seen, the obvious victims of sword cuts. On he pushed, looking for the expected dark patch, itself hundred yards wide that would signify his arrival at the marketplace. It was not normally well lit at this time of the morning, only around the houses at its edges and the vast torches by the great doors of the Temple. The lights hung around the various spires and bell towers rarely penetrated the cobbles below.

As he neared the marketplace, he could hear the clash of metal on metal. His heart stopped, and he took a deep breath, he had no time to stop, as the momentum of his pushing so far would take him to whatever was going on. He could already see a series of barges tied up at the quay. As he rounded the edge the immediate noises of fighting halted, and he could see in the distance by the steps of the Temple, a good hundred yards away, the stone figures. As his eyes adjusted, he could see there were bodies everywhere.

His attention was drawn to one stone monster standing up above a glistening object. He realized it was a Golden Guard laying prone on the floor, he was too late to turn his eyes as the killers struck the prone guard. He couldn't comprehend what he saw. It made no sense. Then from the far right, he saw small figures come running across the marketplace: children.

"No...!" he screamed. Had they not seen the monsters? But they had, as the remaining stone warriors turned to look to where the scream came from, Lilkin and the others pounded towards the canal. The stone warrior began its malevolent walk towards them.

"Run!" someone screamed "Run!". The pace of the warrior increased though he never seemed to break into a run. Gascon was unable to get out of the boat, as the tied-up barges were two or three deep, and by the time he moved it would all be over. He pushed on looking for a gap.

"Run!" Gascon screamed. The warrior was closing on the group. The biggest child and a smaller child were slipping behind, but this was probably because he could see the smaller one's hands were tied. He reached an opening and pulled the barge into it. The main group of children reached the other barges and started to jump into them. He was fortunate that he had moved further down, or they would probably have sunk his barge. As it was some of the children had fallen in.

Realizing his peril, Lilkin let go of Francesca and ran clear of her. The warrior was now a mere foot away from the girl. Gascon looked to draw his sword, but he would be too late, he would never clear the distance between him and the girl. Then leaning down he grabbed the punt like a spear and with all his effort he launched it into the air. The barge rocked throwing him to the floor. Francesca ran as fast as she could, her mouth still bound, and feeling the presence behind her. Ahead she saw the guard in the barge falling.

Gascon hitting the barge floor, looked up to see the pole flying like a javelin and crashing hard into the chest of the stone warrior. The first foot of the pole seemed to disintegrate, unable to penetrate the hard exterior, but he was amazed to see the warrior jerk backwards and fall to the cobblestones beneath him. Francesca reached the edge of the marketplace quay and leapt into the air. Gascon raised himself just in time to be knocked back to the floor as the young girl landed on him.

The warrior was pushing himself back up from the ground. All around Gascon the children, in an assortment of barges, were drifting into the middle of the canal. Some had figured out how to use the poles to push them away. Gascons' pole was gone so he was the nearest to the shoreline, although the momentum of the girl's jump had carried them a yard from the canal-side.

The warrior was on his feet now and approaching the canal-side. Gascon was using his hands to paddle frantically, but with little movement. Then in front of him appeared the barge with Lilkin and Karl. Lilkin was pushing hard on the pole, oblivious to the boats behind him. Karl lifted another pole from his larger barge and extended it out to Gascon. Gascon grabbed it and pulled it towards him.

The warrior had not moved. It just stood looking. Gascon pushed the pole into the water, and soon he was in the wake of Lilkin's barge heading away from the marketplace.

26

The Council session lasted only half an hour, probably the briefest in history. The Duke was dragged away by two Golden Guards and taken back to his chamber. He may as well have been taken to the cells, when his keys were removed from him, and the guard locked the door from the outside.

How had his life collapsed in just thirty minutes? Events in the Council accelerated from a statement from the Guardian on the end of the world, to all the Lords baying for his blood. This time he couldn't have walked out; his legs had given way. He was dragged out by the armpits like a common thief. He had barely managed to hold back the tears welling in his eyes. What saved him was the rage. Confusion, not anger, had been his commanding emotion, until the guard grabbed his arms, and the Guardian had smiled. That smile was burnt into his mind. That smile fed his anger and would feed it until he died.

Once the Duke was removed Rahmin called the Council to a close and thanked them for their service to the Empire. The Lord Justice fell into line, ordering the great gates closed and forbidding any movement back and forward to the city. The Council would meet again tomorrow to discuss other measures, but Rahmin felt he had achieved much today, and started to leave. He was met in the corridor by one of his Golden Guard. "News of the city, sire" he stood to attention.

"Good, where is the Commander?"

"He didn't make it back, sir. We closed the gates, and he hadn't returned. The Temple was stormed, and we know he went in, but that is the last report sir. But...."

"What is It?" demanded Rahmin.

"We have heard screaming from the city, and there are hordes of people at the Citadel gates."

"That is terrible news, but not unexpected. No-one comes in. The order stands. Anyone climbs the walls shoot them, and that includes the Commander...and congratulations on your promotion." Rahmin smiled and walked past. He stopped for a second and looked back. "Make sure everything is secure. There are enough men to hold these walls indefinitely, but no mistakes...oh and can you have the Princess Francesca brought to my chambers. We have a future to plan."

"Yes sir, except no sire. The Princess. She is not in her chambers, sir. No-one has seen her since earlier today." Rahmin's smile fell from his face. "By the gods" he whispered.

Ark made his way across the rooves. The feint noise of battle and pain drifted up to the skies, but no-one followed him. The guards back at the Temple had not pursued him. As he crossed the roofs, he slowed his pace down, looking down into the courtyards, gardens and alleyways to see what was happening. The city had turned red.

He saw bodies, lying but not dead from the plague but baring atrocious wounds. Children, women, soldiers, shopkeepers, merchant, beggar all laid low in an infernal group: the dead. Looking up at the Dam he saw reams of dark figures against the rock of the mountain passageways climbing to the Dam's top. He remembered running up those steps with the same fear, the same senses under stress and torture as death and destruction followed. He had come across the open window of a merchant's house and seen the body of a mother and baby awash with blood, prone on their milk white bedspread.

Atop the Dam he could see figures, the torches regularly positioned under the canopies at regular points casting strange shadows, making them look like strange beastly shapes. Along the interior of the Dam, people had boarded the lifts and were ascending slowly, less smoothly than normal but ascending. Down in the dock people gathered at the bottom of the walkways waiting their turn.

There was no screaming, just shouts, as people pushed their way through, or guards barked orders. Reaching the last warehouses, he joined the dock and Ark stopped a while on his pinnacle surveying the scene. There is no place for me up there. The east steps seemed to be crammed, and the west steps less so, but he could not sneak his way up there.

And what next if he reached the top? Could he calmly amble along the walkway, take his place in the queue for a boat, and be offered a helping hand to get in. He doubted it. How long would it be before the people were pushing their own into the water to get the last few boat places?

He looked back at the city. He could see the Temple towers and spires and beyond it the Citadel. Beyond that the volcano. He wondered if the mountain passes were still open? They had been shut because of the plague, but did anyone stand guard now? What about Francesca? Was she safe, walled up in the Citadel? Did she care that the city was dying? And what of the traveller?

Without realizing Ark had made his way across the warehouse rooves to the wards leading to the east mountains. There he found an old hideaway in the decaying chimney of a shipbuilder's workshop. The chimney was never used, and previously Ark had been able to wedge some planks of wood into its stack as a platform and wedged a makeshift roof in above him. The broken bricks allowed him to still see the Dam.

His body decided his next step for him. His eyes closed and sleep was on him. He was woken suddenly by the sounds of huge splashes and crashes. It was still dark, but clouds had cleared the moon, full and beaming. At the base of the Dam, in the lake were broken lifts and crumpled bodies. Lifts had fallen the hundred feet down the side of the Dam, hundreds would be dead.

His eyes drew quickly up the Dam to the top. Several lifts were half hanging by a few remaining ropes. People were moving more frantically, and then he saw a figure fall from the Dam, a long slow journey to the base. In the space it had vacated a dark, soldier with a sword drawn stepping towards a line of people, all pushing to retreat from him. The whole west side of the Dam walkway was clear except for five more of these figures. Behind them no-one. Down the west mountain staircase no-one; the crowds were gone.

The dark warriors were killing the people on the Dam. All of them. Whoever had reaped havoc in the city was continuing on the Dam. Suddenly a whole cluster of bodies shifted off the Dam falling in a myriad of shapes, some spinning to the lake below. The canopy covering the walkway was aflame. "How many had made it onto boats?" Ark wondered.

The east steps were now crushed with people pushing up the way and people fleeing the monsters. Ark watched transfixed. The screams were barely audible, but his imagination filled the gaps. As the warriors marched on in their deadly manoeuvre, no-one appeared to escape.

A few climbed up the canopy as he had done all those years before, but they were quickly scythed down. With Arks precise eyes he could see the rim of the Great Dam was turning red, making a strange collar to the Dam, with some red streaks racing to the ground as fast as the bodies were falling.

No-one would be getting off the Dam now. He would not be able to leave this way. It was only now that he realized the whole city was doomed. Looking back into the city he could make out bodies and hear the metal sounds of swords and spears. The warriors were everywhere, and no-one was going to survive. And then the image of Francesca come into his mind, and he felt his body shiver with an inexplicable cold. Could these warriors take the Citadel? Take the one good thing in the city, the girl who had seen him as more than a Beast?

He looked beyond the spires of the Temple and tried to see the Citadel. He could not make out the outer walls but could make out a few of the brilliant white towers. One of which was home to Francesca. If I make for the Citadel, and its safe then maybe they both could make for the mountains and the passes. If she was gone, well there were pathways to the passes there and he would go alone. He took one last look at the Dam then made his way quickly across the rooves.

The Temple was silent. The guards who had retreated into the Temple when the stone warriors attacked were now lying dead across the mosaic tiles in corridors, and some in the main hall. Amongst them the bloodied capes of Bursars and Priests. All dead. Pools of blood were beginning to dry. In the Bell Tower lay the body of the traveller. It lay still, a violent wound ran from his ear, across the left side of his face down through his neck and shoulder into his chest. It was like a ravine in a mountain. The head attached by the faintest collection of surviving bones. The brown cape, now dark with his blood and the stones beneath his body awash with his hideous life.

In the Bell Tower, a bell was still swinging but slowly losing its momentum so that each gentle ring became more spaced apart and quieter, like its own life was ebbing away. The traveller had known resistance was futile, so had turned as best he could to limit the damage of the blow. With no weapon he could not defeat this monster, but if he could limit the damage, keep his head on his shoulders then there was a chance. Laying beneath the bell, still, eyes not moving, no more blood to pump out, the traveller's mind was still fighting.

His thoughts were filled with blood, red and flooding into every pore then a light appeared amongst the vermillion. He headed for the light, and his thoughts focused on reaching the growing spot. As he neared it the light became a bluey white. Then suddenly he was soaring through the sky. The Sky was blue, and he floated above the dark powerful waves of the northern ocean. He could not feel his body, but it was cold and the spray from the sea was in the air. He wished it would touch his face and cool the burning fire in his head. He passed over the seas and over the dark stones, a causeway of stone slabs made by the long dead giants. He would be reaching the great walls, higher than the even the Dam of Kursck.

And then the mountains of ice and snow. He felt the cold again, deeper, but the not enough to halt the burning of his mind. Across the mountains and then the gardens. The great greenery and orchards of the gods and there he slowly descended to the earth, landing amongst the flower's gold and red petals. And then he saw a light above his eyes, and a felt a warm hand on his brow, and the burning rescinded.

A thousand lives passed through his eyes. He saw the city; he saw his death. Ark. He tried to talk but nothing happened. Around him rising into the air from the golden flowers were a thousand butterflies, rising up and blocking the sun. Hovering just above him. He closed his eyes and thought hard, though perhaps his final thought. "I have found him" and then the butterflies swarmed around him, and his mind was awash with a soothing feeling like nectar poured from a cup.

Beneath the bell, the body remained still, but from beneath his robes a stream of butterflies emerged spinning in the air in a flock. Soon the small chamber was thick with the swarm, a fire of red and gold. The body of the traveller was no longer visible, hidden by the mass of colour. Then slowly a dark shape appeared at the centre of the swarm.

It took on more of a form, a dark shadow becomes the form of a man, and then stepping clear, came the figure of the traveller, alive, untainted, the wound gone. He raised his hands to the sky, and the swarm of butterflies flew around him like a whirlwind and slowly disappeared as quickly and mysteriously as they came in the folds of his brown unstained cloak.

■■■

27

Gascon reached down to remove the gag from the girl's mouth, whilst the boat drifted along with the momentum from his last big punt. They were clear of the open spaces and now back in the narrow avenues with houses creating ominous cliffs either side of them. Ahead he could see the older boy's barge slowly creeping further ahead, and behind a collection of children on at least three barges. He didn't feel safe, and they were making too much noise.

As the gag came clear, the girl let out a scream, and Gascon reacted by quickly putting his hand over her mouth, raising his other hands finger to his lips "Shh!" The girl stared wide, open blue eyes at him and then sunk her teeth into his hand. He screamed and yanked it away.

"Sometimes you just have to scream!" she yelled at him. The wound was minimal. He reached down and undid her bound hands and then picked up the pole and pushed off again before the momentum died off. "Are you some sort of thief?" he asked. She was looking away from him up, ahead at Lilkin and then along the rooftops. She didn't answer him.

"Where are we going?" she asked. Her accent was quite refined, and although her dress was ripped and her feet bare, he figured she must be the daughter of one of the rich merchants. Beneath the dirty marks, her skin was also very pale, and that was common for the newcomers to this city. His own skin had become a deep tan from the years of living beneath the sun. "My name is Gascon. And I accept your thanks for saving your life" he said.

She stared at him. "Yes. You did. Thank you." She seemed deep in thought and distant. The children behind had quieted down and the canal was silent with just the gentle lapping of the water around the barges and against the canal sides from their boats wakes. Gascon smiled. Francesca found his smile reassuring. It was a kind face, she thought.

"Francesca. My name is Francesca. That boy" pointing ahead, "kidnapped me".

"Yes, I think I recognize him. It looks like Lilkin. He is a street thug, a wild child. Burglar, pick pocket, mugger, but not really a kidnapper...." He left the inferred question hanging. She turned sternly saying, "Well he is, and I demand you arrest him" she recognized he was wearing some kind of uniform." You're a guard, aren't you?"

"City Guard, yes. Right now, I'm more concerned with saving our lives than arresting Lilkin. The city has turned to hell on earth." He took a guess, "You're from the Citadel, aren't you?"

She looked up at him. Do I trust him? "Yes" she said. But give him no more.

"Good. That's where were going. Hopefully you can get us in. It may be the only safe place in the city." She didn't answer.

"Why were you outside the city, my lady?" Gascon thought he better be a bit more polite; she was obviously someone with and used to power, even at her tender years.

Do I trust him? It's the guards who were hunting Ark. She thought, finally saying "I got lost."

"Really?" Gascon shook his head. They rounded a bend and came to a straighter portion of the canal. They could see Lilkin in a barge ahead. The canal once more opened to a large concourse on the left, the area in front of the Citadel. This canal and its sister on the eastern side ran around the walls reaching a series of locks that took the canal up to four stories high, to small reservoirs fifty meters square imbedded in the mountains. The locks were guarded, normally by the Citadel Guard, and few ventured this far up unless carrying goods from the Citadel.

From the concourse there was a huge noise of a mass of voices shouting. They could see that in front of the main gate had gathered a huge crowd, probably a thousand people all crushed together facing the gate demanding to get in. "Are they all trying to get into the Citadel?" Francesca asked.

"I think so, but I don't think they are going to have too much luck." The guards on the walls were all looking down on the crowd with spears pointing down; if by some miracle some managed to scale the twenty-foot wall they wouldn't be getting over it. Francesca looked across and saw that the crowd was obscuring the small stable from view but could see some people climbing it. There was a cluster of guards pushing the climbers away with their spears.

"Why don't they let them in? Francesca asked. "They are going to get crushed". She pointed at a mother falling to the ground with a small baby in her arms, as someone stepped over her.

"They can't" Gascon said. "It's the plague. There all scared of the plague. The Duke has abandoned the city."

"But those monsters, they will get them if they don't let them in." Instinctively they looked across at the edge of the concourse that joined the city, looking for signs of the monsters. Gascon slowly pushed on the pole to move the barge away from the side. He looked behind and could now see that in three barges were huddled five children, all boys by the looks of it. They stared longingly at him. He looked up the way and could see Lilkin's barge at the first lock, but the boy was not in sight. He must have climbed out.

"Look!" shouted Francesca pointing at the city away from the crowds. Then she wished she hadn't reacted so. It was not the monsters she saw but high on the last row of rooftops a black shape moving along the tiles.

"What?" Gascon quizzed.

"Ark! He must not know" she realised and so whispered the words under her breathe.

"By the Gods" he stammered. On the edge of the city, he saw the stone figures emerging from alleyways and thoroughfares stepping into the square. The crowd had not realized.

"Run!" Gascon instinctively screamed, but the crowd were too loud and too far away. The stone warriors made their slow march forward. Francesca had not taken her eye off Ark. She was convinced it was him.

The shape moved slightly back from the edge of the roof to be less obvious, but it was him. Had he seen her? "We have to get out of here" The urgency in Gascon's voice broken the spell for Francesca.

Gascon looked back down the canal. There was no hope in the city. They had to get into the Citadel. Then he saw a red material waving by the locks of the canal. It was Lilkin. He was waving a piece of cloth at them. He stood above the first lock turning the wooden wheel that would shut the first lock doors. "Over here!" he seemed to be shouting.

Gascon pushed hard on the pole and the barge edged forward to the lock. He shouted for the other children to follow. It would be a squeeze, but the boats should all be able to get into the lock. From there they could climb up to the last lock that took them into the great reservoir that touched the edge of the Citadel and cut into the mountains. He had never been in there but there must be a route to the inside of the Citadel. He pushed hard, as Lilkin slowly shut the doors. If they didn't make it, they would climb. They could hear Lilkin now.

"You must bring the barges. We will need them in the reservoirs!"

He reached the lock doors just open enough to let them in. The children were behind. Gascon shouted up to Lilkin: "We will need to move the children into just a couple of barges. That will be quicker."

"Yes", shouted down Lilkin "and me".

Francesca scowled at him. "You can't trust him" she growled.

"He is all we've got. It's a good plan." Gascon said. Francesca looked away back at the concourse. Ark was gone and the slaughter had begun.

* * *

Ark backed away from the edge of the roof, instinctively not wanting to be seen. The same warriors as on the Dam seemed to be here at the Citadel, and they were wading into the frightened masses outside the Citadel gates. The sight was sickening, more so, than that of the Dam. He could see each blow struck, the faces of the fallen. There was little resistance from the people, most turned their back pushing the crowd in front to get away. The warriors had encircled the mass and were slowly chopping their way to the gates. The flagstones normally white and glinting with the sun were red.

The Citadel Guards did nothing to help. He could see the people at the very front of the mass were completely crushed against the gates. The pressure had forced a small child above the heads and was floating on a sea of hands and heads, crying.

Heads were disappearing like they were sucked down beneath the waves. The Citadel Guards looked perplexed. They had ceased pushing people away with their spears. The stable building's roof was a mere island in the mass. A lone man had made it onto the roof, but rather than trying to climb the wall had curled into a ball covering his head. Then with a huge rumble the stable roof collapsed, dragging the man violently down into the quagmire of bodies.

A brief respite appeared for those at the rear of the crowd, in the path of the warriors. So many had died that the warriors had had to stop and chop the bodies up and shift them to be able to move forward. A woman and a child attempted to make a break past the warriors. Seeing the gap, she pushed her daughter ahead of her and they both leapt over their slain companions. They were clear, the young girl making it clear of the bodies, her feet living bloody red footprints on the remaining white flagstones. The mother just behind, was suddenly halted in her tracks as a warrior swung his sword at her back and brought her down.

The daughter was unaware and kept running. The warrior stopped and seemed to consider for a moment before turning back to the main mass of people and continuing with his carnage. Ark swung his eyes to movement on the canal to his right. It was some distance, but figures were standing on the canal, on barges he assumed. One was in a bright red dress. He squeezed his eyes and concentrated. Francesca!

***

"It's a slaughterhouse." Rahmin stood on his balcony overlooking the Citadel and the concourse. Behind him stood the new Commander of the Golden Guard. Then he saw a child running from the mass across the cobblestones. Is that Francesca? "How is the search of the citadel?

Have you found her?" He yelled at the Commander, not talking his eyes off the running child.

The concourse in front of the gates was now a hill of bodies, making a ramp to the last few remaining survivors who stood atop a pile at least four foot high. He saw a Citadel Guard walk away from the Citadel battlement holding his head making for the stairway down to the inner courtyard. Then he reached the ground he just sat on the floor and removed his helmet, laying his spear by his side. "The guards are finding this difficult, sire" stated the Commander nervously. Rahmin appeared not to hear. There was a long pause. The slaughter was now complete. During its course the concourse had filled with more warriors. There must have been fifty now, with around ten standing in front of the gate atop the hill of dead.

"It won't be long, now." He said, calmly. "The worst will soon be over." He was interrupted by a violent knocking at the door. Rahmin nodded, and the Commander opened the door. In walked the Lord Justice.

"Guardian, I have summoned the Council again. We are under attack." Then with less authority and almost like a pleading child, "What the hell is happening?"

"Well done! Yes." Rahmin shook the Lord Justice's hand and led him out of the room. "To the Council."

28

From the prison of his bedroom chamber, the Duke watched the slaughter. He had thrown his fists at the door until they were numb, pleading with the guards to let him out but to no avail. He had never seen anything like it. He had never been so helpless, so useless.

His head was a blur of questions. As he struggled with one, another would charge in and he would be lost. The events of the last few hours were incredible, shocking. He was the best swordsman in the city, by far, what he could have done if he had been in charge, face to face with an enemy, not hunting a ghost!

He could see that the Citadel Guards were struggling with the events in front of them. Very few had their family in the Citadel, those who weren't bachelors would have wives, children, and parents in the city. How many of them were buried amongst the concourse's masses?

The Duke leaned over his balcony. Could I climb out? The drop was at least fifty feet. He looked up. He was in a tower that had no upper floor, so all he saw was the start of the conical roof. The Duke, though no longer in the flush of youth, was still strong and fit, but he would need to be a monkey to attempt either. Or the beast.

Some of the stone warriors who had arrived in the concourse had turned and made their way back into the city but a few remained with their eyes on the Citadel. The Duke noticed that the sun had just broken above the Dam spreading its light through the streets and alleyways and beginning to illuminate the concourse. Was there anyone alive in the city? It was too far to see, but something made him doubt it. He sat back on his bed and buried his head in his hands.

**

Two barges had made it into the first lock, and they were slowly rising as the lock shut as Lilkin opened the flood gate to let the water from above in. He now had two small boys, perhaps five or six years old in the barge with himself and Francesca. In the other, four boys, all older, probably ten years old. They all looked the same, in that their hair was long and scruffy, some with charms sown into them, a fashion he remembered last year. Their faces were all brown, from the sun and the grime of the streets. The clothes were rags, which once may have been colourful but now were just a faint shade of grey.

Lilkin was still balanced on the top of the lock. He was different, his clothes were worn but more flamboyant. Up close he could see he was wearing a vermillion blouse with a fusilier's dress jacket. He was significantly older, almost a man. His hair was a striking blonde, wild uncut. He smiled down on the group. Francesca scowled back. When they reached the maximum height, Gascon switched his attention to Francesca. He expected her to launch herself at Lilkin, and she did. He caught her by the waist and pulled her away. "Not now!" he whispered forcibly. "His time will come. For now, he has saved us."

Gascon could see into the next lock. It was empty. He jumped up onto the gates and helped Lilkin to slowly open them. "Thank you." Gascon nodded to Lilkin.

"You're welcome...." Lilkin smiled back. "I always preferred the City Guard." The lock filled, and slowly the barges rose.

"One more lock to go and then we are into the reservoirs. Have you ever seen them?" asked Lilkin.

"No" Gascon replied.

"Well, it's not huge and it's still outside the walls of the Citadel, but at its far end is a dock, with a door that I'm sure leads you into the Citadel. There's usually a guard and Citadel officials, so we will need to watch for that. If we stay in the barges you can drift into the caves under the mountain, but I've never been there, the guards won't let you do that. I assume therefore that there may be another way to the Citadel."

"It's a good plan" Gascon said. "If there is a guard let me do the talking." They exited the final lock and drifted into the reservoirs. They were now quite high in the city but couldn't see into the concourse as the Citadel walls blocked the view. Down to the city on their left everything looked normal. The sun was rising, and the sky was clear. They punted slowly to the other side of the reservoir. There was no one on the dock, and he could make out a small wooden door in the

Citadel wall. He instinctively looked up to the top of the walls, but there were no sentries.

The two barges touched the dock, and Gascon helped the children out. The dock was wide enough to stand two abreast and had wooden beams to tie the barges to. Gascon approached the wooden door. It was firmly closed, and he pushed it with his hand, but nothing moved. "It's locked" he said.

"No such things as a locked door!" laughed Lilkin as he pushed past Gascon. "Felix, come here". Lilkin beckoned to one of the smaller boys. "Have a look at that lock will you." Felix stepped forward and knelt down in front of the lock and stuck his eye to it.

"Can you, do it?" asked Lilkin.

"Yep, should do, But there's people on the other side. I can see them."

"Are they guards?" asked Gascon.

"Could be." The boy replied.

"Why don't we just knock?" Francesca said. Her voice suddenly sounding very refined compared to the boys. Before anyone could answer she gently moved Felix to one side and robustly battered the door with her two fists. "Let me in!!!!" she screamed.

Once again Rahmin was sat in the Duke's chair looking out at the Council. It was not a full Council, about half of those who were there last night had not turned up. Were they hiding? Had they fled the Citadel somehow? Had they died? "Where is everyone?" Rahmin opened his arms to encompass the whole Council.

"It seems some of our peers are absent, my Lord" The Lord Justice stated with a slight hint of distain.

"Yes, I see that" answered Rahmin. "Is this a good thing? Can I use this?" he thought, then said: "I suggest we push on with those of us who care, don't you Lord Justice. So, summarise the situation, Lord Justice."

"The city has come under attack from a force unknown, that as far as we can tell has captured and decimated the city. That force has surrounded the Citadel. We have no news of the City Guard but assume that it is defeated. Access to the Dam and the docks is lost, including the warehouses. The Citadel Guard is seriously depleted. We have just fifty guards watching the walls, with support of around twenty of your Golden Guards. Finally, the mountain passes are sealed and there is no sign of any attack from beyond the mountains."

"Thank you, Lord Justice. Let me also add we have limited food and supplies in the Citadel, I assume. We have lost the Princess Francesca. We have lost half of the Council and the Duke is under arrest." added Rahmin.

"Yes", replied the Lord Justice. The few Lords who were in attendance also nodded.

"Our priority is to hold the Citadel and protect the remaining lives we have. We must ration our supplies in the Citadel, and potentially prepare for exit through the mountain passes," Rahmin continued.

"Yes, sire. May I suggest that we start a dialogue with the enemy? See their demands"

Rahmin mulled that over. "You can try. From what I saw of the slaughter, I don't think we have a talkative bunch of warriors out there, and I have seen no sign of a leader. Maybe you should go out and ask, Lord Justice?"

The Lord Justice squirmed a little. "No, sire." Then Rahmin. "But we do need to go out there. One, we made need supplies. Two, someone needs to find the Princess." The Council was now silent. "Do we have a military Lord here? Someone to tell us how to do that?"

"No, my lord. The Duke served as commander of the Citadel Guard." Replied the Lord Justice, "The City Guard reports into me through various commanders...based in the city."

"So, you are our General, Lord Justice?" teased Rahmin.

"I think not, sire. I am just an administrator..."

"Yes, I see that. Anyone a soldier here? A couple of warrior priests amongst the clergy?" Rahmin gestured to the other lords, all who had their heads down.

"Captain Delks of the Citadel Guard is the highest-ranking office left in the citadel." The clerk spoke up.

"A captain? No, we can't send him. That will leave us with just the guards when his head gets chopped off." said Rahmin. The room then fell silent. Rahmin was happy to sit tight, he had food and could wait out the attack. It was hard to tell how long the magic of the warriors would last before they returned to their toy like state, but it would probably be no more than a few days. He couldn't care less about anyone going outside, except perhaps to lower the number of mouths to feed. But there was Francesca; he really needed her to ensure the long-term plan was strong. Finally, he spoke: "I have an idea. Lord Justice what is the Duke's penalty for his crimes?"

"Well raiding the Temple is really a religious crime. So, death" he looked round at the priests and their heads hung low avoiding the gaze.

"Yes, of course." asked Rahmin. "I have a plan gentleman and if you have no clear thoughts or are nervous of this, just bear with me. Someone bring me the Duke, and clerk hand me some parchment and a quill."

Ark started to make his way across the rooves to get to the far canal. Sometimes he had to head further into the city and sometimes climb down almost to street level to make any progress. He was in a race against time.

It was clear Francesca was fleeing the Citadel as it was under attack. There was at least one man in a guard's uniform with her. If they were using the canal then she must be heading for the docks, probably to escape via the sea.

He leapt from roof to roof only stopping when he heard the march of the warriors beneath him. The screams were less frequent now, but each one still scarred his soul. He reached the edge of the Temple and saw that the only people there, were dead guards scattered across the marketplace. The Great doors were open. He thought of the traveller.

There was so much he was still to learn from him. He had thought him special, but he was so easily slain.

***

Francesca continued to bang at the door and eventually a head appeared, fifteen feet higher over the lip of the wall. "Begone! Begone!" the guard yelled at them. He was an old man, his face worn with the sun and the passage of years. His helmet was loose and when he moved his head it slipped slightly. At its back was a huge dent that must have made for very uncomfortable wearing. The point of a spear protruded over the edge.

"I am the Princess Francesca!" she yelled up at him. "I order you to let me in!"

"None shall pass! None shall pass!" he yelled back. "Orders are none shall pass!"

Gascon joined in "Listen here, this is the Princess, I am a City Guard. Let us in!"

"Bloody City Guard! Look at you. You're a rabble, a bunch of peasants. I bet you're riddled with the plague; you certainly look it."

"Idiot!" yelled Gascon. "She is the Princess, just look at her" and in doing so Gascon looked at her too, and the children behind her. They were a mess. Francesca in a torn dress looked as much a beggar as the rest of them. "This is madness!" he cried. "Go get the Duke!"

The Citadel Guard shook his head. "There is no Duke. Duke's gone! Head chopped off! Now get away before I share this spear with you!"

"The Duke dead?" Francesca was shocked. "What of Rahmin, the Guardian?"

"I don't know, my orders are from the Lord Justice and he says none shall pass." In fact, the Citadel Guard had no orders since the rest of the guard left for the Temple. The Captain left in charge had come into the infirmary where he had been recovering from a fall that had severely battered his head. Being next to useless he had been sent to the

203

storeroom to guard there. He hadn't seen anyone for ages.

"Is Rahmin dead too?" Francesca thought, crestfallen and looked lost at Gascon. Gascon waved the group towards him. "He is obviously mad, but he is not going to let us in. Here's my plan. We will take the barges into the cave and search for another way in. If by night fall, we are no better off then we will come back and I will climb the wall and let us in."

"What makes you think he will let us in then?" asked Francesca.

Lilkin answered "He won't, but then again, he won't be alive either. Your boyfriend the guard here will kill him." They made their way back to the barges and boarded them and pushed their way towards the entrance into the mountain. It was wide and cavernous and ominously dark. They passed through the overhanging rock and glided their way into a huge cavern. It was like the inside of the Temple, the caves ceiling easily sixty feet above them, but the darkness made it unclear. The dawn's light had lit enough of the cave, but not the furthest corners at its back. They pushed on further. The air was now suddenly cooler. All were struggling in the dark but looked desperately for walkways along the sides but could see nothing.

"It's too dark!" said Francesca.

"Yes, but we have to push on towards the back." Said Gascon.

"Let's just go back and kill the guard" Lilkin blurted out. For the first time in a while Karl spoke up. "This might be better actually. Who knows what is going on inside the Citadel? No Duke, warriors attacking. How long before they break in and massacre everyone there? These caves might be a haven."

"He's right" Gascon said. "You seem smart, lad, what do you know about these caves?"

"Not much, but I know about the mountains. They are volcanic you see and most of the mountains round here are just giant heaps of rock-hard ash."

"So what?" Lilkin gave him a push.

"Well, it means that every time there was an earthquake, or the volcano erupted then the ground would split, and caves and channel would open. My mother said that the mountains were riddled with caves and tunnels….and stuff living in them."

"Stuff?" said Francesca.

"Just ghost stories, your highness. Spooks and ghouls."

"Excellent. Violent killing monsters behind us, and ghosts and ghouls in front, all wrapped up in complete darkness." said Francesca.

"That's all nonsense but let's at least see what's ahead…" Gascon pushed on into the darkness.

"See what's ahead? Is he joking?" whined Lilkin, but he pushed on as well but keeping his barge a little back from the guards.

The Duke was dragged into the Council for the second time. "Just let me walk!" he screamed continuously at the guards. The Council, this time was a lot emptier. He wondered where they were. Hiding in their chambers? Attempting the mountain passes, and there sat on his throne was Rahmin. He waved a piece of paper in the air. "This Lord Duke, is your death warrant!" cried Rahmin.

The Duke was stunned. "What?"

"Silence!" Rahmin's roar echoed around the chamber.

"The sentence for your crime is death, at this hour, by the severance of your head from your neck." Rahmin dragged the last words out slowly like he was pulling the Duke's head off there and then.

"By the Gods, Rahmin! Death, not never" The Dukes mind raced. This was insane. "Has there not been enough madness?" was the plaintive cry that escaped his body. The chamber was silent.

"Perhaps." Rahmin had paused for maximum dramatic affect. "Perhaps. There is still a chance Duke that you can redeem yourself. Many of your peers in the Council have pleaded for leniency, and I am of a mind to listen to those pleas. You are a soldier at heart, aren't you?"

The Duke nodded. "And you love this city, your city. Is that correct?"

"Of course,", the Duke stood to his feet.

"Yes, I know that is true. Do you love your Empire? Your Emperor?"

"Yes, of course" although Rahmin could sense the slight pause in the Duke's voice. He knew the Duke couldn't care less for the Empire.

"Your Emperor and the city - the survivors of the city, need a soldier, a general, Duke. I can pardon you, remove the warrant if you agree to a task...a very dangerous task. But an essential task." The Duke was confused. He made no commitment and just stood.

"The Princess Francesca is missing in the city" he held his had up to stall the Duke's response. "Missing in the city. Possibly taken or just lost I don't know which. She was seen leaving, fleeing the concourse not long ago so we are sure she is still alive. We need you to lead a handful of men –all we can spare – into the city to find her and bring her back."

"That's suicide" whispered the Duke.

"Maybe, but as you say you love your Emperor, and I am sure he will reward ...or punish in this regard. You have the chance to be a hero Duke."

"And if I am unsuccessful?" replied the Duke.

"Then you are to raid the warehouses for as much provisions as possible and return to the Citadel." The Duke looked around at the Council. "Agreed". He raised his bound hands and nodded towards them. "Free me now, the girl won't have much time."

***

In the silent eerie darkness Gascon and Francesca's barge had finally hit the end of the cave. Gascon studied the barge whilst Francesca and the two boys felt along the wall. He moved the barge slowly along the wall. They were hoping for an opening, and their eyes were no use. The sunlight did not penetrate this far, but Gascon knew there was an opening. They had all crouched in fear when a huge howling was heard just before they reached the wall. It had come from the back of the cave.

All the children had screamed, expecting some monstrous ghoul to have attacked them from the darkness. It was Karl who spoke up and told them that this was the wind. It was rushing and squeezing down through a tunnel and bursting out into the open cave. It meant there was a tunnel at the back, a tunnel that led to the open air.

Lilkin had pulled his barge up alongside his on the opposite side to the wall. "How much longer before we go back?" he asked, with the cynicism that Gascon was learning to expect. He ignored the question.

"Your Lilkin, is that right?" he asked.

"Yes, the King" replied Lilkin. Gascon laughed. Who calls you that?"

Lilkin smirked. "They do" he nodded towards the boys in the barges.

"And who are they?" asked Gascon.

"My boys. My soldiers." He replied. Gascon laughed.

"You can laugh, solider, but we are what we are. I report to no-one, no one is king of me. These boys look up to me, I saved them, you see." None of the boys looked up or away from the wall they were feeling.

"They are the unloved. The orphans of those that you guards lock up or kill for just trying to survive in this hell hole. They get protection from me. I keep them alive."

"And do they have names?" chirped in Francesca.

Lilkin smiled. "You know Karl – his the smart one." Karl looked up.

"The two little 'uns are Frezco and Grimes. They are new. Just off the boats. They came alone with just a letter to their name and a bag of clothes. Their food had run out just before they docked. The letter was addressed to Gorge Grimes the boy's uncle, but Gorge Grimes was long gone. A family from an earlier arrival had moved in, and probably done away with Mr Grimes. I found 'em and I helped 'em.

This other one" he bent down a pulled up the chin of a boy, who in attempting to smile showed he had no teeth "this one here is Dudum on account of him not ever saying a single word, but by God he can pick a pocket. And Felix, well Felix I've known a long time. His dad fixed and made locks, until he was arrested when a rich merchant got robbed. All the evidence pointed to an inside job and Felix's dad was the inside job. With his dad in prison...well they all find their way to me eventually."

"And what about you, Karl" you're no son of a thief" quizzed Cascon.

"No..no I'm not. "Karl began to say.

"Let's just say his an odd 'un" interrupted Lilkin "and leave it at that." Before Gascon could comment, one of the boys in his boat suddenly fell headfirst into the water. The splash covered the barge, and the loss of weight rocked the boat.

"Get him!" Gascon shouted, and he plunged his arm into the unexpectedly cold water. He grabbed at water, Frezco was gone, and then suddenly he appeared above the water, his head just breaking the service. His face was shocked, his hair clinging wet to his head. The water was apparently shallow enough for Frezco to stand! Gascon pulled him into the barge, a shivering wet mass.

"He must have found the opening," Lilkin chimed "Hold fast and push forward." He pushed forward on his pole and straightened Gascon's barge into the space where the wall should have been. Frezco continued to shiver at the bottom of the barge. The barges banged against walls and each other but soon were drifting down a channel, blind but with a soft coolness on their face.

29

Rahmin and his Commander stood with the Duke and three Citadel Guards in a storage area at the far eastern corner of the Citadel, the door behind them would open onto the lock system and the eastern reservoir. It had been the idea of one of the Guards with him. He had served duty here many times and he meant that they didn't have to open the front gates. In the corner was a battered old guard, trying to stand to attention, but looking slovenly. Rahmin ignored him.

"Best of luck...your highness" Rahmin extended his hand. His admiration for the Duke had gone up. He was after all a brave man, and chances were that he would never see him again. The Duke just nodded, before opening the door and stepping out onto the walkway, where a few hours before Francesca, and the group of survivors had stood before. Rahmin watched the Duke get into a barge and push away to the lock system across the reservoirs.

The Duke pulled the door shut and lowered the barrier. "Stay here Commander. If he returns, only the princess gets back in. Do you understand?"

"Yes, my lord." The Commander nodded.

Then an old voice in the corner "Princess?" The old guard was a mess, shown more so by the full figure of the Golden Guard.

"What do you know of the Princess?" the Commander grabbed the guard by his arm. The old guard looked at his arm then at Rahmin.

"There was someone outside a while back. She said she was Princess. But she was just a peasant. She was with a gaggle of thief's and dockyard scum."

"And where are they now?" demanded Rahmin grabbing the guard by the throat.

"I don't know. I watched for a while. They drifted into the caves, but who knows?"

Rahmin dropped him to the floor. Get some men and search the caves!" He yelled at the Commander.

"What about the Duke, sir? Shall I call him back?" Rahmin paused. His brain was working overtime. "I don't think so..."

* * *

The Duke and the three guards slowly descended the lock in an ornate barge. One of the Citadel servants managed the various lock mechanisms. Nobody said a word, but the tension communicated the fear and trepidation that all four were feeling. The Duke looked at the two men. He only recognized one of them: the tall one with the grey hair. Not the grey hair of an old man, this guard must have been in his early twenties. He had been in the Council chambers a number of times. His face showed no emotion, but the white blood drained hands gripping his sword, showed the true emotion. Was he a good soldier or just a glorified doorman?

The other two were older, their faces more chiselled with experience. Their skins both darker, perhaps more duties on the Citadel walls than the grey. There was not much to distinguish the two, until one opened his mouth in a broad but toothless smile. The man wouldn't stop looking at him and smiling. The Duke thought of saying something. Something pleasant, bonding, but in the end just looked down into the locks below.

When the final lock opened and the barge began to drift into the canal, he turned to the three, handing the tallest the barge pole. "That's yours." He ordered. "You other two: one look forward, the other to the left, I'll keep my eyes on the right. See anything moving, let me know."

"Sir" the smiling one nodded and verbally acknowledged. The Duke looked out over the concourse in front of the Citadel gates. There were none of the violent assailants, just a pile of bodies. A small cloud of feint black hovered above them: flies.

"Where to sir?" asked the tall one.

211

"Just stay in the main canal. We will listen for anything on the way but were best to make it to the docks and then work our way in. Find some survivors…if there are any."

***

They had drifted in the dark for probably just a few minutes, although it felt like an hour. Fresco was shivering in the bottom of the barge, whilst Francesca tried to comfort him. "He'll die of the cold" she said. No-one responded, and even Francesca realized that there was not much passion in her plea. The darkness was easing as ahead there was some sort of light. It was very dim and high up, but they aimed the boats for it.

Thankfully they had not encountered any ghosts or ghouls, though the wind made them shudder as every now and then it strengthened and brushed their faces. As they drew closer the light became two yellows orbs, each no bigger than a fist. They seemed to flicker and move.

"What is that ahead?" Francesca asked.

"That's a pair of eyes that is" whispered Lilkin. "We should go back."

"Don't be ridiculous!" Gascon returned. "Who has eyes that give off light. And whose head is way up there?" None of the children answered, but the thought spread like a disease. Lilkin gave in first. "Ghosts and ghouls, that's what."

The yellow lights suddenly went out and then appeared again as if on cue. "Just keep low in the barge" Gascon said turning to look at the children behind him and in the boat with Lilkin which stayed a few feet beyond his aft. They were already laying low. The eyes got bigger and brighter, and they all screamed in unison as Gascon's barge hit something on the left and the barge behind rammed them. The boat shuddered then there was a loud screech as they were suddenly surrounded by a myriad of flying things, hitting their faces."

"It's just bats!" yelled Gascon, as the beast disappeared in the dull light, obscuring the two eyes for a while before they brightened once more. Gascon suddenly leapt from the boat to his left with his sword in his left hand and his right clasping the rope. His movement was a blur in

212

the dim light and shadows. They all expected a splash but there was none.

Gascon had landed on a stone platform dug into the walls. He seemed to run towards the lights ahead and above his head. His shape obscured the lights for a few seconds and then they burned fiercely. Francesca cupped her head beneath her arms waiting the violence to follow. But there was nothing.

She felt a gentle hand on her shoulder and saw Gascon lit up by two flaming torches in his hand." Take one, whilst I tie up the barge." He handed her a torch and in the lower light she could see they were next to a small dock cut into the mountain, the size of a small chamber. At the end was a shadow of blackness. An opening?

"The eyes, they were just torches." Said Gascon. Come on, let's get off the boats, but tie them up in case we need them."

They were soon all sat around the torched laid across each other on the stone floor. They had sat Fresco as near to their heat as possible, but he still shivered. The platform was wide enough for all of them. Gascon and Lilkin were next to the dark opening. It had turned out to be an alcove with a wooden door. It was locked but already Felix was sticking small objects in the lock. Somehow the other children had gravitated towards huddling around Francesca. They had got use to the silence. Gascon came over.

"Felix thinks he can get it. I'll leave them to it." Gascon said. "Are they okay?" he asked of the boys huddled around her.

"Just scared and tired. Fresco though…. He needs to get warm; we need to find some dry clothes…soon" Francesca replied. Gascon just nodded and stared at the boy for a while, before walking back to Felix and Lilkin. Francesca had got use to the silence, but she felt it like an ambivalent force attacking her. She heard the odd noise down the tunnel they had come from, perhaps just flotsam and jetsam hit the sides or the weird effects of the wind winding through the tunnels.

She knew this was unnerving the boys. Without realizing she had started to sing. Softly, a gentle lullaby from when she was small.

"When the wind blows

Through the mountains away

And the trees whistle sweetly

At the end of the day

We should all close our eyes

And think of the grace

Tomorrow will bring us

Here in this place."

She stopped, there were noises in the tunnel, and it wasn't the wind. She strained her ears and shushed one of the little ones who was sobbing. There was a light. A wide glow coming up the tunnel. Someone...or something was coming.

"Gascon!" she raised her voice just beyond the whisper. "Gascon!"

"We nearly have it, Princess. Nearly there." He responded. The sounds were now splashing, the glow, lots of lights, and the voices of men.

She jumped up. "Gascon!" The children jumped up too and instinctively made for the door in the alcove, where Felix was huddled with Gascon and Lilkin looking over. Gascon spun around and picked up the sword lying on the floor. "Is it the monsters?" he asked, his eyes straining in the dark.

"I don't know..., I don't think so." Then she shouted out "Over here!". Her instincts told her it was not the army of death. Gascon grabbed her arm to hold her back, he was not convinced. But she knew and she was certain, when out of the darkness, surrounded by a halo of light were four or five barges with human faces peering out, and standing at the back was the Guardian, his arms behind his back.

***

Ark reached the last roof, overhanging the east canal. He was a few buildings down from the concourse, making sure to keep clear of that killing ground. His was plan was to leap across the canal to the other

214

side and thus have the body of water between himself and the assassins, but it was a substantial leap of over twenty feet. Substantial even for him.

As he travelled the city had been quieter. He had not encountered any more of the assassins and was feeling safer than he had for a while. He traced his steps back along the roof to prepare a run up and took a long look at a water buttress hanging off the roof across the canal. He would look to land above that in case he slipped down the tiles. Below the roof was a small quay for the barges. The building was a warehouse of some kind, its large wooden doors matching the width of the quay: a loading bay. The warehouse doors were ajar.

He began his run up, hit the edge of the roof and threw himself into the air. As he did so, he saw the glimpse below of a barge floating down the canal with a group of soldiers, just coming level with the edge of the quay. Ark set off and hit the edge of the roof pushing off into the air. He felt like he was flying. He landed hard against the tiles above the buttress. The tiles were old and came away from under him cascading like a waterfall of terracotta. He slipped with them but landed squarely on the buttress. The tiles continued their way to the ground, smashing on the quayside and some into the water. Ark looked down, as the barge of soldiers looked up. Instinctively he threw himself flat against the sloping roof beams. A hole had appeared where some of the tiles had been and far beneath him, he saw more bodies amongst wooden barrels.

The Duke and the three soldiers all looked up instinctively, whilst also holding their hands up in case tiles hit them. "What was it?" Shouted the tall one.

"I'm not sure" the Duke said quietly under his breath. "Take the boat into the quayside. Its maybe a survivor who could help us." 'Toothless' nodded and jumped onto the quay and tied up the barge. 'Tall' laid down the pole and drew his sword in unison with the Duke and the remaining guard.

Ark looked down and saw the guards. Then he sensed movement below in the warehouse and looked down. A stone warrior, no two warriors and they were making for the warehouse door by the quay.

Ark looked down at the men. Something inside pulled at his emotions. He should flee but his body wouldn't move.

"Watch out!!" he screamed. Just as he did so the warehouse doors burst open, and the stone warriors were onto the quay within a few steps. 'Smiler' spun round as a sword descended into his head from above and clove him in two. Ark looked away, as the two parts of the man fell like tree trunks to the ground.

'Tall' and the other were off balance as they had begun to step out of the barge and the second assassin swung his sword into the side of the smaller man. The momentum carried him into the tall man who fell out of the boat onto the quay his sword clattering to the ground. As he reached to recover it 'smilers' assassin drove his sword down into his back with both hands grasping the hilt.

The Duke was still in the barge. The assault had started the boat rocking, and he was struggling for balance, but fortunately it seemed the two assassins were unsure how to step onto the barge. Ark looked back, and without realizing had grabbed a tile in his hand. One of the warriors tentatively took a step over the water and planted a foot on the barge. As he did so Ark launched the tile at his head. By some strange sense the warrior realized something was coming and turned to look, still straddling the water.

The tile hit him full in the stone face. Ark was sure stone chips flew into the air. The warrior wobbled and stretched out its hands to balance. The Duke had thrust forward with his sword, crashing into the chest of the warrior, but not penetrating the stone, but doing enough to further unbalance the assassin. It spun around and lifted its leg off of the barge, but the damage was done. He had overstretched and was falling into the gap between the canal side and barge. The splash soaked the barge, and then the warrior was gone. The second warrior stood and looked at the barge, which had drifted away from the side. Then he turned to look up at the source of missile from above. Ark looked straight at it. There was no emotion. It was like looking at a statue. The figure spun to face him directly and seemed to be calculating how to get to him.

Ark should have run, but he didn't. He pulled at more tiles and begun to throw them one after the other at the figure. Each one hitting and seeming to chip at the stone. The figure stood looking. Then it raised its sword and grabbed it like a spear. He leaned back with his right arm extended. He was going to throw the sword. Ark instinctively turned, but looked back as he heard a huge thud of metal on stone.

The Duke had reached the quayside and whilst still standing on the barge had swung his sword into the throwing arm of the warrior. The keen blade wedged itself an inch into the arm of the warrior and its assault was halted. The Duke pulled the sword out, but nothing happened. The sword was wedged tight. The assassin turned its head slowly, mechanically and stared at the Duke. The Duke fell back on the barge, landing hard on his side against the pole. The warrior with the Duke's sword still wedged into his arm, took its own sword and made for the barge. This time the water did not appear to be a barrier and the assassin prepared to leap from the quayside into the boat...but a shadow appeared like an eagle behind and above him.

Ark had leapt from the buttress and crashed down feet first onto the back of the warrior. Both crashed into the water smashing a wave over the side of the barge. The Duke rushed to the side, jumping back when a strange looking child burst through from the water scrambling for the barge. The Duke rushed to help him, stretching his arms out to pull him over the side. Ark's hands grabbed at the arms of the Duke, and in a rapid movement the Duke pulled the child onto the barge.

What he saw was no mere boy, but a strange beast, full of hair and with almost Klarion like features. Whatever it was he owed it his life.

***

Rahmin urged the barges forward towards the collection of figures on the small platform. He could see Francesca amongst the collection. An armed guard stood by her.

"Get the girl!" he yelled at the crew, as two of the barges surged forward ahead of Rahmin. Their barges crashed into the platform and three guards leapt onto it. Francesca suddenly felt afraid and turned her back. She felt arms grab her back and pulled her backwards towards the barges. She screamed and tried to fight but was overpowered. Gascon held his sword and hands in the air, but soon realized that he was under attack. He was pushed backwards by a guard and saw him raise his sword to strike him. "No, no" Gascon yelled.

Francesca was already in a barge that was pulling away from the platform. Watching the guards on the platform swinging swords at the children and Gascon. "Kill them!" yelled Rahmin. Then under his breathe, "They will be riddled with plague." Francesca made a series of screams and sobs that were intelligible, as the platform disappeared into the distance.

Gascon was now wielding his sword and biting into the armour of one of the guards. He saw one of the boys, Grimes he thought, fall into the water. Fresco appeared dead a bloody gash across his face.

Gascon managed to position himself between the back wall and the three guards, pulling the remaining children behind him. Holding the sword out in front of him, he yelled "Get back! Get back!"

"Is that door open yet?" he asked.

"We're in! "Lilkin shouted back.

"Run!" he shouted at the remaining children who rushed to the alcove. Gascon followed them. Walking backwards still holding the sword out in front of him. He reached the alcove. From behind him he was yanked backwards through the gap, and then the door slammed in front of him. They were back in the dark.
∎∎

30

The Duke sat looking at the boy in front of him. Who the hell was this? "Thank you" said the Duke, and then extended his hand offering a handshake. Ark just looked at it. His hands were almost black with the dirt of a lifetime. He looked at them and extended his slowly. The Duke took it forcefully and gave a solid shake. "You're not from the city, are you? I mean not originally. Your features are …. well. I guess. From the east? Klarion?" Ark, still not speaking. Nodded. There had been no movement from the water and their barge had drifted slowly down the canal towards the docks.

"Do you have family here? Are they okay?" Ark sized the man up. He was not a guard. His armour was light and well-polished, the clothes beneath, smooth and shiny. Then he spoke. "Are you a Lord?"

The Duke smiled. "Yes…of sorts. Yes, just a minor one. I've come from the Citadel on a rescue mission."

"I'm not sure who is left to save." Ark interrupted. "The city has been massacred. What are those things?" he said referring to the stone warriors.

"I don't know" the Duke replied "But the good news is they don't seem to like water. "He laughed. Ark liked his smile.

"I'm not new to the city." Ark volunteered. "I have been here since I was a child. My parents, my family…. they died a long time ago."

"I'm sorry for that." said the Duke. He grabbed the pole and pushed the barge on, as they passed under a bridge staying to the middle of the canal. "You have done well to survive the massacre," the Duke asked. "Are there others?"

"Yes, a few" said Ark. "Many fled to the Dam, and they are all dead. The Temple – all dead." Ark paused picturing the body of the traveller. The Duke hung his head too, and Ark thought he must be a believer.

"A few may be hiding in their houses, but I have seen the warriors cutting people down in their beds." The Duke seemed to be taking this on board. "Why have you left the Citadel? The assassins seem to have stopped there. You would be safe there. I was heading for there."

The Duke nodded. "I fear nowhere is safe." He waited." I am looking for someone...maybe you have seen her. If you help me, I can bring you back to the Citadel." Ark nodded.

"The city is a big place. Where do they live?" asked Ark.

"They lived in the Citadel but were caught outside." How much does he say? Does he trust this boy? "It's a girl...my daughter". A lie, but easier to explain.

"She is a bit adventurous, and I took my eye off of her. She has blonde hair, blue eyes yes, wearing a red dress. Ark thought. "I have not seen her. Is she smart? I mean, would she be able to survive?"

The Duke considered it. "Yes, I think she is...." They suddenly opened into the dock surrounded by the Dam. The dockside was covered with bodies, but no warriors. "I'm not even sure where to start? You know the city, where would you hide?"

Ark, thought, "I don't have time for this. I can't help this man. It's a fool's errand. But Francesca was in the Citadel and I could use him to get into the Citadel.

"If I were her, I'd head high. I mean keep clear of the ground. I have not seen any on the rooftops. I would head there. We could climb high and look across the city. What places would she know? She would probably be trying to get back to the Citadel?"

"The Temple." The Duke said. She can see it from her room. It's the highest point.

Ark nodded. "I can take you there. Can you climb?" The Duke nodded.

***

Francesca did not stop screaming as she struggled with the two guards who had locked their arms around hers. The lights on the platform quickly dimmed as the barge she was on floated quickly down the tunnel they had originally come from. She could not see the Guardian but knew he was behind her. She could see the platform now more and the sounds of fighting had stopped. She stopped screaming and sunk to the floor. Only then did Rahmin speak. "Thank the gods you are safe, Princess. You had us all worried there." He was very calm, not angry, not reproachful.

She could spin her head to see him now. He looked like a ghoul in the eerie light of the torches and his hood covering his head. "They were my friends! What have you done?"

"I'm sure you thought that, Princess and I'm sure they made you feel that way, but they were not. Why bring you to these caves, why not straight to the Citadel? Those boys are criminals; thieves and cutthroats."

"They were just boys!" she yelled." We tried to get into the Citadel, but the guards wouldn't let us in."

"Of course, but you are safe now." The tone of the Guardian's voice didn't change. Calm and unemotional.

"The guard, Gascon, he rescued me. In the city."

"Then he will be rewarded, your highness. I am sure he will help with the...dismissal of the vagabonds, then we can bring him to the Citadel.... he will be a hero."

"But he won't! He will help the boys. He is a good man...he saved them." The Guardian paused, looked in her eyes. "Then he will need to save them." The barge came into the sunlight as it emerged from the darkness of the tunnel and the back of the reservoir cave.

"I will send my men back to check, but right now the priority is getting you safe." They reached the quayside that they had been on earlier. Francesca had no more strength in her voice to argue. The guards lifted her out for the barge.

"You guard take the barge back, make sure the children are spared and the soldier. Bring him to me." Francesca mouthed the words "thank you" as she was carried in the arms of a particularly large soldier through the now open doors of the Citadel. She saw the guardian hanging back to give some last few orders to the guards. He looked up at her and smiled.

***

Gascon felt his way through the darkness. None of them had torches and all stumbled over uneven ground. No-one seemed to have followed, although they could still hear voices far behind them. Gascon couldn't be sure who was with him or not. There was definitely movement ahead, and as far as he was concerned, he was the last one through the door. He stopped for second and got his breathe. "Whose here?" he whispered.

"Whose asking?" that was Lilkin.

"Lilkin, who else is here?" Gascon asked.

"Felix and Karl were ahead of me". Lilkin was behind him he could just see the shape a few feet away.

"They must be ahead of me" Gascon replied. "Stay close and we should catch them up."

That's assuming there is only one way to go in this tunnel..." Lilkin said. Gascon was pretty sure he had not missed any openings. The tunnel was only a couple of metres wide. It had steadily climbed upwards, and he was guessing that they'd travelled at least one hundred yards. There were no voices ahead, though. Gascon still had his sword but didn't use it to prod ahead in case the boys were closer than he thought.

"You lead" Lilkin whispered, and Gascon felt the boy's hand on his shoulder. They keep going fumbling in the dark always heading upwards. The incline was mild most of the time, only going very steep at one point before levelling again. The voices behind had gone. The air was close, and for the last few minutes Gascon could sense a strong odour reminiscent of the smells from the tanning warehouses.

It was warmer as well, but that might just have been his mind playing tricks on him. The ground had become more uneven, and he stumbled a few times almost twisting his ankle.

After another half an hour of fumbling a small arc of light appeared ahead. It was enough for Gascon to make out Lilkin's face. He stopped and rested.

"Look a way out!" he grasped Lilkin by his collar.

"Slow a minute," Lilkin grabbed his arm. "if it's the Citadel but I seem to remember us not being very welcome. Just step carefully."

"Yes, of course." Gascon held his sword up and stepped forward. He could hear voices but could not make out the words. He hugged the side of the wall hoping it would give some protection. A few more feet and he could see a bright light. The tunnel was ending. The voices were louder, but he sensed they were trying to be quiet.

A few feet further and he could make out rocks and tufts of weed or grass. The brightness was almost dazzling. He paused and leant slightly forward moving his shoulders to try to get a different view, but he could not see who owned the voices. He squatted down and with his hand felt the ground ahead of him. He was only five or six feet from the opening. The ground seemed firm. "That's it, I'm charging" he decided.

"Lilkin, there's more than one person there. On three, lets charge and hopefully surprise will win the day. Lilkin?" He looked round Lilkin wasn't there. "Damn!"

He set his feet firmly and charged out of the opening. He was shocked by the blue sky and bright light of the sun, he could see two figures huddled on a rock in a corner and charged for them, his sword above his head. "No!" Screamed one throwing his hands in the air. Gascon swung his sword down and to the side, well clear of the two figures. Two figures who were obviously Felix and Karl.

Gascon halted his charge and exhaled pent up air from his lungs. "Thank the Gods" he said. He spun round behind him and checked his position. There was no-one else. The two boys jumped at Gascon and hugged him. "We're safe. We're safe" he said. Then a noise behind him as Lilkin slowly emerged from the tunnel.

"Everything seems okay behind us" he said.

***

Ark led the Duke across the city via the rooftops that had been his home all his life. The Duke found it slow going and Ark kept stopping to ensure he was not leaving the Duke behind. A few times they both had to descend to street level and climb back up again, as the gaps between buildings was just too much for the Duke to jump. On every descent they discovered bodies, but not a living soul.

The Duke initially would make conversation but, on each descent, and with each body he became quieter. The Duke had doubts that he would find Francesca. He had seen many dead children, but none dressed as she would have been, and that gave him some comfort amongst the sorrow.

The boy didn't seem to flinch at anything and by the gods how he could move. He must have been an acrobat or something, and he had a vague memory of seeing a circus troop who performed in the market square. He considered that he had never seen them for years now. At least five or six summers. He had just taken over form his father, and then he remembered: the cleansing.

His father and the Council had attempted to gut the streets of vagrants and beggars, and he remembered hordes of people being locked in warehouses and eventually placed on ships to depart the city. He had taken little interest, in those days all he cared about was the sword and socialising. He would either be found in the training rooms or in the inns of the city. Is this what had happened to the boy's family?

Within a few hours they had crossed the best part of the city, and he began to recognize the streets and alley was that were distinguishable from the view from the Citadel. The tributaries of the canals were narrower, sometimes lost amongst the houses, but ahead was the Temple and the only true space in the city: the marketplace.

The boy was like a cat. He knew he was slowing him down. And those features, unlike any of the myriad other races that had swarmed into the city over the last few months. Halfway on route the Duke had ditched his armour, including his helmet, but not his chest plate. The climbing was hard enough without the weight of another person pulling him down. The objective was to avoid the assassins.

Finally, they reached the edge of the houses overlooking the square directly opposite the Temple. He could see the bodies of the Citadel Guard and the Golden Guard of the Guardian in an arc parallel but fifty feet on from the Temple steps. It looked like the guard had barely moved when they were cut down. He could see no assassins, but he could see a neat line of bodies on the top step of the Temple. The doors were closed. The horror almost overwhelmed him, and he struggled to stop himself being sick. He had sent them too their deaths.

Ark saw the scene differently. The great doors were closed, and the bodies on the top step were laid neatly in a line with their arms crossed above them. Most were monks and a few Golden Guards, but he remembered no monks making it outside. Someone had placed them there. He strained his eyes for every detail, every clue. There were no weapons. The swords and spears that were previously scatted were gone. Looking back at the soldiers further into the market square he could see although not lined up that they had no weapons.

"There are people from the Temple" Ark said.

"You think so?" said the Duke.

"Yes, someone has closed the doors. Your girl might be there."

The Duke pulled himself to the edge to get closer. "Let's join them, then." He patted Ark on the back and jumped down the two storeys to the square below.

"No!" yelled Ark. "we should work around the roofs, get nearer." But the Duke had gone. He landed with a crunch on the cobbles, and it was then that the Duke realized his mistake. He caught the cobbles awkwardly and his left leg buckled under him. He felt the stone send a shock through the nerves of his right side and felt the leg give way completely. He crumbled to the floor whacking his left side and helmet against the cobbles. Then the pain shot through his body like thunder following the lightning.

He screamed in pain and looked to see his leg looking like a foreign object. Twisted at the wrong angle. Then a sharp white object sticking out from the skin. Ark saw the collapse, saw the bone rip through the soldier's shin as the he sprayed across the cobbles. The crack and scream made him sick in the stomach. He began to climb down swinging from drains and beams until he reached the cobbles.

Up close was no better. The sight was horrendous. Amongst all the death and blood lining the streets and alleyways this seemed more real. He clasped his hand over the soldier's mouth. He had to stop the screaming, but it didn't work. He looked across at the Temple. He tried to lift the soldier, but he was too heavy.

Then grabbing the soldiers two arms he began to pull him across the marketplace. He was moving, slowly but moving, but the screams did not stop. The busted leg battered the cobblestones, each one like a dagger in the Duke's side. The Duke found the pain unbearable and was losing consciousness, only to be jolted into reality by the sharp pain every few feet.

The backplate of his chest armour was almost drowning out the screams with its metal screeching. It was catching the cobbles and slowing Ark down with every step. He reached down and undid the four buckles that held it and threw the breast plate and back plate to one side. Their painful journey could then continue.

It seemed like an age, but Ark and the Duke reached the steps of the Temple. Ark left the Duke and ran to the doors. He started banging on them, but there was no answer. To the side were stone pillars with a cornice above the door and above that a dark window. He decided to climb the pillar to the window. He would get someone's attention and if not break in and open the door from inside.

He pulled himself up from the window and managed to edge onto the cornice. Standing above the door he leant on the large dark window and peered in it. The glass was opaque, and it was hard to see. He bashed on the glass, but he saw no movement.

He looked back down at the Duke. He was deadly still. With both arms he banged on the glass with all his strength, hammering and hammering, then suddenly the glass seemed to shift, and he was falling inward. The frame seemed to scream and the wooden just split like the bones of the Duke's leg. He was falling, the window had caved in and he was falling the twelve feet to the ground with a glass sheets leading the way.

The glass hit first, and he followed, hard. The glass shattered around him cutting his hands and his face. It was like an explosion. He lay still aching from the fall when he saw dark figures coming towards him. Hands pulled him up, their feet stamping and crushing the glass around.

"What have you done?" it was a mix of voices shouting all at the same time. But one voice was clear, as tow firm old hands grabbed his shoulders.

"Thank the Gods, it's you, Ark." It was the traveller. Ark was stunned. The face was old and worn, and it was beautiful. He hugged the old man, and then realised he'd forgotten the Duke.

"We must rescue my friend, a soldier – he is outside." A host of voices said "No" in a cacophony of noise. There were many people here and a number had moved to block the door.

"We must help him." yelled Ark.

"We will" spoke the traveller, and he looked up at the bodies. "I opened the doors for each of you" and he raised his hand and waved it to the left and right. The figures seemed to move with the hand motion, leaving the doors available. Ark rushed for the door and threw himself at it pushing it open.

The traveller joined him and pushed. As the door swung open, Ark looked for the Duke. There he was, still lying where he had left him. Standing above him was the stone assassin, his right arm extended pressing a long sword into the chest of the Duke. Ark could see the end piercing him through the back.

31

Francesca was back in her room. Somewhere between the barge and the room she had passed out in the arms of the guard carrying her and she woke up on the bed. At first, she thought it was all a dream, then she looked down at her sore, bare and muddy feet. Her dress was ripped and her hands grubby and red raw. Her hair felt like straw, and when she tried to run her fingers through it clumps of dirt and dust fell into her lap.

She closed her eyes, and a series of images flashed though her mind. Bodies at the gates, monsters chopping people down; the stables and the cellar; the run across the market; the guard, the blonde boy, the barges, the darkness; the children, Gascon, Ark. She leapt up and headed for the door. She rattled the handle, but it was locked. She rushed to the balcony, but this time the doors to the balcony were firmly shut, locked and the key nowhere to be seen. She screamed out loud, and found her throat was aching. She felt faint and a little dizzy, so sat back down on the bed. She was so tired and was soon asleep again.

Rahmin had let Francesca sleep. Her return was a great relief and he felt that he was back in control again. The Council was down to a handful of Lords, including the Lord Justice. As the day progressed, he had camped out at the Council chambers as had most of the Lords. Those missing had been looked for and a few had been found in their apartments and chambers declining to attend the Council. Some, it could only be assumed had somehow got out of the city and headed for the mountain passes. Their average age and health would make that a futile, deadly escape. Two passes cut through the mountain and had been sealed shut with rolling stones. The two stairs over the mountains were open but the terrain was impassable unless you were a mountain goat. No doubt some would make it, but most would become abandoned heaps in the high cold altitudes.

It was time for him to seize real control. He met with the Lord Justice and they agreed that in the absence of the Duke and with the Council and shadow of its former glory that the Lord Justice would resign his position. Rahmin would be nominated and voted in within the hour, and martial law declared; this place would be his.

The seventy or so guards at the Citadel would suffice to keep back the assassins he had set in play. The fact that the city population had died by the blade should halt the effects of the plague, the effects that none here had truly seen but that he had witnessed across the cities of the Empire on his journey south.

The Council chamber was next to the outer wall of the Citadel and he stood on the balcony here overlooking the concourse. The guards were mostly sitting leaning against the wall not bothering to look at the city. The pile of bodies was still wedged against the gates like a small hill. He could see no sign of his assassins. Perhaps the magic was already wearing off. Once he was sure he would send out some servants to hunt for the figurines they would become and collect them in. He imagined a small boy picking one up and carrying it off as his plaything not realising the devastation they had caused.

The sun was beginning to set. There had been no return of the Duke. The naive fool wouldn't survive long he imagined. Francesca was back safe, and now it was a question of waiting. Waiting out the assassins, waiting out the plague. He walked back into the Council chambers. Some of the Lords were sat in their seats, whilst some were walking about or in small groups. A merchant lord stopped him as he walked in and asked about sending men into the city to recover some of his stock from the warehouses on the dock.

"Are you willing to show them the way?" he asked him. That put an end to that. As he walked around the chamber studying the faces, listening to conversations, he heard a debate on who had attacked them. Where this army had come from. Was its part of a bigger campaign against the Empire? Should the Emperor be warned?

Others discussed opening the mountain passes. Then talk of the dead who lived in the passes; talk of climbing mountains, breaking out of the Citadel for the boats and sailing north.

Rahmin made his way to the Duke's chair and sat down. He closed his eyes and pictured the future. He had seventy men left, the remainder of the Golden Guard and the stone warriors. He would wait out the plague. Send messengers out to see what was left of the Empire. He would, of course, announce himself Duke of Kusrch. Then it would be time to leave the city. Ride North rally the survivors to his banner. Rebuild the Empire.

He opened his eyes. The sun was low now, and the clerk had lit the inside torches. The Duke was probably dead by now.

***

Gascon, Lilkin, Felix and Karl were huddled together as the sun set over the city. The tunnel had led to a clearing on the side of the great mountain that overlooked the city below. The view was incredible. The Citadel was directly below them and for the first time in the children live they saw the sea beyond the Dam.

The sun looked like it was being eaten up by the sea and already most parts of the city were shrouded in a darkness slowly creeping towards the Citadel. The clearing was flat around the side of a small garden. The floor was paved and there was a series of benches against the mountainside looking over the city. "This must be some kind of retreat for the Citadel. A viewing point to watch the sun come down." figured Karl.

They had had a good look round and along with the tunnel down to the reservoir, there was also a series of very narrow steps heading down. The foliage had overgrown its beginning and some of the steps were badly damaged.

"Obviously, not used for a while" said Lilkin. They had also found a track leading further up the mountain. This was not a man-made construction but rather generated over time probably by some wild animals. The mountain was still ominously big behind them. They could see a further twenty feet or so, but then the rest of the mountain veered away from their line of sight.

A cold wind blew, and the group remained huddled together. They were all tired and conversation became limited. No-one had followed them up the tunnel, although Gascon had stood ready for what seemed like an age before conceding to the comfort of the benches.

"So, what next?" Felix asked. No-one rushed to answer. When eventually someone did it was Karl. "The way I see it, we have three options. "One, we head back down the tunnel and make our way back into the city. "

"What about the guards?" chipped in Felix. "They will be long gone, "said Gascon. "They will be back behind the walls as soon as possible. They probably even told the creepy guy that we were killed."

Karl nodded. "Second: We head down these steps. My guess it takes us into the Citadel…."

"Where, we will be captured, and the guards job finished". Lilkin's first contribution.

"Probably. But my guess is the exit for these stairs is long forgotten. It might lead somewhere where we can hide out. We will be safe from those…monsters." Karl responded. Gascon nodded. "We couldn't hide out for ever, though."

Felix coughed, his voice horse, "We really need some food, I'm hungry."

"Starving!" said Lilkin.

"And then there's the mountain." Karl continued. "We follow that track up the mountain and see where it goes. We leave this crappy city behind." They all looked up at the mountain.

"Where would we go, cough, presuming we make it over the mountain." Asked Felix.

"I haven't a clue." Said Karl. He looked at Gascon. "The Empire I guess?"

Gascon shrugged his shoulders. "I've never been out of the city, that's the first time I've even seen the full vastness of the sea." The group was quiet for a while.

"You won't get me going over the mountain." Lilkin was adamant. "The only thing up there is death, but there's another option." They all looked at him.

"We stay here. See what happens. No point rushing headfirst towards three different ways of dying." He drew in his breathe. "The way I see it, all those goings on in the city, well there must be an end to it. Either the Citadel gets captured, or the monsters pack up and go home. I mean it's not like this city is anything worth staying for?"

"What about the gold?" Felix said.

"The gold?" Lilkin asked.

"Yep. The gold. The legend of the city. The stuff buried a millennium ago." Karl said.

"Oh, the gold!" laughed Lilkin. "of course. I've been pinching pennies on the streets when I should have been digging!"

"I'm just saying." said Karl. The others laughed for the first time in a long time. Gascon thought for a while and then said. "Lilkin is right. At least for now. We should stay here tonight. It will be too dark soon to tackle either the stairs or the mountain. Let's sleep as best we can and see what the morning brings. We'll take turns to watch the tunnel just in case. I'll take first watch." He got up and sat next to the dark entrance, sword between his legs. It would be cold tonight, and he wondered whether this was the right decision, whether they would survive the night, but no-one had had the energy to disagree.

***

Ark rushed out but was pulled back by the traveller grabbing his arm. "No." he said forcibly. Still holding Ark, he closed his eyes and raised his right hand out in front of him. His face clenched, his eyes tight shut, his lips slightly parted his teeth tightened. The warrior was drawing his sword from the prone body of the Duke and begun to look at the pair of them.

Ark couldn't explain what happened next. The air in front of the travellers outstretched hand started to wobble, like a heat haze. Like the air had become a still water, and the travellers hand a disturbance sending gentle waves out. The waves filled the air expanding out towards the Temple steps and the warrior. The traveller continued to strain, sweat appearing on his brow.

The air waves hit the warrior, and like a cape in the wind the warrior was swept up into the air. He was hanging in the air but slowly moving away from the steps. The wave got bigger and bigger until its edges the side of the market. The warrior was now twenty feet in the air and halfway down the market square.

Then he dropped. The travellers arm dropped, and a huge sigh fell from his lips. Ark looked at him, and then the traveller spoke in a voice full of exhaustion "Get him, there isn't much time."

Ark didn't wait he ran to the Duke. His chest was mess of blood. He grabbed his arms and resumed his pulling. It was hard, his arms bruised from the fall, but he soon had the Duke inside the doors. The traveller pushed the doors closed, Ark's last sight being the crumbled body of the warrior in the distance, and the long smear of red leading to the Duke.

The traveller was down beside the Duke, the others had gathered round. Someone said, "By the Gods it's the Duke!" Ark stood and stared. The traveller was stripping the clothes clear of the Duke to get at his chest. Then with the same intensity that he had just seen he crossed both of his hands outstretched over the chest of the Duke. The wave burst forth again, but more intense and focused around the upper body of the unconscious Duke.

The Duke's body shook, and it felt like the air around Ark and the group was moving. He stretched out his hands to balance himself. The faces of the crowd showed fear and amazement. He heard "Gods!" and other exclamations and saw some turning their heads away. The air above the traveller, became red with the blood. Ark could see each droplet swirling like a tornado around the traveller's hands. And then slowly the pressure around seemed to ease. The droplets were filling the air and then slowly disappearing like flakes of snow dissolving before they reached the ground. Then it stopped. The air was clear. The traveller fell backwards to sit from his previously kneeling position. His arms lay limp at his side. He mumbled to himself with his head hung between his shoulders.

Ark stepped forward and looked at the Duke's chest. There was nothing, there was no wound no scar, just fresh healthy pinkness. Ark looked at the traveller again then at the crowd of survivors. They were all kneeling, gesticulating.

The next few minutes were a blur. The Duke was still unconscious, so two men from the crowd came forward and lifted the Duke s body. They carried him to one of the empty monks' chambers and lay him on a cot. The traveller remained sitting. Someone from the crowd rushed to the great doors and made sure they were closed. He was shouting orders to others, and he saw many rushes off to bring objects and furniture to pile in front of the doors.

Some of the women lay there hands gently on the Traveller and lifted him so he could walk. They led him slowly, carefully, respectfully to the chamber next to the Duke and helped him into the cot. Ark stood staring into space.

***

Rahmin returned to his room. The sun had fully set now, and the longest day was over. He was not one to need much sleep, but the last two days events had left him exhausted. He longed for his bed and had decided to leave the Council chamber. The Golden Guard had escorted him to his room and two waited outside, they would guard him all night. He had no doubt of their loyalty. One had left for a few minutes to check on Francesca, and he had returned to say that she was asleep in her room, though she hadn't touched her food.

He had personally worked with his Commander on positioning the guards for guarding the Citadel through the night. Everyone had fallen into line and he felt confident that there would be no further attacks. He closed his eyes and sleep came easily.

32

Ark wasn't sure how long he had been asleep, but he woke under the cot that the traveller was asleep on. He crawled out and looked at the traveller, he still slept. There was no sunlight coming through the windows, so he knew it was still night. He left the cell and looked out across the Temple. Most of the Priests and Bursars had retired to the empty cells. A couple of men were sleeping on the stone by the barricade built up in front of the door. All was very silent.

Not far from the door an old, well-dressed man sat on the floor. He was bent over as if reading the flagstones, but as Ark neared, he could see that he was writing with chalk on the stones. White marks surrounded him. Ark couldn't read so he had no ideas of the markings, but he walked up the man. The man looked up. "Ah, the mysterious flying boy!" the man spoke with an accent Ark didn't recognize. Ark didn't answer, but just pointed at the markings.

"Ah, yes, I didn't aim to be a be a vandal, but It does seem to have got a bit carried away." The man scratched his head bearing his hand into a swathe of black hair. My name is Terrico, he stretched out his hand and offered it to Ark. Ark kept his by his side. He looked at his hand and decided that it was the chalk that had stopped Ark from fulfilling his courtly obligations. "Ah, yes the chalk. And you are?"

"Ark", he sat down clear of the markings opposite the man. "Well, Ark. These monsters aren't real men! No. There some sort of puppets, puppets without strings, I suppose. They are made of stone, here" he showed Ark a few shards of a shiny stone, like slate from the rooves.

"You see, stone, and an incredibly strong stone. Not from our mountains, not even from the Empire!" Ark looked on.

"Very strange, but stranger still: what makes them move? Maybe some sort of wind power, or furnace, but I'm guessing magic…"

"Dark magic…" the traveller completed the sentence. He was standing behind Ark and smiled at him as he looked up. Next to him was the

Duke. The Duke was whole, complete. His shirt ripped but no wound. His leg fixed. He was standing and looked the picture of health.

"And here is the man of magic, himself...," said the inventor. He jumped up, "How did you do it? Is it magic? What is it?"

The traveller grimaced. "That is a very long story." He volunteered no more.

"A gift from the Gods, is who he is!" The Duke patted the traveller on the back. "How he does it I don't care about, how we use him that's the question". The Duke stepped forward, and in doing so scuffed the chalk drawings on the floor.

"And you my ...strange, peculiar lad, I must thank you again for saving my life and bringing me to this saviour." He shook Ark's hands, whilst continuing to pat the traveller on his back.

"His name is Ark...in fact he is the Beast". The Duke looked on stunned. Then laughed out loud, "Of course, the Beast! Of course!" Ark looked at the traveller, who gave a strange smile.

"To the point, though. How many of us are here? Are there any soldiers?"

The traveller seemed to disappear into the background, half lurking in a shadow. Ark could tell he was uncomfortable, but somehow the Duke had glossed over his miracle survival and was just thinking about "what next?"

Tessisco filled the Duke in on as much as he knew. The Duke stood nodding.

"I came to the temple about an hour ago. I had been hiding out in my workshop not far from the Citadel, as you know. After the slaughter at the gates, I kept low. Eventually I decided to move. I came here, the doors were open, and I found these other refugees, but no monks or Priests. Our friend here was tending the sick. More came, and we have about twenty of us hiding out here. No soldiers."

The Duke nodded but said nothing. He had all he needed to know, and almost as if he had forgotten something he turned back to the traveller. "Yes, and by the way who are you?"

***

Francesca woke from another long sleep. She could barely lift her head off the pillow, and her body ached. She felt cold, but when she touched her head, she found her hair was soaking wet, and her face moist and damp. She had a headache and when she opened her eyes the room appeared to be spinning. She tried to sit up, but she was so tired. She tried to recall the dream she had had, but it was like a feather in the wind, she couldn't quite grasp it, the images gone but the feeling of fear remained.

She leaned back and reached for the servant chord that hung by her bed. It was too far away; she would have to get up. She managed to swing her legs around and lift her upper body upright. She took a deep breath and leaned on her elbows. The room really was spinning. Fighting the pain in her head she pushed herself up. She seemed to hover for a second and then collapsed to the floor in a heap.

***

Gascon didn't sleep. He had woken Lilkin to relieve him but didn't trust the boy not to run off once he slept, so he tried to stay awake and keep an eye on him. The city and the Citadel had merged into one body of darkness, but he could see the Dam, with its ring of torches and the tower of the Temple. The rest of the city was in darkness, not a single torch though the Citadel had a few more lights and two or three lights could be seen moving where the Citadel walls would be. They must have been guards walking the walls.

The boys slept. What dreams they must be having, he thought. He had been like them once, though they seemed more fragile and he had lived on the streets for a while. He had never known his mother, dying when he was very young and then his father had been in the City Guard. His memories were vague of him too, he had never really been around much. His older brother made sure he was fed, and he would see his father late at night when he came home, not from work but from the local inns. Gascon spent the days sitting on the docks, like many children. School was not an option and of little interest to him.

Garik had been an old family friend, close to his father. One day, Garik had come to the house and told him that his father had died. He had just keeled over on duty one night. Gascon had felt nothing. Garik was kind and "matter of fact" and said, "You're old enough to come and work for the guards, and maybe one day you can be one." It had been a few weeks later that he finally went to see Garick, but it wasn't for him. He had instantly rebelled against the guards, and against what his father had been. Yet after time and the patience of Garick, boredom and hunger drove him to stick with it. His brother had signed up a few months before to serve on a merchant ship and it was just time to grow up.

Had these children once been loved or just only known the streets? He looked across at Lilkin. He was asleep. At least he hadn't run.

***

A rag and bone of a guard walked the Citadel walls, holding his spear and a torch. Earlier, he had a cushy number guarding the reservoir doors and the stores. No-one had bothered him until earlier today, and life had been easy. Somehow now he was on the cold, dark walls and hated it. The cold was bad enough, walking was hurting his feet, but the real bugbear was the smell. A few feet below him was a pile of bodies, rotting away.

He was a Citadel Guard and had never seen war, not even a fight. He'd never seen a dead man, and below him were enough bodies to fill the reservoirs. The city was weird as well, dark and quiet. He was guarding a bleeding cemetery! Rations had been cut as well, and if he was stuck out on this wall, so he wouldn't be able to pilfer anything from the stores.

Then he heard something. A squelch, a sound like a hand being pulled out of a wet glove, long and squelchy. Then more of the same, like a dozen hands. It was coming from below the wall. He made his way long the wall nearer to the gate. There was another guard there, and that made him feel a bit more confident. "Can you here that noise?" he called out to another guard who was now only a few feet away.

"My hearings not great, Jasper, but yeh it sounds like a fish barrel being stirred." He knew the guard, it was old Crow, and probably the oldest guard the Citadel had, but remarkably fit for his age. He could stand to attention for hours with his chest sicking out.

Where was it coming from? Jasper knew, he just didn't want to think about it. It was coming from below, in front of the gate, but there was only one thing there. Dead bodies. Crow tilted his head towards where the noise was coming from and pulled a quizzical face. Suddenly Jasper felt very vulnerable. The guard's torches were casting a strange small area of light and the dark beyond seemed suddenly uncomfortable. "You need to look," said Crow.

"I don't think so", replied Jasper. "It's your bit of wall, not mine."

"Let's both do it..." compromised Crow. They slowly leaned forward over the parapet, holding their torches in front of them, but high to give maximum illumination. At the edge of the light's perimeter was the top of the pile of bodies, strange shapes of grey in the weak light, bundled like a pile of old rags. They moved slightly to the right. The squelching could still be heard. Then they saw it, both of them, a movement from amongst the rags.

"There, hang your torch there", Crow pointed to the movement. And then they saw it. An image that they first doubted and then wished they had never seen. From amongst the rags a long thin, bloodied hand and then wrist and then arms burst through like a swimmer gasping for air. Crow and Jasper jumped back, not before Jasper had let go of his torch. It fell in loops to the pile of bodies below and lit up the mound it grew closer.

The guards last image as they fell back was a field of arms sprouting from the bodies in its gruesome light.
■■

33

The Temple was silent except for the four people sat around a makeshift fire that Tessico had constructed in the middle of the apse. It illuminated the traveller, the Duke, Tessico and Ark as they sat around it.

"I am a traveller." He paused. "I see that mean nothing to you, but if you had the true faith and knew your histories it would mean a lot. If you look around these walls you will see the image of travellers amongst all the images of the Gods that are carved or painted up here." The traveller waved his hands towards the distant walls.

"A thousand years ago the Gods believed the world was drifting away from them. They had lost touch with the ways of man. So, they sent travellers to walk among the men. When the need arises."

"You are a God?" Tessico, jaw dropped.

"No, I am definitely not a God." the traveller halted him. "The Gods do not live alone on the island kingdom. There are men, there are women, that reside there. They are the Godclose. Close to the gods, pretty simple really."

"But your powers..." the Duke began to ask.

"They are gifts. We serve the gods, tend the land, guard the islands. When asked we serve the Gods. I was asked."

"You have seen the Gods?" Tessico asked.

"Yes...and no... I have been in their presence, but you don't see them. It's strange but you hear and feel them. The message is there in your head, and its simple. Your questions are answered, you have a new knowledge."

"And the powers?"

"They just come to you. You are not told or handed a spell book; you just have an ability. I have not met any other travellers, I don't know what they can do, but I soon learnt that I could heal."

"...And destroy," said the Duke.

"That I don't know. What I did at the door, I have never done before." The traveller stopped talking.

"And why have they sent you here?" asked Ark "What is your mission?"

The traveller smiled. "All I know is that the world needs a saviour. This plague is not from the Gods, nor is it from man. The Gods cannot save mankind. I just heard two words in my head 'Save them'."

"You have been sent to heal mankind; you can heal the plague?" Tessico was excited.

"You have not listened. The plague is not from the Gods, I am from the Gods, I cannot heal the plague! By the Gods I tried. My hands can heal, and I thought the answer was helping the sick or the dead, but I made no difference. The plague was stronger. My mission was not to heal."

"How will you save us then?" asked Ark.

"I don't know. Truly I don't know, but after months of wandering from city to city, I prayed to the Gods and in my dreams, I saw this city. The answer would be here." He looked up at Ark. "This city has the answer, I just need to find it." Silence again, each taking this incredible knowledge in.

"Who are the warriors? What part do they play?" asked the Duke.

"They are God-made. I don't know why or how and which God, but they are old God-magic. Someone has brought it to this city, someone powerful."

"Rahmin" said the Duke. "We have a Guardian here, could he be the one."

"Which God does he serve?" asked the traveller.

"I don't know, but he's an evil sod. Close to the Emperor." Replied the Duke.

"If we knew which God then maybe we could defeat them, they are not that powerful."

The Duke pulled a face. "You're jesting".

Ark spoke up "They are unstoppable. They are relentless. They have killed the whole city."

"Our swords bounce off them, with just the merest chip of stone..." the Duke continued.

"Stone, you say?" queried the Traveller.

"Well, I think so." The Duke tried to think.

""Keep going" the traveller said.

"I mean we fought two of them by the canal and they fell in the water and didn't emerge." The traveller smiled.

Tessico interjected. "It's like slate, if I was to guess I'd say Kabat. It matches the description of the Mountains of the Gods. No-one has ever seen it, it's just a guess but ..."

"...is as hard as iron, and as heavy." Finished the traveller. It is used to pave the Gardens of Ezkebel, the darkest of the Gods. Your God, Tessico, I believe?"

"Yes, the Maker, the Maker God. He creates everything, and is the patron of all scientists, inventors and blacksmiths."

"Yes, the Maker God. In the east they call him Maker."

"So, these are from him?" asked the Duke.

"Made by him, yes, but wielded by his followers."

Ark voice was slow and concerned "Traveller, has Ezkebel, Maker, sent them to kill all mankind. Have the Gods given up on us?" The thought hung in the air for a few moments.

"I don't feel that. I truly don't. the Gods love mankind, Gaal made them remember and infused you all with essence of each of the Gods."

"Perhaps they want to start again?" asked the Duke.

"Maybe."

"What can we do traveller? How do we stop them?" asked Ark.

"Fire" said Tessico.

"Fire, yes," said the Duke. The traveller looked hard at Ark, like he was testing him.

"They won't burn, will they?" he said, "no they are fed by fire, they grow strong in fire, they came from the fire of the Northern sun." answered the traveller, he willed Ark to keep going.

"The water. It doesn't rain in the Isle of the Gods. Can water kill them? They don't seem to like it." The traveller slowly nodded. The there was silence.

"Then I know how to kill them, all of them!" announced Tessico. And as he said it there was a thud at the Temple doors

**

Repeated thuds at the door, woke Rahmin from his first good sleep-in ages. He slowly dressed and rummaged through his belongings to find a good-sized knife, before reaching the door. "Who is it?"

"Commander, sir...there has been a ...development". Rahmin relaxed and opened the door. Through the windows he could see it was still night. "Explain."

"It's the Princess sir, she is …. sick." Rahmin was stunned. "How do you mean sick? Take me to her" he began marching down the corridor, the Commander following.

"The servants found her on the floor of her chamber. She has a fever...and..". The Commander seemed to stall in his description. What was he not saying? He was not saying about her eyes. The reddening of her eyes was a sign of the plague.

247

"Her eyes, man, her eyes? What of her eyes?" They reached the stairs leading up to Francesca's room.

"Red, sir. Red" They reached her door, to be met by a group of physicians. They all instinctively held their hands up to ward him off. "Stop, your Lordship. It's not safe!" There was true fear on their face." Are you sure it's the plague?" he asked. "Have you been in and examined her?" The physicians looked at each other. The Commander answered. "They opened the door and looked in on her, sir."

Rahmin bit his lip. "Open the door." The Commander pushed past the physicians and opened the door. There was a strange aroma in the room, the smell of sickness. On the bed lay the princess, but her face could not be made out. Rahmin grabbed the collar of the nearest physician and dragged him to the door, then with an unexpected strength shoved the man into the room. "You have fifteen minutes. Diagnose." He then pulled the door shut and left the man to it.

Francesca was aware of the commotion. She was barely awake but sensed the noise and the movement. She had never felt so bad. Her body was useless she could not lift her head. The headache had gone, but she was left with a dull pain above her eyes, and her eyes felt like they had broken glass rubbed into them. It was easier to keep them shut. But she felt a breath on her face, and she forced them open.

Through a blur of colours, she saw the man leaning over her. His mouth covered with his hand and a cloth. He was looking straight into her eyes. He could here muffled words but couldn't understand and couldn't answer. The head moved away. She tried to keep her eyes open but couldn't.

After fifteen minutes Rahmin opened the door. "Well?" the physician started to walk towards him, wiping the sweat from his brow. "Stop!" Rahmin held out his hand, and the Commander drew his sword a few inches from its sheath. The Physician stopped. "It's the plague, your lordship. I'm very sorry."

Rahmin knew it would be. He had bought time to gather his thoughts. "Thank you for this service, "he said. "And thank you for your continued service. You will stay here with the princess and do what you can for her. Food will be brought and left at the door. Thank you once

248

again" the last words were drowned out by the exclamation of the physician.

Rahmin shut the door and turned to his Commander. Round up the guards who brought her in. Isolate them...although it may already be too late.

***

If Francesca died then that would put a huge dent in his plans, thought Rahmin. What to do? He had no immediate answers. It never ceased to amaze him that when all seemed calm and on course the Gods would send something to throw his world into turmoil. I suppose that was all he could expect from the time of Ezkebel, which meant that he would have to find the opportunity from the chaos.

He made his way down to the courtyard of the Citadel, thinking and thinking. "Sir, the gates...we are under attack... I can't quite explain...." A guard ran up to him and the Commander, wheezing out of breath.

Rahmin stared at him. "Under attack? Have you gone mad?"

He and the Commander rushed to the gates, collecting along the way various servants, and guards and some of the Lords. He raced across the courtyard, and saw on the battlements, guards crouching with the heads below the parapets. He could hear a low humming noise...no it was moaning ..he could hear a collective moaning.

He raced up the first set of steps that he could to the walkway and stared over the parapet. Across the concourse, the whole concourse, into the streets and beyond was filled with people. Not soldiers, people. Not an inch was spare from the walls to beyond the first houses of the city; from the east to the west canal. But this was no army, the people were standing still, all facing the walls. "Who are they?" Rahim asked anyone.

One of the guards spoke from below, a quivering wreck. "It's the city, the people of the city."

Had this many survived? He could see wounds on their bodies, many without limbs. It slowly began to dawn on him as he looked at the severity of the wounds and then the stare of their lifeless eyes. "They are dead" he whispered. "It's the dead of the city." And that was what it was: the dead of the city. Those slain by the warriors. Rahmin knew exactly what it was, but it shouldn't have been. He had seen it across the Empire, the dead of the plague rising, but this was not supposed to happen when killed at the hands of the warriors. Ezkebel. Chaos. He held his mouth to his hand.

■■

34

The banging at the door would not stop. Tessico, Ark, the traveller and the Duke stood and looked. "The assassins!" yelled the Duke. He drew his sword. The traveller held his arm. "No, wait. Your plan Tessico what is it?"

"It's the water. We need to drown the assassins, and I know how to get lots of water into the city."

"Go on," said the Duke.

"The Dam has sluice gates. They have not been used for hundreds of years, but they exist. They were built after the Great Drought, when the mountains no longer fed the canals and the lake. They allowed water to be released from the sea beyond the wall into the lake. Incredible machinery. There are four gates along the Dam, and the mechanism is by the east corner of the Dam. It will release them all."

"But that will drown the whole city?" said the Duke.

"No, we just open it enough, enough to flood say ...what do you think traveller?

"Probably four feet or so should be enough. Enough to dampen the assassins maybe knock them into the water as well, but not too deep to drown the survivors." The Duke thought for a few minutes, the doors creaked as if someone or thing was pushing it. The other survivors were emerging from the cells and coming to see.

"And you can control how much is released?" asked the Duke.

"Of course," and Tessico knelt on the floor with his chalks and began to make calculations on the floor.

"The Duke took control. "Okay, you people, head to high ground, one story should be enough, go onto the roofs if you need to." The people stared and slowly nodded, some already moving to the stairs at the back of the Temple. "Traveller, Tessico, we will head for the Dam."

"And me," said Ark.

"No, you must finish my search. You must find the girl, she is very important" he paused, considering whether to say it. "She is the Princess Francesca, the Emperor's daughter, we must find her and get her to high ground. If you are the Beast then, well you can do it, you owe the city..."

"Francesca?" asked Ark. The girls is "Francesca from the Citadel."

"Yes, what do you know of her?"

"I know her, and I know where she is..."

"Go on..." the Duke leaned forward, eager.

"She is, or was climbing the canals, on the east side to the mountain reservoirs."

The Duke sighed, "Then she is alive. How odd you know her..." Ark started to explain but the Duke shook his head, "No, no time. You must check that she made it. Head for the canals, I came that way and she was not there but perhaps we passed at different times, perhaps she made it in. "There is a door, but it will be guarded at the top of the lock, you will get through, I'm sure. If not travel deep into the caves, there are tunnels that lead up the mountains and you will find paths down into the Citadel." The Duke explained. "Have you got that?" Ark nodded.

***

Ark led the Duke, the traveller and Tessico through a small opening onto the first roof of the Temple that covered the main length of the building. This point was still a couple of stories higher than the market square, and so by edging forward along the tiles they could see down into the square. Ark led the way but when he reached the edge, he was surprised not to see the warrior figures banging on the door but rather the dishevelled form of around thirty people huddled against the great doors.

"We should let them in," said Ark.

The traveller looked over. "They are not what they seem, Ark."

"What do you mean?" questioned the Duke.

"They are the dead." the traveller said. The traveller rolled back from the edge. "I hoped this city would not see this and assumed that perhaps the death by the assassins would not lead to it, that it was just linked to the plague. You see, the plague doesn't just kill its victims. It does something to them. Across the Empire I have seen this. The victims die, but within a few days rise as these reanimated carcasses, revenants. They have no personality or life, just empty shells."

"By the Gods", said the Duke, and he leant over the edge to look again. "Are they dangerous?"

"I have not seen any violence from them. In the Empire they just roam, heading north like migrating cattle, sometimes in groups of hundreds, but I also saw just the odd one walking past, ignoring me as it headed north."

"Where are they going?" asked the Duke.

"North, but I'm not sure where or why. Perhaps their body is trying to find their souls which have crossed over to live in the Northern fields. All I know it that they are no harm to us."

"Will the assassins kill them?" asked Ark.

"Probably not. They are dead no matter what your eyes tell you, and I guess whatever drives the assassins will think that too."

"Will they stop the assassins?"

"No, they have one goal; the north and they will literally climb the mountain to get there. I'm not sure why these few have come to the Temple, though. Perhaps there is something confusing their compass." The traveller looked at Ark.

"Could it be you?" asked the Duke. "You are from the North."

"Yes, perhaps" but the traveller did not seem convinced. Ark made his way back to the east tower and climbed quickly up it. He called out. "I can see thousands at the gate of the Citadel, and some climbing the locks. There is no sign of the assassins....no wait there are one or two...just standing amongst the crowds..."

The Duke gently seized the traveller's arm. "They will be converging on the Citadel. We must move quickly." Ark was back with them. "The...people seem to be putting a lot of pressure on the walls and gates; some have tried to climb up."

"As I feared" said the Duke, "The assassins haven't gone, and if the weight of the dead can create a way in for them then the assassins will take the Citadel, and our last stronghold. We must proceed with the plan. Ark, show us the way."

And so, they moved across the rooves. The traveller was surprisingly agile and moved quickly and confidently. The Duke showed no signs of the physical damage of the day before, except perhaps for some hesitance. The scientist was slower and kept needing help across the wider gaps.

Eventually they had run out of rooftops and had come to the point where they would have to climb the mountain stairs at the sides of the Dams. The scientist had headed them westward, as the main chamber was near the centre but on the west side. When they were finally looking up at the Great Dam and the docks and lake ahead of them all was silent. There were no dead, and no warriors. Dark patches of obvious blood lay everywhere. And the water had the flotsam and jetsam of the fight on the Dam floating amongst it.

"Hundreds tried to flee by boats" said Ark, "but the assassins cut them down. Some died on the spot...others fell."

"It's a long way to fall" said the scientist with no obvious sympathy in his voice.

"So, to the west stairs", said the Duke, "come on, we must move quickly." And have begun climbing down the front of the warehouse that they had stopped on. It was about a hundred yards to the entrance to the mountain stairs. Ark suddenly felt nervous, walking on the dock felt wrong. The scientist was soon down with the Duke, and they were making their way across the dock. The Duke had drawn his sword.

The traveller looked at Ark. "What is it?"

"Something's not right." Ark closed his eyes, and then turned to look towards the Citadel. He opened his eyes, and through his vision the city flew past his eyes, roof after roof, Temple, roof, concourse, citadel, courtyard, tower, until he was seeing a girl, Francesca lying on her bed. And then he was back.

"Francesca is dying. I must go now" and with that he hurried away into alleyways beyond.

***

Rahmin just stood and stared. The dead were now clambering at the walls, and he could see to the east and west they were finding high ground around the canal locks. He knew they weren't threatening, but the pressure was building on the walls and in the distance the glint of warrior's armour could be seen. Why weren't they gone? Had his spell been too strong? They would need to leave sooner than he thought.

The mountain passes could be opened, through the mountains. He would take the soldiers, and the useful Lords. Some servants to carry the provisions, his chests, all must come. He leaned close to the Commander. Gather the men all of them to the square. Bring horses and carts. Tell the servants to get my things from my room and load them up. We will need food and provisions, and winter clothes, blankets. We must leave the city.

"What of the princess?"

"The gods will see to her,"

***

Gascon woke with a start and seized his sword. Dawn had broken, the three boys were gone. He jumped up and began to look everywhere. Then he heard movement on the path that led down to the Citadel. He stepped slowly with his sword poised towards the path.

Then through the leaves and pushes burst Lilkin. "Ah, you're awake!"

"Where in hell have you been?" demanded Gascon.

"Have you not seen it?" Lilkin said, turning and pointing down toward the Citadel. "Some sort of army has come in the night, and is attacking

256

the Citadel." Gascon looked down and saw a mass of thousands of bodies in the concourse in front of the Citadel walls. They were just a mass; he couldn't make out their uniforms or features. "What's going on?" he stammered.

"God knows, "replied Lilkin. Suddenly behind him appeared Felix. "Reckon it's more of those warriors. Full scale invasion of the Empire, when it's at its weakest!"

"We must help them, the Citadel," Gascon didn't realise that he had such a commitment to the Empire, to the city, even, but something stirred in him.

"That would be right, like they helped us by letting us in. You're on your own soldier." Lilkin blurted out. Gascon looked at the three of them: they were skinny, hungry, cold and dressed in rags. "What were you doing down the pathway?" he asked Lilkin.

"We reckon our future is on the mountain, for a while. See who wins the fight, then high tail it north over the mountain."

"Over the mountain? You'd never make it; you'll freeze, get eaten, or get lost. There's a reason no-one goes that way." responded Gascon.

"Reckon that's right, but there's a path, and they say the old tribes crossed the mountains in the old days." Lilkin argued. Gascon just shook his head and looked at the two smaller boys. "You're crazy."

"Reckon it's crazier to go down there and fight, but you're right, we would freeze and probably starve, and if we're going to be eaten, we better give those mountain wolves something to feed on, so we started to clear the path down to the Citadel. Reckon we can borrow some clothes, weapons, food without anyone noticing, especially if there's a battle on." Gascon nodded. They were right. Lilkin wasn't daft; he'd survived this city for a long time.

"Okay, let's go down together. I won't be taking the mountains with you. You can stay with me but if you don't want to, I won't stop you."

"Reckon that's right...you go first" and Lilkin pointed down the path.

***

The traveller felt for a moment that he should go with Ark. He knew Ark had to go, there was something in the air, an energy pulling all of them to the Citadel. But he couldn't lose Ark; he knew the answer was tied up in him or those around him. The Citadel would be dangerous, and he had hoped that once on the Dam he could shepherd the child onto a boat and make for the land of the Gods and let them figure it out, but that was never to be.

He looked at the Duke and the scientist who had started to make their way up the Dam. Yes, the Citadel would be dangerous. The traveller took one last look at the Dam, and then having made up his mind he headed after Ark. The Duke looked back and saw the two disappear. He decided not to shout farewell, He took a deep breath and headed onto the Dam.

Then the Duke saw them: two warriors. One at the far end of the west side of the dock, the other had emerged from the mountain stair a mere fifty yards ahead of them.

"Run!" yelled the Duke, and he backed away from the direction he had been moving in to spin and head to the centre of the dock. Tessico followed suit. Instinctively the Duke made for the dockside and the first jetty that led to the base of the Dam across the lake. He looked up, many of the lifts had been broken and were hanging half in the air or half sunken in the lake. "We'll take the lifts. That one looks like it works. Do you know how to use them?" he said as he grabbed and dragged the scientist behind him.

"Of course, probably it just pulleys, but you need to be strong..." The Duke ignored him and kept running. The nearest warrior had reached the start of the jetty, when the Duke and Tessico reached the lift. It was intact. They hurdled the side and grabbed at the pulleys.

To the Duke it looked like a spider's web of cables and rope. The warrior was closer, not changing speed but gaining on them. Tessico screamed and then grabbed the pulleys – "This one, this one! Pull It! Pull It!"

They both yanked down on a rope, the roughness cutting into the Duke's hand. But he kept pulling, and with a jerk the lift raised itself from the platform. The Duke kept pulling, he had knocked Tessico to one side and he fell into the base of the basket. It was easier for one person, but by the Gods the lift operators must have been strong.

The basket reached head height as the warrior swung his sword into the basket, cleaving a slice through the wicker and ropes. The basket shuddered and swung forcibly against the Dam side. The Duke kept pulling. They were clear, before the second swing could do any damage. And for a second, he paused, and they just hung there. He looked around. The second warrior was nowhere to be seen. He took a deep breath, and with bleeding hands and arms that screamed with pain, he continued to pull, and the lift slowly climbed the Dam.

35

The pain was extraordinary, but somehow, she raised herself from the bed. The old man was waving his arms at her, but she struggled to her feet. Her hands were grey like the blood had been replaced with swamp water. Each vein on her arm was pronounced and proud, looking fit to burst. She was no fool, she knew she had the plague. She had seen it all over the Empire, although Rahmin had tried to keep her from it. She saw the bodies in the streets; she saw soulless revenants wandering aimlessly.

How long did she have? She told herself she wasn't afraid of death, but she was.

The old man was standing well clear of her. He obviously didn't have the plague, or at least thought he didn't. If he came near her again, she would sneer at him and wave her arms like a cat, if she could lift them. He was staying well clear, anyway.

She was able to stand. If she was going to die, she wanted to see the sun one more time. The balcony was on the other side of the room, beyond the old man, and she was facing the door. It was only a few feet away. She would head for the door.

She lifted her legs. They were heavy, like they didn't belong to her. She took a step and then another. Then another. It was slow going. The old man was screaming something. Another step. Another. Another. Another. Then she was at the door. She grabbed the handle and turned it. The door opened inwards and wasn't locked. She managed to pull it. It slowly opened and it was at this point that she felt the fresh air; she hadn't realized how thick and obnoxious the smell had been in her room.

There was no-one on the other side. She sensed a movement though, from behind her. The old man was rushing towards her. She raised her arms in the air, but the old man just brushed past her and through the door. She steadied herself as the man disappeared down the stairs.

She stepped through the door. She felt a little more energy coursing through her and was able to take slightly fuller steps. The stairs looked daunting, but she would make for the rail. She could here noise from the bottom of the stairs, of horses, and movement of people. The courtyard was only a hallway from the bottom of the stairs. She took a deep breathes of the clean fresh air and took her first step down the stairs.

***

The courtyard was filling up with people and horses and carts. The great mountain pass doors, wide enough to allow two carts to pass by each other and still not have the drivers touch hands, loomed in the western corner. They had been sealed long ago, and now there was an army of guards wielding axes to break the great wooden beam that held the doors shut. There was no shortage of volunteers, as only Rahmin now stood up on the wall, the guards realizing that this was their escape from the army of the dead.

Rahmin knew the dead were no concern, but the warriors behind them maybe. He continued to wonder "Why had they not returned to their miniature form? Had his god abandoned him?" He caught a glimpse of his chests being loaded onto a cart. Most were those he had arrived with, but many there were a number that contained food and provisions, although carefully stored under clothes and blankets.

The darkness beyond the great door was emerging and thick chunks of wood flew from the impact of the axes. He looked back over the wall. None of the dead had cleared the parapet yet, but he could see a thin line of silver appearing behind them: the armour of the assassins.

He looked up at the balcony where Francesca's room was. It was a shame she would not survive this; he would pay her one last visit before he left, but not until he was sure everything was ready to go.

He saw the Lord Justice and a few of the other Lords, there carts were piled high. There would be plenty of coin if it was needed.

***

Ark and the traveller made their way across the rooves. The traveller watched the child move like lightning, and he was soon lagging behind. They reached the rooves above the concourse and looked out on the incredible scene. From the gate into the alleyways were thousands of people, or at least thousands of animated bodies. They were shoulder to shoulder with no spaces, from the canals on either side to the gates of the Citadel. By the gates and at the canals, the slow laborious bodies were attempting to climb the walls, but with little success. The stable was gone, lost amongst the bodies. A route across the rooves was impossible, there only way in would be to cross the concourse somehow or visit the locks.

Amongst the bodies were the glints of the metal warriors. Ark moved his head back instinctively, as if they might see him, but the warrior was amongst the dead trying to squeeze towards the gate and had not seen him.

"They don't know what the dead are," said the traveller. "It's like they are inanimate objects to them. Like moving through a forest."

"Why don't they use their swords?" Ark had noticed that they were struggling to get through the crowd.

"I don't know. The spell that drives them must have limitations. If their creator has said "kill the living", then that's all they can do."

"Could you change the spell?" asked Ark.

"No, no" he shook his head "it's not my spell to change."

Ark pointed to the eastern canal. "That's where I saw Francesca when she was heading back to the Citadel. There are no assassins there, we should head that way." He started to move to the east. The traveller having had those few moments of rest, managed to keep up now. They crossed an alleyway using a piece of wood that Ark had placed there many months ago on one of his previous explorations.

Ark stopped and looked around him. He was standing tall; the traveller had so often seen him almost running on all fours like a cat. He stared at the traveller. "I fear for your friend, Ark, and I fear this could be a bad move for us. Stop and consider whether this is worth it. She is probably in the safest place she can be, what more do you expect to do?"

"She will be saved!" Ark shouted. His eyes were red, the traveller hadn't noticed that before; he had been crying for a while.

"Of course," the Traveller said. They continued on, reaching the canal and slowly lowered themselves down to the ground next to it. Ark's crying had stopped, but the two were no longer exchanging words.

* * *

Gascon and the boys made their way down the stairway. Most of the steps were crumbling and deteriorated in some way, but still passable. Every ten or so steps the path would be flat for a while. Gascon thought this must have been a difficult walk for anyone. Perhaps that was why it was in such disrepair. The children had stumbled a few times, and he had had to slow his pace to ensure they didn't get hurt. They had made good time and at the next flight of steps he would reach the level of the first Citadels rooftops. At this point they took a break. There was a stream running under a small wooden bridge, where they were able to quench their thirsts. At this position they could no longer see what was going on in the Citadel or the city.

Gascon was impatient, "Let's get going" he ordered. He was surprised when they all got up with little complaint, especially Lilkin who had been puffing and blowing. They would never make it over the mountain, he thought.

"We should reach some sort of entrance to the Citadel soon, so you need to be quiet."

"You won't even know we are here" Lilkin replied. Gascon thought it sounded a bit sinister, but maybe he was just being sarcastic, after all these boys were thieves, after all.

The foliage was covering most of the steps quiet heavily now, but mostly they could just push branches and leaves aside. Every now and then they would come across a tangle of branches, and Gascon had to snap them or cut them with the sword. They finally came to a mass of branches that looked almost like a hedge had formed as a barrier to their progress. Beyond it Gascon could make out a wooden door. The foliage went high, and it was easy to see now that it was climbing a wall. The four stood and looked for a while, whilst Gascon started to cut away at the branches.

"Why don't we climb up the branches?" asked Felix.

"And what would we do on the other side?" Lilkin teased. "Grow wings and fly down?"

"He is right, "said Gascon drawing a stern look at Lilkin. The wall might have a walkway but probably it will be a sheer drop or a leap onto nearby roofs. No Felix this is a job for you and those magic hands!"

Gascon had soon cleared a narrow gap, wide enough for him to squeeze through if he bent down. He could see the lock. "Come here Felix" he beckoned the boy, whilst he leant down to peer through the keyhole.

"Looks clear." He moved away and let Felix in. Felix reached into his pocket and pulled out a collection of keys, some looking like pins of different lengths. He proceeded to work them into the lock one after the other. One seemed to fit, and with his tongue gripped beneath his teeth in concentration he rested his ear against the door close to the keyhole. Gascon couldn't hear anything, but Felix began to smile.

"It's done!" Felix cried after a few seconds.

"Well done, "Gascon pulled Felix back and he used the end of his sword to slowly push the door inward.

***

The Duke's arms were almost useless by the time the carriage reached the top of the Dam. Tessico had given up even attempting to help. He looked as far along the Dam, to his left and right, as he could but saw no signs of the warriors. The pathway had the remnants of violence but no bodies. Climbing onto the Dam he could also see the ocean side.

He had no concept of whether there were more or less boats than normal, but things did look calm. There were a few bodies on the boats, but not many. Amongst the boats and barges were scatterings of belongings, the signs of people abandoning their possession as they fled. On the horizon he could see sails in the distance. He felt a yearning to be with them, for their safety. He had never sailed a boat but the desire to climb onto the boats was almost overwhelming. Tessico had joined him and he could see from his face that he obviously had the same thoughts.

The Duke looked back over the city and the view was incredible. He had seen it many times, and it never ceased to amaze him. The whole city was visible, clutched in the grip of the great mountains encircling it. He could see the Temple and the Citadel, the highest points. From here the courtyards and open spaces were obscured, so he could not see how the death of his city was progressing. He could not see any warriors or people and yet another doubt crossed his mind: perhaps it was all over. Tessico then pointed back down to the lake at the foot of the Dam. The warriors that had pursued them had left the causeway and were almost at the mountain stairs.

The Duke's resolve come back. "You are sure this will work?" he grabbed Tessico by both arms.

"I'm sure, but it has been a long time since the sluice gates were ever opened." The Duke nodded slowly. "Let's do it."

Tessico led him along the walkway to one of the four buildings that stood on the Dam's top. Each had an arched tunnel to allow people to walk through. The Duke had been in one or two before and he seemed to remember that one had quite an ornate sitting room above the arch on its second story.

They entered one of the arches and approached a door on its hinges. The Duke used his sword to pry it open a bit more and looked inside. It was lit inside with torches and was obviously some sort of guardroom. The floor was covered with blood, gore, fallen weapons and shields but there was no sign of bodies. Tessico pointed to a square hatch in the floor.

"There. The mechanisms are below us." The hatch had a large ring in its centre, and the Duke pulled it up. The hatch was not on a hinge, it just came free. He manoeuvred it to his left and looked down into the hole. The space was lit, but not well. It looked like a large basement, perhaps fifty feet by thirty feet, roughly the size of the Council Chamber. In its centre was a huge round pipe the size of two cart wheels that ran from the sea wall to the lake side wall. Surrounding the room was a series of wooden wheels cogs and pulleys.

He lowered himself down the steps followed by Tessico. Tessico was beaming; the world of cogs and levers was heaven to him. The Duke ran his fingers along the dust. "Over here," Tessico called, climbing across the pipe, the main mechanism is on the other side. The Duke could see in the far corner another set of steps leading up the way. He figured this was to the second building on the Dam.

Climbing over the pipe he saw Tessico was standing in front of a giant wooden wheel. It was as tall as the scientist and as wide. It stood out from a wooden wall; the gap made up of smaller wheels. The wooden wall was a box of some kind from floor to ceiling that had a series of long metal rods that appeared from its sides and ran parallel to the lake side wall. They disappeared deep into the walls.

"You see this is the mechanism for all the gates. These rods link up to each of the four gates. This pipe is just one of them" He patted the pipe with a sense of pride. "This wheel opens all the gates and you can see by the marking on the wall it shows the amount you want the gate to open."

The Duke saw that the wall was like a clock face, with 12 points marked out. It mirrored the size and shape of the wheel. He could now see that the wheel had a large metal arrow like a clock had, from its centre to the perimeter. It was pointing at the 12 o'clock position.

"We just need to turn the wheel, until the point is at the required number."

"Do we need to open all the gates?" the Duke asked.

"We have no choice. That's what the mechanism does. It's designed that way. It spreads the water pressure out over the whole Dam. It's a huge amount of power...I've often thought that we could use it somehow, have the gates always open at it turn a waterwheel of some kind..." Tessico had drifted briefly off into another world.

The Duke seized the wheel. "Let's do it then. What number do we turn it to?"

"By my calculations, I believe just level two will be enough, and only for a minute! No longer!" he was looking up at the ceiling, as if he was looking at an invisible question written there." Yes, a minute."

The Duke laid down his sword and grabbed the wheel. There were two clear handles near the centre. The system was obviously designed for two people to do it, but his arms stretched far enough, and he believed he would still have purchase. He then slowly began to turn it. Nothing happened. He tried again, exerting more force. Within, the cogs joining the wheel to the wall, he saw layers of rust and grime fall away. The wheel moved at little easier and slowly he began to move it. The wall and the pipe seemed to groan like a sleeping giant. He could feel the pressure straining the room.

"This doesn't sound too healthy. Are you sure about this?" asked the Duke.

"It has not been used for a long time, but it was well built...." Tessico responded but seemed to trail off. The wheel reached the "2" markers, and the pipe shuddered with the water flowing through. The Duke turned to Tessico:

"So, a minute, we'll need to count out..." but he didn't complete the sentence. Tessico was stood there, his mouth wide open, a look of terror on his face. Protruding from his chest was the end of a black blade, blood dripping to the floor. Behind him stood the unholy form of a stone warrior.

36

Ark and the traveller had managed to climb across a series of barges until they were on the opposite bank of the canal to the concourse where the dead were massed. Even on this side, though there were people moving and they were heading in the same direction as they were: towards the locks. Ark could see that many were climbing up the side of the lock, but strangely he did not feel threatened. He and the traveller made their way to the first lock and started to climb. The traveller found this hard. "We could just use the barges and the actual locks" he said.

"No" he replied, as he lowered his hand to help pull the traveller up. As he did so he noticed something strange and unnerving. A line of the dead below, by the walls of the Citadel, across the canal turned to look at him. The effect was like a wave on the ocean as beyond across the concourse more heads turned. Above him on the next lock one of the dead had stopped climbing and turned to look down at him as well. "What are they doing?" Ark asked himself. He climbed over the first lock and was on his way up the second. The traveller followed but looked back. Many of the dead were falling into the water, no stepping into the water, as if they were following them.

The traveller looked up at Ark. Who is this boy? More than ever the traveller knew he had found something significant; he would stick with the boy and not let him out of his sight.

Ark passed one of the dead who seemed to just stare at him. Up close he felt he was looking at a corpse. The face was sunken, with the skin stretched across the skull. The eyes were dark and bloodshot. There was no colour to its skin, just a tired greyness. The torso was shirtless, and clearly his stomach had a gash at least a hands length long, although it looked neither fresh nor healed. It was a deep red with a crust like edge.

The man didn't touch him. His arms just hang at his sides. Ark tried to read his eyes, but there was no emotion, not even sadness. Ark moved

271

on, believing he had left the man behind, but he began to follow Ark. Ark looked back and saw him ahead of the traveller, and there he saw that the lower lock was awash with bodies attempting to follow them. Even down on the concourse there was a wave of movement towards the canal.

He kept climbing. The traveller's reassurances that they were harmless were dissipating. He could see that the traveller was having to push some away from him as they got in the way of his climb. They reached the reservoir at the top of the lock. The dead man had become an uninvited companion, and he stopped when they stopped. No dead had made their way beyond this point. The water seemed to be a barrier to them, although there had been plenty wading across the canal. The reservoir was deeper no doubt.

"Can you swim?" asked the traveller.

"No need." Ark pointed to a barge floating nearby, not moored but close enough to reach and pull in. The traveller did this, being taller than Ark, and they both climbed on board. The dead man tried to follow, but the traveller uses the pole to push him away. Other dead were now appearing above the locks: old, young, men women, soldiers, cooks, traders, rich and poor.

"Make for the door", Ark pointed, and the traveller set the pole in the ground and pushed off against the side and then against the ground. The water was not as deep as he thought, perhaps four foot or so. Already the dead follower was lowering himself into the water.

They reached the other side of the reservoir as more dead entered the water. It reminded the traveller of the seals along the bay of Harlecot, heads just bobbing above the water.

The door into the Citadel was locked. "Here give me a push up," Ark beckoned the traveller. "I'll climb over and then I will let you in." The traveller was heartened that Ark's mood had seemed to mellow a little from earlier. The traveller readied his grip and pushed Ark up. The hall was still higher than the two of them, but after pushing hard, Ark seemed to fly in the air. Covering more feet than humanly possible he landed on the top of the wall.

Below was a courtyard. This was all he could see of the Citadel. There were crates and boxes and then an open door into a roofed building. He jumped down and reached the door. There was no key, but there was a wooden beam across the door. He lifted the beam and shouted through the door "I'm in. I just need to find a way to open the door."

He searched about and still couldn't find a key. He tried the room opposite that led into the building. It was more storage space, but he noticed a fireplace with kindling and a bucket of fire starters. He shoved the starter into his pocket and grabbed the kindling. He made his way back to the door and piled the kindling up against it. "Stand back" he yelled.

On the other side the traveller moved away from the door. The bobbing heads in the water were closer and, in a few minutes, would be climbing out of the water. "What are you doing?" he called out to Ark. Then he saw the smoke billowing from under the door. Then flames flicker around the bottom.

Ark found some oil in a jar in the storeroom and threw it at the door. With a huge roar the flames spread up the door. He watched it burn. The kindling was gone now, and smoke was billowing out. He coughed and stood back. Then he heard the crack of wood, and then the sound of metal hitting the ground.

The traveller had now been joined by the dead man and new companions. Before long, it would be too crowded. Flames were roaring from the other side of the door, and a huge split had been rent near the lock. He could see through to the smoke on the other side. He took a few steps backwards and then charged the door. With its weakened lock the door flew inward swinging to the right. The traveller fell into a dense cloud of smoke and felt the flames catch his cape. He hit the floor and rolled into space arriving at the feet of Ark.

* * *

The main beam that kept the Great Gate through the mountain locked shut had been drawn back to allow the gates to be opened. Rahim had overseen the whole process. "Commander, we need to organize ourselves for reaching the gate so line up the wagons, my one first. We will lead with the Golden Guard as a vanguard and when the great

273

doors open cut down the.... Them. Them. We will drive the wagon through and keep cutting down until we have a clear way to the Great Gate. Circle the wagon whilst we push the doors inward."

"What about the rest sir?" The Commander pointed to the Lord's servants and wagons.

"Make sure that the Citadel Guards are behind us and then they can follow. If anyone disagrees kill them. The Citadel Guard won't put up a fight; they're going to be amongst the first out of this hellhole. Now follow me", he took the Commander's arm and made his way up to the steps to the parapet. I have an idea for a diversion." They marched up the wall, the Guardian still talking. "There must be something in the gate tower that can be dropped into them and maybe clear the way a bit." They reached the parapet and Rahmin's words stopped in his mouth. The scene in front of the gates and Citadel walls had dramatically changed. The mass of bodies had shifted over to the eastern canal, almost clearing the Citadel gate and creating a clear pathway to the Great Gate in the mountain on the west.

He looked to the east but couldn't see what was causing the shift. "Is there a breach?" he asked. And then Rahmin saw the smoke: it was coming from behind a series of buildings that adjoined the outer wall that climbed next to the lock system.

"There!" Rahmin pointed. "That's where they're heading!"

"I'll get some men over there, sir!" the Commander started down the steps.

"No! It will be pointless. Gather the men, now is our chance to leave the gate!" Then suddenly the screaming began. It was down in the courtyard. Expecting to see the dead, Rahmin rather saw the crowds backing away from a door into the main Citadel. They were backed away from a figure emerging from the door. Dressed in a torn and worn red dress, was Francesca stumbling out of the doorway into the daylight.

She looked like one of the dead, although the way she shielded her eyes, he knew she wasn't. Panic ensued, and the crowds veered away from her. Some of the guards formed the start of a semi-circle surrounding her but with at least twenty foot or so space. They drew short bows and aimed arrows at the girl.

Francesca was monetarily blinded by the light as she walked through the door. Her vision was already blurred, and all she could make out was the flagstones beneath her feet and the blur of movement. The smell of horses was overpowering, like smelling salts. She staggered forward.

Her mouth was dry, and her lips cracking but she managed to say "Help me! Help me!"

Rahmin saw the Princess staggering towards the men, their arrows now pointing stoically towards her. Suddenly a voice screamed "Stop!"

Gascon led Lilkin, Felix, and the other boys through a series of elegant rooms looking for a way into the main Citadel. Lilkin and the boys kept stopping to pick things up. "Remember you have come for provisions, not ornaments!" Gascon reprimanded Lilkin. All the way down he had seen that these boys were under Lilkin's spell. Perhaps they would need that if they were to survive the mountain. He knew they wouldn't though, perhaps that's was why he was not rushing to the battle at the walls.

His sense of duty had not diminished, but he knew he owed something to these boys. Somehow, they had become his responsibility. Even Lilkin. As they had walked down, he had continually challenged Lilkin on his plans, stressing the dangers. The world had turned upside down and if he could convince the boys to stay at the Citadel, he was sure he could save them. Then again, maybe he was leading them to their deaths. Maybe he should go with them, lead them over the mountain.

He decided he would stay with them until at least they found the right resources. They moved on until they had found what appeared to be a storeroom, but it was pretty bare. It was obviously the storeroom for a guardroom, he had seen many of these before. There wasn't much in there only a few crates and sacks. They went further into the Citadel and he could look out on the courtyard through a small window. He saw horses and carts and people milling around but no signs of a battle.

The three boys were already rummaging through the sacks and crate, pulling blankets and weapons out. Lilkin had grabbed a bow. "Do you know how to use that?" asked Gascon. Lilkin just smiled. "You'll need arrows" Gascon grabbed at a quiver on the wall and through it towards him.

"That'll help" Lilkin smiled.

Felix had found some provisions. Being guard's rations, most of it would be foods that would last a while and not perish: dried fruits, meat, bread and some preserves. There was panel of backpacks on the wall as well, and they all instinctively started loading them, Gascon too. Had he decided to go with them? Then the door opened and a Citadel Guard stood there looking at them.

"Thieves!" he yelled, but before he screamed another word, Lilkin had charged into him and knocked the man to the floor. Lilkin was on him, punching hard into his face. Gascon yelled "No" and pulled Lilkin back of the guard. Lilkin fell away and stared with fury at Gascon as he reached for a dagger.

Gascon turned to Lilkin as if to say "Wait", but before he could the guard was up and had charged into Gascon. Gascon fell against the wall but kept his feet. The guard drew his sword and made for the dagger wielding Lilkin. Felix cowered behind a chest. The Citadel Guard swung his sword at LIlkin, and Lilkin narrowly avoided its blow by falling backwards, but now he was down. The guard swung again, but Lilkin managed to grab a shield and block the blow with an almighty clang. The shield fell away though, with Lilkin losing his grip.

Gascon again screamed "No!". He was stunned into doing nothing and the guard looked at him and swung his bladed towards him. The guard was good, and Gascon only narrowly avoided the blow, but the guard threw a kick at Gascon that sent him sprawling to the floor. Gascon spun round expecting the next blow, whilst his hands scurried for his fallen sword. But the guard had changed tack. He was heading back towards Lilkin, who hadn't stood up, but rather had manoeuvred himself to being in front of the two boys, protecting them and himself with the shield.

The blow fell on them, and the shield soaked most of it up. Then Gascon decided: his hands found his sword and he charged at the Citadel guard, his back to him. Then in a smooth sweeping motion brought the sword down on the soldier's neck. The sword passed through bone and wedged into the guard releasing it from Gascon hands. Gascon stepped back, shocked. The Citadel guard appeared to be turning, but he wasn't, it was just the prelude to his collapse to the ground.

Gascon stared. Lilkin was up and, on his feet, though. He threw the packed bags at the boys and pulled them to their feet. "We go. Now!" he then turned to Gascon, "Are you coming?"

Gascon just stood there. He had killed one of his own. Chosen these street thugs over a guard, like him, doing his job. What was he? A traitor? But they were just children, trying to survive. Lilkin didn't wait and was out the door they came through with the two boys, leaving Gascon standing motionless staring at the dead guard.

* * *

Slowly the body of Tessico, dead but with his face still locked in a silent, agonizing scream, fell forward releasing itself from the sword. The Duke stepped back as the body fell forward, landing with the scientist's head at his feet. The warrior stared coldly at the Duke, as his sword was pulled back from the body ready to strike again.

Quickly the Duke grabbed his sword as the warrior raised his over his shoulder. The Duke didn't have time to swing his weapon, so opted for a charge into the assailant, hoping this surprise action might buy him some time. He hit what seemed like a solid wall and bounced back only just recovering enough to avoid falling to the floor and to avoid the downward swing of the warrior's sword. The Duke rolled to his right and threw a kick at the warrior's leg whilst he did so. His heel hit the figure, but he may as well have kicked the wall. The warrior spun around and swung his sword down again in a doubled handed chopping motion. The Duke continued his roll and avoided it again.

The warrior wasn't fast, and the Duke saw this was his only advantage. Its attack was easy to predict, but he could do nothing unless he was standing. He scrambled to his feet and by running a few yards managed

277

to get upright before the warrior attacked again. In doing so he had made his way to the steps on this side of the giant pipe. A quick glance at the step made him consider running up them and away, the hatch was open, and this must have been how the warrior hand got in. The warrior approached more cautious. His stance was textbook fighting, he knew the style well. Over the warrior's shoulder he saw the wheel shuddering slightly; the pressure of the water was shaking the room. Was that the two minutes up?

What would happen if he went on for more than two minutes? He couldn't run. He would need to shut off the gate or the city would drown. Then he had an idea. He needed to get water into this room, that would stop the warrior. Then the warrior lunged a forward attack at the Duke and the Duke turned sideways to avoid it whilst swinging down with his own sword striking the head of the beast. Chips flew away, it was a good hit that would have killed a normal man but was not going to stop the warrior.

He took two paces back towards the wall, all the time looking for a pipe he could break. The giant pipe was too huge and made of cement. He had managed to get himself back between the warrior and the wheel. He had to be quick and find a way so that he would have time to turn off the wheel.

Then he saw it. The step exit was further away now, but he saw something that made the decisions simple, coming through the open hatch was another warrior.

37

"Run boys run..." Gascon began to whisper under his breathe. The boys were long gone but he repeated it like a mantra. "Run." He looked down at the body of the guard. He was finally finding clarity in his thoughts. "You were saving the children, saving the innocents." He paused and stepped towards the door the boys had left through. Then he heard the screams, coming from behind him, out in the courtyard. He stopped and turned, picked up the shield and his sword and stepped into the courtyard.

The courtyard was full of horses and people who were all gathered by the Citadel wall, shouting and pointing at a small figure to his right. He recognized her: Francesca. She looked sick and lost. She was crying and clutching her eyes. Around her a few feet away were more Citadel Guards, swords and bows drawn.

The mantra continued to pound in his head: "The children; the children" and in his loudest, commanding voice shouted "Stop!" The guards spun to see the city guardsman who had defied them. Rahmin was already starting to jump the steps back down to the courtyard, whilst Gascon stepped in front of Francesca and raised his shield so only his eyes could be seen above it. "Don't worry child, it is Gascon. I am here."

Francesca felt relief wash over her, a brief wave of euphoria to drown the pain. Then she collapsed to the floor.

Ark and the traveller rushed through the storeroom; behind them the fire had started to spread. The traveller again struggled to keep up with Ark, not because of his own tiredness, just because of the sheer speed of the child. He was truly miraculous.

Ark rushed down the corridors, he knew they were on the opposite side to Francesca's chambers and had to cross the whole Citadel. He took wrong turns and dead ends and soon he knew he was lost. He rushed to a window to look out and see if he could figure out his bearings. Then he saw her. She was lying on the floor behind a soldier, who seemed to be guarding her from a rabble of people and guards surrounding them. A tall figure strode through the crowd and stepped into the open space between the guards and the lone soldier.

By now the traveller had caught up with him. "Ark you must see this" he grabbed Ark's arm.

"Later, I have found her, but we may be too late."

"No look "and he spun Ark to see down the long corridor they were in. Packed into the corridor were the dead. Steam eked from their clothes. Some looked burnt, all were bearing wounds. "They have followed us. You, they have followed you."

And they stood just watching Ark, waiting, staring at him. Ark just shook his head and grabbed the traveller's arm. We must get to them", his other hand pointing.

***

Rahmin stood in front of the guards and looked at Gascon. Gascon didn't move holding his post without flinching. He would kill all of them if they approached.

Rahmin considered the scene before him. Time was running out; it was time to leave. There was no saving, Francesca. She was just a distraction. He turned to the Citadel guards, walked level with them and without looking back said "kill them!"

But before they could move, he felt a gust of a airy ferocious power hit his back. The men either side of him fell to the ground, some flying back a few feet. Rahmin kept his balance, but it took all of his strength. The carts even lifted onto a few wheels before crashing back to the floor.

Rahmin spun round, and saw Ark crouched over Francesca, the soldier still protecting her, and the traveller's arms outstretched. He has power. He thought. He has gifts of the Gods!

"You have great strength; my friend and you have come to us at our hour of need. We are not the enemy; they are beyond that wall." Rahmin bellowed loudly, whilst pointing to the walls.

The traveller looked exhausted; his head hung low on his shoulders. He slowly lifted his head. "I am the traveller. It is true the hour of need is truly upon us all. Whether you are my enemy, I do not know, but right now this girl will not be slain."

The guards who had been blown of their feet began to gather themselves and slowly stood. Ahim spoke "She has the plague, my friend, and my men must protect the people. We are the last of the city, and we cannot allow this deadly assassin amongst us."

The traveller stared. "You are a charlatan! Blah blah blab. My power is too great for you, stand back and let me help the girl." The traveller briefly half turned to look at Francesca. The decision seemed quick but in Rahmin's head a thousand calculations had been carried out. Who was he? Was he a guardian? Would he save the day? What was he too the girl? Answers never came but all his thoughts came to on conclusion. Kill him!"

And with the simple words twenty arrows flew from their bows, all striking with a short-ranged ferocity into the back of the traveller. The repeated thuds, making the traveller stumble.

The traveller fell. Gascon threw his shield back up to protect Ark and Francesca. Rahmin stepped back, his body touching the cart behind him. Half the guard readies their swords the other readied the next onslaught of arrows. Suddenly, Rahmin was yanked back. This time not by a supernatural force, but by a yank on his cloak, but then by hands grabbing his arms and something sharp squeezing his neck.

Lilkin emerged from the top of the cart with a knife, Felix had pulled Rahmin back whilst Lilkin held the knife to his throat. At the same time from the right bursting form multiple doors surged the dead towards them.

Lilkin shouted. "Stand back or he dies." Ark rushed to the traveller who had managed to pull himself up from the ground with his front arm and looked at Ark. Ark went to him and grabbed his hands. The traveller gripped them tightly and whispered. "Lay you hand on her. Quickly! Now!"

Ark felt the tightening grip of the traveller on one hand whilst his other stretched for Francesca's. She was almost gone. He couldn't see a breath.

Rahmin tried to move but couldn't. His assailant was strong, but what Rahim lacked in physical power was more than made up for in true power. He began to whisper a soft incantation as the blade pressed against his windpipe.

Meanwhile the dead had swarmed into the square but had stopped a few feet from the chaotic scene before them. His guards were retreating away from everything; one even turned and ran from the gate.

Then everything seemed to stop, time slowed to almost a standstill. All heads turned to the three figures on the floor, one of them Francesca.

Suddenly a burst of colour emerged into the air surrounding the figures: butterflies. They seemed to come from within the clothes of the prone traveller and spread along his arm and up the arm of the small girl. Soon the small child was completely obscured by the multiple colours of the butterflies. Gascon was pushing them away, as up close he could see them swarming around the boy and Francesca. To Rahmin's and Lilkin's eyes the small group had become engulfed by the swarm of insects.

Rahmin was stunned by a magic he had never seen before, an incredible power. Yet, he continued his incantation and with all his power and a final coughing of words, his body expelled an energy that blew Lilkin and the cart to the wall. Rahmin was first to react and spun round, ready to finish his assailant, when they all heard the noise. The mountains around them seemed to roar.

***

The Duke stared at the two assassins slowly approaching him. He knew he was going to die, and for a split second his mind become a cloud of regret. Then clarity: I can at least save the city, he thought. He dropped his sword and turned his back on the assassins, as he started to turn the great wheel back to its zero position. He would at least stop the flood, but each moment he took to move, allowed the two warrior blades to reach his back.

The wheel inched closer to the shut position, when the Duke felt the first blade pass through his back into his stomach. It was not as painful as he expected, but almost immediately he could not feel his legs. Where the first assassin had thrust his sword through him, the second was swinging down with a huge amount of force.

The Duke could see it out of the corner of his eye and closed them knowing that the pain of this blow would be beyond his senses but it never reached him. His legs buckled beneath him and he collapsed to the floor. His sight was blurring and everything fading to black, but the movement had led to the blow missing him and violently slamming into the wheel.

The Duke rolled back, and he saw the shattering of the wheel and its bits fall towards him. The mechanism that was linked to the wooden unit cracked with a scream louder than the sound of the blade on the wood, and the room seemed to shake.

The Duke was dead by the time the room had shaken so much that the two assassins were rocked to the floor. Within the spruce gate, the mechanism had collapsed, and each gate had dramatically opened to its fullest level. The four sluice pipes were now sucking in what felt like the whole sea. What had been a gentle waterfall out into the great lake, became a torrent of incredible power, hitting the lake below with the force of a mountain collapsing.

In the Citadel courtyard the noise of the waters was accelerated around the mountain bowl surrounding the city so that it sounded like the Gods themselves had roared. The noise was greater than thunder. All were rocked momentarily. Lilkin and the boys were already taking the opportunity to flee. Gascon clutched at the floor.

Then the roar increased. At the Dam the pipe inside the sluice chamber exploded filing the room within seconds, the assassin and the Duke's body in a whirlwind of water and stone. The whole chamber seemed to shift as the pressure of the water on ancient mechanics had proved too much. The water found its exit by bursting through the Dam wall joining the torrent already hitting the lake below. This was repeated in two of the other gates.

Rahmin could see where the roar was from now: the city. He looked up but the Citadel wall blocked the view. He broke free of Lilkin and ran to the steps, followed by his commander. The concourse was still filled on the eastern side with the dead, and the city looked the same, but his eyes looked up at the top of the Dam that appeared above the buildings. It was gone, there was no top, there was no Dam, and all he could see was a wall of water. The commander was the first to react. "Shut the gates, shut the gates!"

Ark squeezed hard on Francesca's hand. The butterflies were everywhere, swarming around him and Francesca, but seemed to be leaving the traveller. He felt the traveller's grip loosen and in equal measure Francesca's hand felt warmer.

Then he felt himself being pulled up as Gascon lifted him to his feet. He heard Lilkin shouting "Run!" and saw him pass through the swarm into the building. Gascon had now lifted Francesca and was following Lilkin. It was all a daze. He felt hands grab his. Small boys and pull him after the disappearing Lilkin.

The swarm of butterflies was dissipating. He was now in a storeroom and Gascon was rushing through with Francesca in his arms. He was being dragged by two boys who he followed upstairs and across hallways and then he ran. Ran to keep up with them.

Rahmin looked down at the courtyard. The butterflies were gone. The body of the old man lay on the floor, but he was already disappearing under a swarm of the dead, making for the door to the Citadel.

The noise from the city was deafening. He could see the commander shouting at him but couldn't hear. The Commander was running down into the courtyard. The horses were bolting, pulling carts uncontrollably behind them. The soldiers, servants and others had fled to the far side of the Citadel to be clear of the dead, and now were crouching on the ground in fear.

The gates were still open. The dead were still swarming into the courtyard and there was a mountain of smoke drifting from the eastern side. And then Rahmin saw it. Waves of water were exploding through the streets into the concourse, tearing down buildings as it battered its way through the streets. He mentally calculated: he was high enough the waves would break against the Citadel walls. Except the gate was open.

The commander was pushing the gates shut with the help of a few men, but most had scattered. And then the wave hit the walls, breaking only five or six feet below. The impact through Rachim to the floor, and he was sure the wall moved. Spray fired over the parapet. Waves burst through the partially closed gates engulfing the commander and his me. The water quickly covered the courtyard, all signs of the people there wiped out.

As the waves crashed against the Citadel, a few heads and limbs broke the surface of the water, including a terrified horses head. City doors and broken wine casks contributed to the jetsam of the scene becoming violent weapons when they hit anything before them. Rahmin raised himself. The wall had stood the waves settling a few feet below him, but the there was another roar. An unholy crescendo of noise that sucked the air from his lungs. An unnatural noise accompanied by a wall of air from the city like the southern winds. He looked at the Dam.

There was no Dam. Bursting through the city was a wall of water, so high that it blocked the sun. It was moving at an alarming rate eating the city as it accelerated to the palace. As it hit buildings, they disappeared amongst the water only to appear regurgitated higher up. Rahmin spellbound saw the guts of ships being tossed in the maelstrom.

The only place to run to was to the stairs from the wall to the Council Chambers and from there he could make the Citadel. He ran, shaking off his cloak. His ears were deaf to the sounds of screaming from the waters in the courtyard, survivors clutching wooden beams and parts of broken carts.

He ran parallel to the wall of water, parallel to the death that was chasing him. He made the stairs to the Chamber, climbed and burst into the room. Everywhere was deserted and he crossed the Chamber, now no longer able to see the wall but able to hear the deadly assailant behind him. He reached the throne and kept going to the doors to the main Citadel. They were shut, and he began to pull them open.

Then he was gone. The Chamber, the Citadel walls, the courtyard were all swallowed by the wall of water decimating the Citadel.

***

Gascon was lagging behind the others but eventually he had made the door out from the Palace to the mountain pass. The others were already well up the pass, only Ark hanging back for him. Gascon could feel Francesca breathing but her eyes were shut. She was still very pale. Behind them they had heard a mix of explosions and screaming, and now just a prolonged roar. Gascon's limbs ached and screamed but he had to keep going. Save the children. Something told them all that they had to climb higher.

Lilkin was well ahead of the others, never looking back. He had reached the roof level of the Citadel only its towers being higher. He too was exhausted. After a few more steps he saw what they had been running from.

The Citadel was disappearing, building by building, eaten by the sea, because that was all he could see: the sea. No Dam, no city, just a few buildings of the Citadel, and as the others including Gascon joined him, he saw the last parts of the Citadel swallowed and disappearing.

The last vanguard of waves assaulted the paths they had just climbed, and parts of the trees and pathway were consumed and spat out along with the remnants of tiles, bricks and doors. As the waters settled a layer of waste and destruction floated to the surface.

Lilkin stood and looked out over the new sea. Gascon collapsed to the ground his head sunk into his hands, Francesca lay on the pathway, Ark embracing her. Felix and the others dropped their packs on the floor and looked out across the sea. The city was gone. Its only sign of its existence being fresh flotsam and jetsam in the new bay.

Felix muttered "The Dam was built by the gods..." Amongst the wooden beams, crates, a throne were bodies. Ark stared out to see if he could see the traveller. He imagined him somewhere on a piece of wood waving to him. He stared hard and the sea and the people rushed towards him. He looked at each body, each face, but could not see him, and eventually he could stomach the dead faces no more.

Francesca coughed and Ark looked down at her opening eyes. They were still blue, though bloodshot. Her skin was pale but not sickly. He touched her hair, and it was quite brittle, strands breaking away in his hands. He smiled at her. "Francesca are you okay?". She didn't answer, just laid still.

"We've survived soldiers, the walking dead, the sea itself and were still going to die of the plague, coz of her" said Lilkin, angrily. He was noticeably standing well clear of them.

"She doesn't have the plague" Ark calmly answered." She was saved."

"We'll see, but I'm not carrying her!"

They all sat staring saying nothing. "What now?" said Ark.

Lilkin looked up at the mountain. "That way" he said nodding his head further up the path.

"He's right" said Gascon. "We need to get over the mountain. He stood up and looked up at the snowy peaks. It's getting late, we 'll make it to the garden and rest there, then explore at first light. It's not going to be easy." He started up the path. "I'll carry the girl."

Ark looked up at him. "Thank you."

THE END

Printed in Great Britain
by Amazon

53705834R00165